THE SERPENT

SPIRITS OF THE NORSE, BOOK ONE

KATE ROBBINS

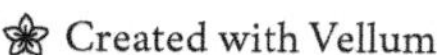 Created with Vellum

CHAPTER ONE

Firth of Clyde, Alba—September 936AD

Raging waves heaved around the ship as if to forewarn him on his quest. Giric MacDomnail gripped the serpent on the galley's prow and leaned forward. Storm be damned. He would not lose his vessel to the violence around them—not when he had such an important task ahead. Too much weighed in the balance.

"We'll never make it!" Osgar MacAlpin said. His greatest ally needed a little more faith.

Giric could barely make out his words or features over the howling wind and sea spray stinging his face. Sailing down the Firth of Clyde had been choppy, but manageable. But this was a sea he'd never experienced. Giric gripped the serpent's head tighter, willing the ship to win the battle. This journey was too important, and he'd put it off for far too long.

The ship groaned and creaked as each wave threatened to

tear it apart. Though quite strong, he was no match for the push and pull on his body as the ship was tossed around.

"Giric, did you hear me?" Osgar tugged on his shoulder. "We must return to Prestwick. The storm is too powerful."

Giric whipped around to face his doubting friend. "We will not turn back. It's taken me too long to acquire men brave enough to make this journey. I won't let a wee storm stop me now."

Osgar shook his head. "Christ's teeth, Giric! You'll kill us all!"

Giric grabbed his oldest friend's tunic. "If we do not make the journey, there will be nothing left of our homes. Do you understand? And I will not allow one more Scot to fall victim to their raids and barbarism." He'd made a vow to his sister, and he intended to keep it.

"Aye, I understand, but the men are scared, Giric. They think the Viking king conjured up one of their gods to bring about the storm."

Giric shook his head. This kind of talk would get them all killed.

"Viking kings do not conjure, Osgar. You know this. Do not let a little wind steal your courage."

Osgar put his hands up in surrender. "I hope you know what you're doing." He stepped away from Giric. He'd made his point, but now Giric needed him to do the job with which he was tasked.

"You worry about the men. Keep them calm. Let me worry about what to say to the Viking chief."

Osgar shouted at the men to row harder. Their rhythmic chant grew loud enough to reach the heavens. Good. Their chanting would help them focus. He turned back to the horizon to scan for land.

Giric had heard plenty of stories of how the Norsemen and Gaels had made their peace on the Isle of Lewis. He had a proposal for Gunnar Haraldson and no amount of bad weather would keep him from it. To hell with superstition and conjuring. He needed the ship and the men to hold themselves together a little while longer.

The sky grew darker as the clouds turned a sickening inky grey. Thankfully, he'd had the men tie the sail up a while ago, else they would surely end up adrift. He and Osgar took turns steering the ship until finally, the wind turned around and pushed them in the right direction. Osgar was a relatively quiet man under normal circumstances, but in that moment he was fierce in his pursuit to keep the men pumping. He was grateful his friend had put his fears to good use. Giric could neither operate the ship, nor make this journey alone.

"Heave!" Osgar shouted.

"Ho!" the men replied.

By the time land appeared, at least half of the men were vomiting over the side of the galley. But Giric was not too exhausted to hoist up a white flag. The last thing they needed was to meet a band of Vikings on the shore whose blood was up from the storm.

Before long, Lagavulin came into full view. The large bay offered excellent protection from the open ocean, but also an unencumbered view of approaching ships from the east. Giric was certain all able-bodied warriors wielding shields and axes had amassed on the beach the moment the ship was spotted.

There was great risk to his approach, of that he had no doubt. He'd sent a message with a man he'd seen in Prestwick but a fortnight ago. Without any way of accepting a response, he was unaware if his message had reached its destination or if Gunnar Haraldson was the kind of chieftain who negotiated or attacked first.

As they approached the shore, a large wooden structure

came into view. Giric squinted to make it out, but his mind would not let him reconcile the image.

"Is that a ship's hull?" Osgar asked.

And then he understood. The structure resembled an overturned ship's hull, but of a size Giric had never seen. He knew a little about Viking ways, but clearly not enough. Was this where they all lived? Or was it some sort of common place like a tavern?

Before he could put any more thought to it, the sea calmed and a single shaft of sunlight shone through the thick clouds overhead, landing on the shore. Something there reflected the light.

"God's teeth," Osgar said.

"Hold steady," Giric said. "We would greet a stranger no differently in these times."

"Are you seeing what I'm seeing, man?" Osgar asked. "That's no welcoming party."

He was likely right. As they sailed closer, the *welcoming party* grew larger and not just in number.

Giric himself was taller than most men he knew, and he'd seen some massively built Vikings. But this lot must surely have descended from the giants in the old tales his grandfather had recited years earlier. Fierce warriors who could slay an entire village with one swing of their axes.

"Steady now," Giric said to the men as they approached the long dock where several moored longships rested. He'd never seen such a well-built wharf in his life. And his lands included several port villages.

As the men secured the ship, the band of Viking warriors approached. Strategically, the long dock was quite clever. These warriors could easily overcome anyone who tried to gain access to the dwelling or even make landfall. The length of it gave them quite the advantage.

Giric stepped off the ship and onto the dock expecting it

to give in some way for surely it would have to float. His legs stiffened when his foot hit solid plank. He wanted to look over the side to view the support posts, but he dared not tear his gaze away from the approaching threat. Drawing a deep breath, he stood his ground and let his arms fall to his sides.

They moved with such purpose, these warriors, their confidence evident in every step. Boots on plank echoed around him resembling battle drums. Giric had to admit they were a sight to behold with their thick, shaggy red, or blonde hair and beards, a mixture of furs and leather wrapped around every inch of their thick bodies and a weapon of some sort sticking out of every nook and cranny. They were made for killing and they made no bones about it.

The largest one stopped but a foot away from him. Surprisingly, he did not have to look up too far to meet the man's icy stare.

"You are Giric MacDomnail," the giant said, in surprisingly clear Scots. "I am Gunnar Haraldson, and you want to talk peace with me."

"You speak our tongue," Giric said.

"Of course. Do you not speak ours?"

That single point illustrated why the Vikings had been able to settle so successfully wherever they chose. They were fearless and intelligent, and anyone who underestimated that might as well pass over the keys to the castle.

"I do not, but not for lack of interest."

Gunnar narrowed his eyes. "You say you want peace, yet every time we reach your shores, we meet with resistance. Why?"

The man was direct. That could make their discussion go much more smoothly—or end it before they began. Giric would take the same approach. "Because you have been known to take without asking."

A big, meaty hand slapped Giric's shoulder. He held his breath as Gunnar threw his head back and laughed.

"You are a funny little man, Giric MacDomnail. Come, let us drink a horn together and talk our business. You may take one man with you. My men will guard your ship and your men."

Giric nodded and looked over his shoulder at a wide-eyed Osgar and motioned him forward with a flick of his head.

"Why is it necessary for your men to guard mine?" he asked Gunnar.

"You have much to learn, Giric. But do not worry, they will be safe, I assure you."

"And me? Will I be safe?" As he asked the question, he noted the clouds had cleared and the calm waters of the bay reflected the deep blue sky above.

Gunnar threw his head back and laughed again. "I like you already. I think I might even offer you my sister."

"Not if she looks like you," Giric said. He wasn't certain where his placidity had come from to offer such a jest, but something told him there was a lot more to these people than their outward barbaric visage.

"You do not think me pretty?" Gunnar asked with a sly grin.

"I own sheep prettier than you."

Gunnar chuckled as they approached the structure that had intrigued him from offshore.

"Is that your home?"

"It is, ja."

"Was it originally a ship?"

Gunnar shook his head. "Have you ever seen a ship that big?"

"No and that's why I'm curious."

"The hull of a ship gives great surface area and most of

my men have spent many years in that trade. When they built it for me, that shape made sense to them. Come, let me show you inside."

Two men opened the large doors allowing the heady aroma of burning peat and fish to waft out. Giric's eyes took a few minutes to adjust to the dark, but when they did, the sight before him only played on his earlier suspicions.

"Your weapons," one of the men guarding the structure said as he pointed to a pile of swords and axes off to the side.

Giric and Osgar removed their swords and daggers and did as they were asked. They would gain more ground with Gunnar if they practiced no deceit at this early stage in the game.

Two wooden tables flanked the sides of the hall with a massive, rectangular fire pit in the middle. Sides of meat hung from iron hooks above and small fish were being smoked on racks around the pit. Several axes, shields, and swords decorated the walls along with various furs, tanned leather skins, and animal antlers, mostly buck by Giric's estimation. If the walls had been stone, he would swear he had just entered a nobleman's hall, though this one was more rustic yet grand in a different way than his own. What might Gunnar think of his home in comparison?

At the head of the hall and on a raised platform, a single wooden chair was adorned with various furs, clearly meant for the chief. Behind the chair and to the side was a doorway and he wondered what lay beyond.

"You do not have a wife?" Giric asked him as he regarded the single chair again.

"You are keen, Giric MacDomnail. Are you proposing to me?"

Now it was Giric's time to laugh. "I assure you, 'tis women I prefer," he said.

"Very well. Come sit at my table and share a horn with me. You have not introduced me to your companion."

Giric turned to see Osgar's slack-jawed expression. "This is my oldest and most trusted ally, Osgar MacAlpin. He owns lands near mine, and we have spent many years working hard to enhance the value of our properties and protect it from—raiders. I might as well come out and say it."

"I am glad you choose to speak plainly," Gunnar said. "We will get along much better that way. Please sit at my table, Osgar MacAlpin."

Gunnar leaned back and motioned for a young woman to come forward with a pitcher. She was quite beautiful with straight blonde hair and high cheekbones, though not as tall as he expected. He'd heard all Viking women were as tall as most Scots men. She wore a long-sleeved fitted green shift with a tunic over it fastened at the shoulders with heavy brooches. By the way the inset stones glinted in the light, he surmised they were some sort of precious gem. But since she served her lord, did that mean she shared his bed, or that she was family? Giric did not know enough about the way their hierarchy established such things as servitude.

"Bring horns too, Aslaug," Gunnar said. "And meat. Lots of meat. Now down to business—"

The door swung wide, slamming against the outside wall drawing Giric's attention to a single entrant striding toward them. This warrior was leaner and less bulky than the others he'd viewed earlier. His silhouette revealed little about his features, but as he drew closer and the light from the fire struck his face, Giric's jaw slacked. *Her* long blonde braids swung around her body as she embedded her axe into the table with a loud crack then straddled the bench beside him.

Gunnar leaned back, folding his arms across his chest. "Saga, is that any way to treat our guests?"

"They do not belong here," she said staring directly into Giric's eyes.

Christ's teeth, he didn't quite know what to do next. She was tall and lean and now that she was close, he could see the icy blue eyes, angular cheekbones, and full lips. He allowed his gaze to take in her furs and the way the leather straps around her body appeared to enhance an ample chest. His gaze shifted back up to the eyes now boring into his. Strength there, aye. Cunning too.

"This is my sister, Saga," Gunnar said, interrupting Giric's thoughts. "Saga, I present Giric MacDomnail and Osgar MacAlpin. They are Scots, come to make peace talks with us."

"There can be no peace," Saga said. "Not now. Not ever." Though she spoke Scot's tongue, her Norse accent was much thicker than her brother's.

"And why is that?" Giric asked.

"Because your king will never allow it. He only wishes to drive us out or breed us out like cattle."

"King Constantine wishes for peace more than anything. He has entered into talks with King Olaf of Dublin to marry his own daughter. You do not see this as a symbol of goodwill?" Her strength of conviction was intriguing.

"He offers his daughter without her consent. Is this the kind of king you support? Are you this kind of man as well? Do you come here to arrange marriages for your own benefit, ignoring the wishes of the people involved?"

"That is a conversation you must have with your chief."

Her eyes grew wide and her jaw set. Giric could not tear his away from her. She was ethereal and untamed and graceful all at once and she drew him in with her power.

"My chief will not force me to marry a man I do not want."

Giric turned to Gunnar. "You know why I am here. I have

one sister and two brothers who are unmarried. You have siblings and are also unmarried. We can make peace between our peoples if that is what you want."

"It is what I want," Gunnar said. "And it is what my sister wants too. But she makes a reasonable point. I will not force marriage upon any person under my care and that includes myself. And what about you?" he said looking at Osgar. "Are you willing to attach yourself to one of ours, possibly sacrificing your own happiness in the process?"

Giric glanced at Saga who still glared at him. It almost made him grin. He wanted to know her better, of that he was certain. He turned to Osgar awaiting his reply. The man was always careful in his approach to any problem, though he knew none braver. Osgar would run through the fiery pits of hell to protect those he loved, but he was careful and calculated in his approach.

"I believe that we must find a way to cohabit. Your people claimed these lands as their own at a time when others lived here. I remember my grandfather telling me stories of the Gaels who escaped the slaughter. You know this to be true. You sit on land that was taken versus earned and you have no intention of leaving it," Osgar said.

Gunnar sat forward, "If your intent is to insult me, Osgar MacAlpin, you are approaching that line."

"It is not an insult to state fact," Giric said. "You asked us to speak plainly and that is what we intend to do. We will get nowhere if we mince words."

"While I would wish to like the woman I marry, I agree with Giric entirely. If we are to live in peace, we must come to some understanding," Osgar said.

Gunnar turned back to Giric. "And you believe these marriages create the path toward peace?"

"Aye, I do. It has brought success on the Isle of Lewis."

"And the king is so confident, he would offer his own

flesh and blood for this peace. And what of your reasons, MacDomnail? Why do you risk yours and the lives of your men for such a treaty?" Gunnar asked. "Am I to assume you are so concerned with humanity to offer your own flesh and blood? Or do you curry favour from your king?"

And there it was. The real reason Giric had, in fact, risked life and limb to cross angry waters and face such an enemy. The truth of it was his sister's reaction to the last time Gunnar's clansmen had landed on their shores. She'd been terrified for weeks and fixated on every possible knowledge she could gain about their way of life. At first Giric thought it was to help him plan a retaliatory attack. He later learned 'twas peace she envisioned all along. She was a deep thinker and over time made Giric see the value in such an undertaking. The king's efforts with Olaf of Dublin merely sealed her argument.

"It may not work in every case, but I believe it is worth the time we take to explore the option," Giric said. "The longer we remain divided, the more likely our relationship will end in bloodshed—as it always has."

"And why did you not list yourself among those seeking a marriage? Do you have a wife already or is this drink not to your taste?" Gunnar asked him.

"My wife did not survive our first year of marriage."

Saga grunted beside him. She would be thinking he had harmed her, and his tolerance would only go so far on that subject.

"She contracted the red fever and was sick for many weeks before succumbing to her illness." The year since her death had been a lonely one.

"I am sorry for your loss," Gunnar said. "But are you willing to enter into a contract yourself to forge this peace?"

Giric drew a deep breath. "Aye, I am. This is too important."

Giric had lost much over the years to the Viking raiders, cattle, farms, and men who had been in the wrong place at the wrong time. Their efforts here would change the face of Scotland for the better. If Giric could look past all the damage done to find a viable path forward, he prayed Gunnar could too.

"We have not raided your shores for two summers or more."

"Nay, but you live on an island with limited resources. I have heard there is another settlement on the other side of the island. How long before your own supplies are depleted because of overpopulation here forcing you to resettle again?"

Gunnar's brows shot up.

"Aye, I know why your people left the North. 'Tis no secret. And I am saying, if you want to stay here, let us join together and forge a peaceful way to do that."

"Do not listen to him, Gunnar," Saga said. "He will poison your mind with his lies."

"Your brother has already said he will not force anyone under his care into a marriage they do not want," Giric said to her. She seemed to be protesting now for the sake of it. "Why do you really not want to see this happen?"

"Because we do not need your marriages and your God sullying our way of life. We are strong and if we need something we take it. You Scots are weak and want to talk and talk." She waved her hand as if to swat away an irritating insect.

"And when you do reach our shores again to take what you need, as you put it, you will be met with an army who will slaughter you. Is that what you want? Would you really prefer to die than find a peaceful way to coexist?"

She smiled without mirth. "Valhalla awaits." With that she

stood and withdrew her axe from the table. She crossed the hall in only a few strides.

Before she left the hall, she looked over her shoulder one last time locking gazes with Giric. There was a disconnect in her words and her expression. He was sure there was a more complex reason for her opposition. And some part of him could not wait to find out what it was.

When he turned back to Gunnar, the man was holding out a horn.

"Drink. I believe you will find Saga among a certain element of our people. However, she does not represent everyone and so I say we toast to a new friendship forged here today. Skol!"

Giric didn't know what Skol meant, but assumed it meant something close to their own good health salute, Slainte Mhath and so he repeated the sentiment. Downing the cool beverage, he could not help but cringe a little at its bitterness. If nothing else, he could teach these Vikings how to make better ale.

CHAPTER TWO

Saga Haraldson slammed the door to her brother's hall as hard as she could. Damned men! They were always up to some scheme. This latest was the most ridiculous she'd ever heard fall from Gunnar's lips. Marry a Scot? Was he out of his mind? She'd been convinced the message Bjorn had brought from the mainland had been a terrible jest. It wasn't unlike something he'd make up, but she would have no such luck. Bjorn had not been jesting and the Scots had landed.

Well Gunnar could do what he pleased, but neither she, nor her sister Vigdis would be forced to marry anyone, much less a Scot. They imagined themselves so much better than everyone else, with their Christian God and their overly decorated clothes. This one she'd just met had been adorned from head to foot in a crimson cape with some sort of gold stitched trim. When he turned, she could make out the leather tunic he wore underneath which spread across his broad chest. She'd sat close enough to note his thick, shoulder-length dark hair and eyes so deep they appeared almost black. And why did he have to smell so good? It was some combination of leather and fresh air that threatened to draw her in, but she would be resolute. Bulging chest and arms be damned. It was true, she admired strength in men, but that was as far as she was willing to go with this man. What he suggested would be advantageous to no one except him.

"Good morning, sister. Saga, does something trouble you?" her sister, Vigdis asked.

Younger by two summers, she was petite and delicate where Saga was tall and strong. Delicate features she may have, the young woman had strength of will if not of hand.

"The Scots have come after all."

"They are here?" Vigdis asked with wide eyes.

If anything, it made her look even more innocent. What would a man whose mind was twisted with political greed do with such a maiden? Saga was not prepared to find out.

"They are and it appears our brother thinks it is a good idea to ply them with our ale and food and negotiate with them."

Vigdis lowered her head and wrung her hands.

"You need not worry, little sister. You will not leave this island unless it is your wish."

"I wish I had your strength, Saga," she said. "But you are the shield-maiden, not I. You must fight against this tyranny."

"I will," she said. "If our brother insists, we shall take a vessel and leave this place."

"And go where?" Vigdis asked with a grin.

This was a game they had played since they were young maidens.

"We shall sail off to live with the gods."

"And how shall we get there?"

"We shall take the Bifrost out of Midgard and cross the rainbow bridge into Asgard."

"And what shall we do once we are there?" Vigdis asked.

"We shall ask Heimdall to send these Scots to Jotunheim," Saga said with a grin.

Vigdis gasped and laughed. "That's a terrible thing to say, even for you!"

"Perhaps some time in a completely untamed land is what they need."

"Perhaps, but I will not have it on my conscience," Vigdis said. "Now, will you help me call the cattle home?"

"But you know they never come for me. For my voice is not as sweet as yours and they know I am not as patient."

"That's because you do not give them time to come before you call them again."

No doubt she was right. Saga followed Vigdis up the path away from the sea and toward the fields where the cattle grazed. The land here was so rich and if it were not for the new settlers on the other side of the island, there would never be a need for them to leave. She was sure they could survive and thrive here, but not with several hundred new inhabitants wanting to work the same land and threatening to go to battle to settle the dispute. It appeared they had enemies on all sides at the moment.

Saga stopped by the fencing enclosure and waited for Vigdis to begin her kulning song. The air was sweet with the scent of late summer wildflowers. The rainfall from earlier and heat from the sun created the perfect recipe for all this beautiful island's growth to display its bouquet. She drank in the fragrance, willing it to help her forget the madness happening at the hall. Saga opened her eyes and turned toward her sister.

"Well, shouldn't you get started?" Saga asked.

"No. Not today. I want to hear you sing today."

"But they don't come for me," she said.

"Just try it today. Please?"

Taking a deep breath, she said "Very well. I will try it, but I'm telling you, it won't work."

Saga squared her shoulders and stood straight.

"Close your eyes and see where they are; then call them. They will come if you imagine them walking toward you. They will feel the energy in your voice and follow it. Let your voice connect with the cattle."

Saga put her hands on either side of her mouth and closed her eyes. She envisioned the cattle grazing on the other side of the hills and let out the first high pitched notes of her call. It was always the same and one their grandmother had taught them. The cattle had heard the same call their entire lives and so knew it was the one to follow home. Saga understood this, but what she didn't understand was how her voice seemed to flow out of her now with little effort.

As she visualized the animals, the song drifted across the field; high notes and long low ones all blending in a special come home message only they could understand. Her grandmother had proved the effect one summer when she tried their call on another's cattle who didn't even look up.

She continued to sing and heard the faint clang of an animal's bell.

"Saga, open your eyes."

Singing a particularly high note, she opened her eyes. Several cows crested the hill and were running toward her. Tears welled in her eyes as she watched them approach and she could not help but laugh while still singing her cattle song.

"You're doing it! Saga, your voice is so clear and strong. They love it!"

Great pride welled up inside her. She had never been able to do this before. What had changed to bring about the effect she could not say, but she was thrilled with the result.

She only finished singing when the last of the cattle joined the herd. Three or four of them nuzzled her hand.

"I did not know you possessed this talent, Sister," Gunnar said from behind her.

Startled, she turned around to see him and the two Scots standing a few paces away. The tall one, Giric, watched her with a curious expression, his dark eyes piercing her. She frowned at them and moved away to secure the fencing to keep the animals safe until the morrow.

"Will you join us for the evening meal?" a male voice said from behind her.

When she turned, he was right there staring down at her. Damned man was a few inches taller than her so she could not even use her own height to intimidate him. She stepped back a pace which prompted a grin from him.

"I always dine in the hall with my brother and today will be no exception," she said, not trying to sound like a spoiled child, but she did not want to stand near him or dine with him.

"I shall reserve a space for you," he said and turned back to Gunnar.

After the men walked back to the path leading to the hall, Vigdis wrapped her arms around Saga's waist.

"He unsettles you," she said.

"I do not like what he stands for," Saga said.

"Are you certain that's it?"

"What do you mean?"

"Ja, he's a Scot, but he is tall and muscular and rather handsome, don't you think? All that dark hair and those intense eyes. He could not take them off you, Saga."

She didn't know what to think when it came to Giric MacDomnail. And she did not wish to entertain his physical attributes.

"I do not care if he is the handsomest man in all of Alba

and the world. I want nothing to do with him and his politics."

"Are you certain you want to be so restrictive in your choice of mate, Saga?"

"Of course I want to be restrictive. Don't you?"

"I do, but I will not dismiss a man without really knowing him."

"I do not need to know him. I know his kind. He thinks he can come here and convince my brother that this kind of change will be good for us, but he is wrong. If we are to preserve our way of life, we need to keep men like him out. I will talk to our brother and make him see reason."

"And what reason is that? Pack up everything we have here and move to Iceland? Is that your plan? Because if so, I will not be a part of it. We can live here in peace. While I am not convinced this plot is the proper solution, I am prepared to hear it through," Vigdis said.

Saga took a deep breath. Vigdis made sense, but it didn't feel like the best solution.

"Maybe if you knew more about these men and their way of life," Vigdis said. "Will you at least listen to what they have to say?"

Her sister always had a way of convincing her to do things to which she was first opposed. Was there any harm in listening to them?

~

To say Giric was impressed was an understatement. Gunnar had not only invited him and Osgar to stay for the evening, he also invited his men to join them and feast at his table. That would begin at sunset, a couple hours from now. Being the onset of the harvest celebration, they were already prepared to feast for the next three days. Now they walked slowly back toward the hall and Giric's interest in the way these people lived was piqued.

"We are well protected here, and we are well stocked," Gunnar said.

"You're wondering how you may gain if you enter into an arrangement with me."

"Ja, that has crossed my mind."

"The other settlement here, are they friend or foe?"

"You already know the answer to that," Gunnar said as they reached the entrance to the hall.

"And what will happen when they discover the lands on this side of the island are richer?"

"They already know that."

"They've been here?" Giric asked.

"They have."

Giric had only known this man for a few hours, but already sensed a common understanding with him. He was worried. For all his burly, invincible outward appearance, the man had insecurities—as any good leader would.

"Are you well defended?"

Gunnar's eyes narrowed. "Do I trust you enough yet, Giric MacDomnail, to show you how well defended we are?"

Gunnar changed direction and walked ahead along a well beaten path to a round stone structure with a grass roof. It was similar to other structures he'd seen but the difference was this one had no windows. Smoke billowed from the top and a clanging sound welled up from within. The smell of burning peat met him as he entered the structure. From the dim light afforded by the wall torches, Giric could make out a thickly statured man hammering away at something on an anvil. A fire burned hot on the ground near him while a young man alternated pumping bellows in the corner of the room to keep the fire burning hot.

"This is Ragnar. He is the finest blacksmith in," Gunnar turned to Giric with a smile, "well, anywhere."

Ragnar ceased his hammering and mopped his brow with his sleeve leaving a black mark in its wake. He took a deep breath and placed both his fists on the anvil. The younger man in the corner ceased his efforts as well and sat back.

"The task is nearly complete," he said to Gunnar.

"That is good news, Ragnar. This is Giric who is a Scot. He wishes to forge an alliance with us."

Ragnar grinned, the play on words clearly not lost on him. "Does he now? And what does he offer for this alliance?"

"He offers peace," Giric said. "It is clear to me you are self sufficient here. In truth I am quite in awe of your feats of structural design between your dwellings and your ships." As he said this, he noticed the hole in the roof of the forge and a small window behind Ragnar. With the window slightly open, the smoke naturally drew up. Clever. "But there are others who want this land."

Giric could not help but notice the irony in the fact that Gunnar's clan was under potential threat from their own kind, not those whom they had presumed to conquer.

"Ragnar, show our guest what you have been working on," Gunnar said.

Ragnar nodded and tended to his fire before leaving the forge. Giric and Gunnar followed him around the back to another stone dwelling with a grass roof, but this one was rectangular in shape and larger.

As they entered, Ragnar flicked something and lit a torch, then another, and another. The illumination revealed what Giric estimated to be several dozen broadswords, axes, crossbows, and hundreds of metal-tipped arrows. Round wooden shields of all colours with various spikes or rounded metal bosses at the centre were stacked in the far corner.

Gunnar crossed his arms over his chest and raised one eyebrow. "I will ask you again, Giric, with full respect. What do I gain from an alliance with you?"

At that moment, Osgar, who had been seeing to the men, entered the armoury. "You had better take some of those," he said pointing to the swords. "We have company and your sisters do not look too happy about them."

"Who?" Gunnar asked.

"He introduced himself as Earl Einar."

Ragnar laughed. "Einar Long-Leg? He's no threat."

"Take a sword, each of you," Gunnar said. "He may not be a threat on his own, but he has managed to ally with those who are. If he is here, others are close."

"Who is this Earl?" Giric asked.

"He was awarded the title and has failed to find the resilience and dedication to turn his barren lands into a lucrative homestead. Instead, he flaunts the title and lives off the forced generosity of others."

Giric grabbed a broadsword. It was heavier than those he wielded, but the balance was such that the weight was not a burden. Once again, he was surprised and impressed with the skill and thought that had gone into something they crafted. Barbarians indeed. They hid their intellect well, these beasts.

$\mathcal{E}$ inar Long-Leg sidled up to Vigdis. He was the worst sort of slithering slime to have ever been spawned from Loki. With one leg slightly longer than the other, his gait was off just enough that he leaned a little forward and to the left. When Vigdis cringed, Saga clenched her fists and stepped in between them. Earl or not, he would not lay a finger on her.

"Saga. The great Harldson Shield-Maiden. Do you want some attention too? I thought your features were too manly from afar. I see, now that we are in such proximity, you are attractive as well. Not as much as your sister, but still pleasant enough to bed. Come, let us find a quiet corner."

At that point something inside Saga snapped. How many times had a man grabbed her bottom or her breasts or assumed she wanted anything to do with them just because they had shown her attention? Too many. She was having none of this man.

"I would rather sleep with the dogs than allow one of your spiny fingers to touch me."

One greasy black eyebrow shot up then his eyes

narrowed. The earl grabbed her by the throat and tried to shove her backward, but Saga had already planted her feet solid, anticipating such a move.

Her height had always served her well in battle. Though this man was stronger than she, he would not overtake her easily.

"Release her," Bjorn said, crossing the hall in long strides.

Einar turned his head at the sound of Bjorn's voice. Clasping her hands together, she used the moment of distraction and swung hard, striking his head with as much force as she could. When he released her throat, she grabbed his shoulders and slammed her head into his then let him go which landed him backward on his arse. She'd have a nasty ache in her head for a day, but it was worth it to see this man put in his place at her feet.

Bjorn stopped short of them and grinned. He smiled showing all his teeth and waggled his eyebrows at her the same way he always did when she'd bested some man. Sweet as he was, she was not interested in his attention either.

"I love you, Shield-Maiden," Bjorn said, in the same doe-eyed way he'd said it for the past several years.

How old had they been the first time he'd professed his love? Six? Seven summers? In any case, he always had a way of disarming her outrage.

A moment later the earl was on his feet and bounding toward her. "I will have you yet, Shield-Maiden, and you will beg for my attention."

"You may try, Ergi, but you do not have the equipment to succeed."

Bjorn stepped between them as the earl's face grew wide with shock and Saga was about to clobber him on the head again. While it was true, to call someone Ergi was a gross insult insinuating effeminate ways, but Saga did not care. She would rather dine with the pigs.

"You will answer for your crimes, Shield-Maiden. I outrank you and your brother, and I will have satisfaction for the wound you have given me and my honour."

"What passes here?" Gunnar asked from the doorway.

Saga grabbed Vigdis's hand and met him by the hearth. "This man laid hands on our sister and attempted to lay hands on me. The bruises on my throat will prove my words and Bjorn can speak to it as well."

"She insulted me!" Einar said as he scrambled to his feet.

"I will do more than that if you ever come near me or my sister again!"

Saga struggled to contain the fury enveloping her. Blood pounded in her ears and her whole body tingled. Vigdis winced and only then did Saga realize she'd been squeezing her delicate hand so tight. She released her hand and pushed her behind and out of the Earl's sight. Saga pulled a dagger from her belt and twirled it to taunt the earl. Her blood was up and she was itching for a fight. Whether the source was the arrival of the Scots, the arrogance of the earl, or the assumption she'd let any of them have their way—she was ready to go.

Gunnar put his hands up. "Saga, take your sister and go to the healer. You have blood all over your face and I want to make certain you are not damaged."

"The blood is his, not mine." As she said this, she noted the slight curve on Giric's mouth. He stood behind Gunnar looking at her not with love as Bjorn had, not with lust, as the Earl had, but something else; something akin to admiration. That was an expression she had not anticipated. She was not in the mood for that either.

"Are you harmed?" Giric asked her quietly as Gunnar walked past her and toward the earl.

"I am well and will be much better when that man is removed from here."

"Your brother will see it done and if he does not, I will." He smiled at her, in a soft, gentle way that made the lines in his face deepen. "I give you my word," he said as he placed his hand on the arm holding her dagger and pushed downward.

She worked to control her breathing. Her hand was still curled tightly around her dagger and the pressure where his hand touched her arm felt good, somehow helping to quell the fire raging in her body.

"Earl Einar, you have insulted my sisters and so have insulted me," Gunnar said. "You are no longer welcome here."

"I came in peace, and I was insulted and attacked. You will treat me with the respect my title demands, else I will strip you of your lands and take it for myself. Everyone will know your shame."

Saga made to lift her dagger, but Giric's hand still held her arm down. He shook his head, locking gazes with her. So much unspoken understanding rested there. If she harmed the earl, regardless of the provocation, she would be punished, perhaps even banished, which was worse than death.

She relaxed a little and only then did Giric remove his hand. Sheathing her dagger, she focused all her thoughts on controlling her breath and not letting the dishonourable wretch before her gain any hold over her.

"And will you really go away and tell everyone you were bested by a woman?" Gunnar asked with a smirk.

Saga was not insulted by the remark. Coming from her brother who regularly praised her, the comment was meant to antagonize the earl rather than demean her ability.

"Not any woman. Her reputation is well known." Einar pointed a crooked finger in her direction.

"But a woman, nonetheless," Gunnar said and crossed his arms over his chest.

When Saga made to insert herself back into the conversation and prove how much of a warrior she really was, Giric placed his hand on her shoulder and shook his head. Its weight was a surprising comfort.

She turned her attention to the earl. His eyes glinted with delight. He appeared to be very much aware of how to evoke her anger. As much as she didn't want to admit it, the Scot's approach would likely irritate him more. Saga drew in a deep breath and let it out slowly.

Saga swallowed the lump that had lodged in her throat and turned back to Giric. "Thank you," she said to Giric, quietly. Then to Vigdis she said, "Come, let us leave the plotting and scheming to the men." She tried to make her voice sound flat.

It was then she noticed Vigdis had found her way closer to the Scot's friend. He had further shielded her from the violence of the scene. Perhaps there was something honourable in these men after all. Either that or they were used to underestimating their women—perhaps both.

"Come, Vigdis."

Saga took her sister's hand and made a wide berth around the earl. When they were outside the hall, Saga touched her head discovering something sticky. She examined her fingers and couldn't help but grin despite the pain that had begun at the base of her neck. It was not yet bad, but as in the past, once it crept from her neck to her head, she'd be in for a rough few hours. She would go to Freydis. The woman was bound to have some helpful concoction.

"You frighten me sometimes, sister."

"I frighten myself sometimes," Saga said with a small laugh that made her aware of the blood pulsing in her head.

It was true, sometimes her anger was such that she would lash out. She didn't try to be so physical, but when she saw someone or something threatened, especially if the balance of power was off, she acted without consequential thought.

"I fear one of these days your temper will get you into a heap of trouble."

"Would you have preferred I let the earl paw at you? Really, Vigdis, I understand what you are saying, but at what point would you want me to intervene?"

Vigdis sighed. "I do not know the answer, Saga. I wish we did not have to endure such behaviour."

"That will never change and so we must be strong and correct them when they overstep."

Saga would never stop believing this. While some men like Bjorn were harmless, there were far too many Einar's out there who took what they wanted.

"I know you are right, but I could never do what you did back there. You knocked that man clean onto his *rumpa*," Vigdis said. She shook her head as if she didn't believe what her own eyes had witnessed.

The thought made Saga grin. She had done that. "Ja and did you see the look on his face? It is worth the ache I suffer to see the look of surprise on him."

Freydis was waiting in the doorway as they arrived at her hut. "It's about time you arrived."

"How did you know we were coming?" Vigdis asked.

"I know everything that happens in this village, sweet one," she said, waving her hand in the air. "Don't you know that by now?" she said with a smirk.

"You mean you have spies everywhere," Saga said with a grin.

They stepped inside the hut. A warm, earthy scent enveloped her as it always did there. A fire slowly burned in the hearth and a pot of something bubbling beckoned Saga. Freydis' hut was a welcoming and fascinating place, filled with clay pots of various sizes containing who knew what. Saga reached for a spoon to sample some of the pot's irresistible contents. Freydis swatted her hand away and drew her to a stool instead. She brought a candle close to Saga's head and examined her without touching.

"I do not need to reveal my ways to you, Shield-Maiden," she said in a distracted tone. "I see you are wounded again. What was it this time? A man looked at you the wrong way?"

Vigdis chortled and caught herself.

Freydis glanced between them both. "Oh, I see. Someone looked at Vigdis the wrong way. Should I go see to him first?"

Saga grinned. "If you treat him, I will never bring your sweets again."

Not one for that kind of thing, Saga always kept squares of honeycomb to bring to Freydis who could not seem to get enough of them.

"I consider that a fair deal. Let the man fester and rot for all I care," Freydis said. "Now let me see that head of yours," she said as she placed the candle on the table nearby and pushed away some hair. "I do not see a cut. Is this not your blood?"

"Nay, it is his."

Freydis leaned close to Saga's face. "Remind me to never get on your bad side." She stood and poked around a little more. "I see nothing but the start of a bruise and a welt. I will give you something to ease your head."

"Thank you," Saga said as Freydis moved away to pull some containers of various items down from a shelf.

"Something troubles you, Saga," Freydis said. How the woman knew her mind had always amazed her.

"We have had visitors. Scots," Vigdis said. "Our brother is talking of arranged marriages and my sister is opposed."

"I imagine she is," Freydis said. "And I cannot say I blame her. The Scots are not like us. They feel they are superior to us and want to change our way of life to mirror theirs."

"That's what I've been saying," Saga said. It was nice to have someone on her side at least.

"Even if their added armies could keep our own foes at bay?" Vigdis asked.

"Since when did you become a strategist?" Saga asked.

"I am not," she said. "But I am a good listener. Most people ignore me and say what they want around me. I pay attention."

Saga gave her a sidelong glance and grinned. "You and I have always made a good team. Now I know why."

Before long, Freydis handed Saga a steaming cup. "Drink it and then lie down. You will sleep for a couple of hours. Vigdis and I will sit with you."

Saga hated these concoctions, but accepted the necessity. She drank the fluid and lay back. Its effect was almost immediate. The room spun for a few seconds and her eyes fluttered shut.

~

Giric took a seat and waited to see how Gunnar would handle the earl. He had seen nobles throw a man out on his ear for far less than the threat he posed to the women. So why had that not yet occurred?

"You will leave my sisters alone, or I will end this arrangement here and now," Gunnar said.

"Why should I not make an offer to them? I am more than your equal and can provide quite well for either of them."

"But they do not like you, Einar. I do not like you." Gunnar's tone was not that of a furious chieftain protecting his people, rather soft as if the earl needed the words delivered slowly in order to understand them.

"You do business with me, but you do not like me?"

"That is correct. Now, tell me your news and be gone."

"But it is late. Will you not offer me a bed?"

"I would have," Gunnar said. "But I do not trust that you will stay in it."

"Please, Gunnar. The hour is late, and I will behave, I promise," Einar said.

"Very well, you will sleep with Bjorn. He can watch you to be sure you stay put."

Bjorn grunted but did not say anything. His loyalty even under such undesirable circumstances was solid.

"You expect me to sleep with a man after the insult your sister gave me?"

"I do not care about the insult she gave you. The way I see it, you are lucky I do not let Saga finish you off. Now tell me why you are here."

"Very well, I will share my news."

The earl shook his head and sat on a nearby bench, clearly having no choice but to concede defeat. Giric found it interesting that at any point, Gunnar could have used brute force, but he crushed this man with words instead. And the effect appeared much more fruitful.

"Snorri Short-Beard plans to claim your lands."

"I know that, but how and when?" Gunnar asked. "He does not have the numbers to win a challenge against me in that way."

"He does now," Einar said with far too much satisfaction.

"How?"

"He says he has King Olaf's support and with that, extra men."

"That's not possible," Gunnar said. "King Harald granted these lands to me after my father passed. Short-Beard knows this and he has no valid reason to plot against me. And how could he possibly secure King Olaf's support when the man is in talks with the Scot's king to marry the man's daughter? Olaf has no cause to work against me."

Giric's ears perked up. What Einar suggested made no sense.

"No reason except his own greed."

"Olaf will not act against King Harald's word. I do not believe you, Einar."

"That is your problem. But he does have more men coming ashore all the time. He is amassing the numbers and told me they were from Olaf of Dublin."

"But why involve him?"

"To make you feel outnumbered, I expect. That and surrounded with no allies," Giric said. It now started to make some sense. "If you thought Olaf supported Short-Beard's claim to these lands, where would you go for support?" Giric was not about to answer the question and give Einar more knowledge than Gunnar wanted. He hoped this would be the defining moment in their relationship. Short-Beard's plot, whether true or not, helped to solidify Giric's proposal.

Gunnar sat back and stroked his beard. "I miss the days when enemies came at me head on."

"Those days are long gone, which is why you need me, Gunnar," Einar said.

At that point, Gunnar stood and grasped the earl by the furs at his neck. "Our arrangement ends now. You may stay here tonight as stated before, but come sun up, I want you gone and I do not want to see you again."

"But I have been loyal."

"And you are spying on me as well as him. This ends now. You may leave of your own accord unscathed, or you will die by my blade."

The shift in Gunnar was abrupt and lethal. What had been a light jesting tone, now turned to something deadly serious and Giric wondered if he was seeing the true Gunnar Haraldson for the first time.

The earl left the hall without further contest with Bjorn at his heels.

"Tell me you have an army, and we are in business."

"Between the both of us," Giric said pointing at Osgar, "we can amass about eight hundred men. That does not include any the king might offer if we have him on-side, which I think can happen. And if the king and Olaf have struck an understanding through a marriage, then you don't need to worry about Dublin, but you will need to find out where Short-Beard's extra men are coming from."

Gunnar nodded then spread his arms toward the table that had been placed in front of his chair. Three additional chairs were placed on either side.

"You will be my honoured guests at our feast tonight. Come join me in a horn of ale. The food will not disappoint."

Giric nodded and turned to Osgar. "How fare the men?"

"They are well. They were surprised to be invited to the chief's table tonight."

"And you?" he asked quietly. "Are you surprised by such hospitality?"

"Aye, Giric. You know I am. I look forward to sharing our thoughts on what we've learned here."

"You are reading my mind, my friend."

"You two can stop whispering and share your thoughts with me," Gunnar said. "I have excellent hearing, you know."

"I think there is much about you I have yet to learn," Giric said.

"And what is your assessment thus far?"

Giric paused for a moment. What was his assessment? The man was a warrior, but kept his temper in check. He was uncomplicated, yet quite intelligent. A contrast at every turn.

"Someone with whom we could grow an alliance," Osgar said. "I have taken in much around your village this day and my impression grew tenfold at every turn. Most importantly, your people are loyal to you. That says much about the kind of man leading this place."

Gunnar nodded then poured two horns and passed one to each of them.

"I was born in this place," he said. "In that chamber behind us."

Giric looked closer at the wall separating the chamber from the main hall. Two long swords criss-crossed behind an enormous shield clearly meant for display versus use in battle. The background was painted black and white in perfect balance, a red serpent weaved its way around the centre, but then protruded in metal form from the centre boss.

"You like the shield," Gunnar said.

"Aye, I do. It reminds me of a story my grandfather once told me about how the serpent Beithir spread his evil, terrorizing coastal villages at night; only lightning reveals his true nature. This shield brings me back to a time when I believed in serpents and dragons."

"And now that you are a man you do not permit yourself to believe in magical creatures?" Gunnar asked with brows raised.

"You do?"

"Of course. What kind of world would it be without magic? We too have a legend. The shield represents Jormungander, the Midgard serpent and nemesis of the mighty Thor. Both our legends are a reminder of the constant battle between good and evil. The trick is to know how to reveal the evil."

Giric shook his head and downed his bitter ale, unable to hide the wince.

Gunnar laughed again. "Our ale is too strong for you," he said with a proud look upon his face.

"Strong ale can be tempered with the right sort of accompaniment," Giric said, understanding that every word spoken now had a double meaning.

"That is true so let us speak plainly. You have men and I need them. I will agree to anything you want, save forcing any woman or man under my care to marry if it is not their desire."

"I agree with that wholeheartedly," Giric said. "The women in our families have dowries consisting of money and land."

"You did not say anything about land earlier. Why not?"

"Because I wanted to sort out the kind of people I was dealing with before putting that on the table, so to speak."

Gunnar crossed his arms over his chest and grinned. "You're going to want my sister, aren't you?"

"I am not opposed to it," Giric said, though the thought had crossed his mind. There was much about this shield-maiden that intrigued him. He had to admit, he wanted to know her better before committing to any woman. His heart had known the twilight of love before and a part of him would always miss Aileen. When he'd arrived here, he was more interested in the business side of a marriage contract for mutual purposes. Perhaps he should explore the personal side as well.

CHAPTER FOUR

When Saga woke the pain in her head had completely subsided. She sat up and tried to stand, but kept going, landing on her elbows on the floor of Freydis' hut.

"Careful, now. You will be groggy for a bit, but you needed that much tincture to stop your head from pounding for days. And what a strong one you are. You have a welt, but no bruise on that pretty head of yours. Nothing a nice wreath of flowers won't hide."

Saga sat back on the bed and held her head in her hands. The room spun quickly at first but eventually slowed. Then something Freydis said clicked in her mind.

"Why do I need a wreath of flowers to hide my welt?"

"Your brother sent word that you and your sister are to dress properly for the feast tonight." Saga's belly coiled at the thought. She'd never been comfortable in a gown and much preferred the leather trews the tanner had made for her like the ones her brother, Magnus, wore.

"Come now. I brushed your hair whilst you slept, and it is almost dry. Come and sit by the fire while I braid it for you."

"Where is Vigdis?"

"She is gone to find a dress for you both. Though she was unsure when you last wore one and so went to fetch the weaver too."

"This seems like an awful lot of fuss. I should wear what I have on now."

"Really?" Freydis asked, prompting Saga to look down.

Instead of her leather trews and fur tunic, she now wore a delicate sleeveless shift made of the finest linen. It was sheer and soft against her skin which was not unpleasant, however quite different from the woollen ones she normally wore to bed.

Saga sat quietly while Freydis worked on her hair, braiding it away from her face. From time to time the woman would compliment her powerful body and beauty and wondered why she insisted on keeping it hidden beneath man-like furs and shaggy hair.

"I found the perfect gown for you," Vigdis said from the doorway a short time later. She stopped in her tracks when she saw Saga. "You are a vision, sister. I wish you could see yourself as I see you now with your hair in neat braids."

Saga was not used to such talk. Their mother had always spent more time fussing over Vigdis, so much that it had turned her from spending so much time on her appearance. She would much rather learn how to properly shoot a crossbow than how to plait her hair.

"Show me the gown," she said.

"Here. It was our mother's. I had forgotten about it until now. You and she were close in height."

Saga took the blue sleeveless gown and tugged it over her head. She had to admit, she liked the way the garment fell to the floor at the perfect length, something that had always seemed like a problem. Vigdis produced two heavy golden brooch pins containing sapphires that glinted in the light to pin the shoulder straps. With a couple more tugs and a few pokes and prods, the woman stood back from her and smiled.

"Where have you been hiding those breasts?" Freydis asked.

Saga looked down to see her bosom spilling from the gown, revealing her deep cleavage. "There is no way I am entering the hall like this," she said, tugging at the shift to cover herself.

"Stop that," Freydis said, swatting her hands away. "You don't need to cover it all. Just a little. There's nothing wrong with showing off your assets, Saga. Think of it as one more weapon you have to keep a man distracted while you bring him to his knees."

Was that what everyone thought of her? How wrong they were. She did not want to best men, she wanted to be treated with respect.

The whole thought of entering the hall and all eyes falling to her made her head ache again. She did not object when Vigdis and Freydis placed golden arm bands on her upper arms, though they had to stretch them a couple of times to get them to fit properly. They placed earrings in her ears and a small wreath of hawthorn on her head.

"There. You are perfect," Vigdis said.

"It is you who is the perfect visage, sister," Saga said. "I feel ridiculous in this kind of clothing," she said and made to grab her trews, but Freydis was too quick.

"Nay! You may have these back on the morrow with a full report of every conversation you had with those attending this evening."

"Do not worry," Vigdis said. "There is only one man who will be able to keep her attention tonight."

"Who?" Saga and Freydis both asked at the same time.

"A certain Scot who has not been able to tear his eyes from you all day," she said.

"Ridiculous," Saga said, scoffing at them both. That man was a schemer, and she wanted no part of him or his political aspirations. She shook off the image of him standing close to her with his strong hand on her shoulder.

"Is he attractive, Vigdis?" Freydis asked her.

"Ja, he is tall and very muscular. He has dark hair and even darker eyes. He looks at her like she is something delicious to eat," Vigdis said and laughed.

"That is not true. The man and his friend have come here to arrange marriages. For all we know, they are poor men looking to take our lands."

"You know that is not true. They are rich Scots who want to marry us and marry their sisters to our men to make peace."

"They want to take us away from here," Saga said. "I will not leave. I do not care how the man looks at me. He will lose his bollocks if he tries to take me from my home."

The more she thought about it, the more furious she became.

Vigdis took her hand and held on tight. "No one is taking anyone anywhere against their will. We have Gunnar's word on that. I was only jesting with you. Please can we go to the feast now? I am hungry and wish to talk more with your Scot's friend, MacAlpin. He is a kind man and said he would tell me all about the great city of Edinburgh and the markets there. He says there are fabrics there of all colours."

Saga had underestimated her sister once again. Instead of looking for someone to love her, she had been looking to learn more about the world and there was surely nothing wrong with that.

"I am sorry for getting upset, sister. Thank you both for

helping me prepare for this evening. Come, let us make our way to the hall and hear all about this Edinburgh. Maybe they have new weapons there as well and I can visit you?"

Vigdis laughed. "He does not live there, merely visits. He lives in a castle, though not as large as Giric's, but he says the weavery where they make the tapestries is quite large and employs many weavers. I am quite fascinated with their commerce."

Saga wondered if she had not bumped her head harder than she first thought. She now wore a gown, and her sister was talking Scottish commerce. Perhaps she was still dreaming, and the effects of Freydis' concoction had not yet worn off. Or perhaps she was about to experience an entirely new world.

They thanked Freydis and made their way to the great hall. The smell of roasting wild boar made Saga's belly rumble its approval. The din emanating from the hall told her it was already full of people. She drew a deep breath as Vigdis squeezed her hand.

"You have nothing to worry about, sister. Tonight shall be wonderful."

Saga nodded and entered the hall with her sister. Within seconds the room fell silent, and all heads turned their way. Gunnar's jaw dropped which made Saga want to turn the other way and find some place to hide.

She scanned the tables, and it wasn't until she had thoroughly viewed both sides that she realized the face she was looking for was two seats away from her brother at the head table all along.

Gunnar stood and pulled out the two chairs on either side of him. Giric MacDomnail stood next to one and Osgar MacAlpin stood next to the other chair.

Saga swallowed hard and locked eyes with Giric. No one could ever accuse her of being a coward. As her sister walked toward MacAlpin, she walked toward Giric. His gaze never left hers as she approached. He was adorned in his crimson velvet fur lined cloak again, but now she could see the crest on the tunic underneath. It was that of a white serpent. She glanced at the shield behind him and back to his chest. When she met his eyes again she saw something else there for the first time. She saw true strength of mind she did not always see in other men.

~

Giric watched as she accepted the chair her brother offered. He caught her scent as she moved closer. Wild and untamed, like fresh mountain air, making him want to bury his face in her hair and nuzzle her neck. God's breath she was a sight to behold either dressed as a warrior, or as she was now. He couldn't help but stare at her as she took her seat. She glanced at him with wide eyes as though she did not know how to process the situation either.

Giric leaned in close to her. "You are the most enchanting woman I have ever met."

Her cheeks pinked which only added to her charm. "You like the cut of my gown," she said.

He wasn't sure whether the comment was in jest or not. "I like the way you walk into a room caring not for what anyone else thinks, even though you think your gown is cut too low."

Her eyes widened again. "How do you know that?"

"I didn't until just then, but I suspected it."

"You think you know me?"

"I do not know you at all. But you have an expressive face, and I am usually very good at reading people's impressions at a given moment."

"I accept your compliment, Giric MacDomnail, and offer my thanks," she said and turned her head toward the crowd.

If he'd been ensnared by her warrior's power, he was enchanted by her elegance and grace. His brain appeared to sputter to a stop when she looked at him with all the regal countenance of a queen. Would he survive an evening with her without stammering over his words like some green lad?

"Welcome honoured guests and friends," Gunnar said, momentarily breaking the spell as she turned to watch her brother address the hall.

"Tonight we celebrate the beginning of the harvest and new friends. You may not know the man sitting next to you, but I encourage you to remedy this tonight. We gather in peace. Skol!"

Servants milled about them filling goblets and horns. The boar that had been roasting on the spit was sliced into large chunks and trenchers of it were brought first to the head followed by the side tables. At his own table at Castle Domnail, he would pick the best pieces of his meat and feed it to his lady.

Was it too soon to consider making an arrangement between him and Saga? If he asked for her, he was fairly certain Gunnar would agree. Though he still knew so little about her, he had to consider that he knew more in these last few hours than he had his first wife before their marriage. That arrangement had been carved in stone by his father years earlier and had helped to secure their claim on their lands.

This time around, he was obviously more concerned with the peace these contracts secured, but the thought of something more developing from it made his heart beat a little faster. Aye, short timing or no, his heart and head were racing in a direction leading straight to Saga.

He did not know the custom here and there were no couples to observe, so he went with his gut. Breaking off a piece of juicy meat, Giric offered it to Saga. He realized his mistake when she merely looked at it and blinked.

"You wish to feed me?"

"Aye," he said. "'Tis custom for a laird to offer the best cuts to his lady." He held his breath when she glanced from the meat to him then back again.

"Do you expect me to feed you too?" she asked, her brows drawing tight.

"No, of course not," he said, pleased when her expression relaxed, and she smiled.

"Then I respect your custom, but I decline. There can be nothing more insulting than one person feeding another like an animal."

Giric received the point loud and clear. He would not try that again. Glancing down the length of the table he noticed Osgar shaking his head and grinning. Bastard.

He watched as those around him enjoyed their meal, taking in everything he could about their customs. It appeared that much like at his own table, except for the honour of offering the lady the best meat, they ate like he did, with their hands. Someone had told him that they did not formally sit at tables, rather sat around the cooked meat and pulled it off as they needed. And perhaps in some less-formal gatherings they did just that.

"Do you not like your food?" Saga asked.

He had not realized he'd stopped eating altogether. "I do enjoy it, thank you. I am interested in learning your culture and where better than at a feast where people converse freely and are enjoying themselves."

"For what purpose do you wish to know our culture?"

"I know you have your reservations, but if we are to make

these alliances work, we must understand one another. Do you not agree?"

"I wish it were not necessary," she said and gazed out over the crowd.

"Does that mean you are warming to the idea?" If she answered yes, he would consider it a major advancement. Was it possible for her to see the value in the alliance?

"I did not say that. I believe our culture will be lost if we ally with you in this way."

"Do you not see the benefits?" He held his breath.

"My sister does. She is curious about the world. I am interested in keeping it safe."

"We have the same goal, you and I."

She turned to him. He put his food down and let his breath out slowly as he hooked the ale horn in its iron stand and wiped his hands. She did not speak right away, rather her gaze fell across his features. He tried to slow his increasing pulse as she examined him, but in truth her scrutiny excited him.

"You are an attractive man," she said.

He chuckled. "Thank you."

"You must have women at your home who are good enough to marry. Why come here?"

It was a good question. He did not come looking for a wife for himself specifically, rather an arrangement that would benefit both sides and encourage peace.

"My intentions are to form a peaceful alliance to avoid further bloodshed. Is that not appealing to you? Do you not want the same thing?"

"But why does it have to come from marriage?"

"Because that way we are forced to have a better understanding of one another, and with that we can build peace."

"That could come from talks, could it not?" She shook her

head. "You do not need to answer that question. I already know that men do not talk, they take."

"Saga, may I ask you a question?"

He had to bring this up, but there really was no way to do so without offending her or her people. But she contradicted herself at every turn. She wanted to fight to protect, yet she criticized peaceful efforts to negotiate; she wanted to preserve culture, yet her people had forcefully claimed the land on which they sat at this very moment.

"You want to know how I can justify my feelings considering we are on conquered land."

He nodded. She was not offended, yet. But this was a delicate subject.

"We are a proud people, Giric of Alba," she said. "We work hard for what we have. When we came to this island, the people here were barely surviving. We built homes, halls, and farms. Those people blended into our culture and are living better now than they did before."

"But they were not given a choice," he said quietly.

She opened her mouth to speak and closed it again. Her cheeks turned red again as she turned back to the crowd.

"My intention is not to criticize your customs or culture, Saga. I am merely trying to understand and say that there may be a way that we can marry our cultures and preserve both."

"That's impossible," she said, turning back to him quickly. "If I married a Scot, I would be taken from the home I love and forced to live amongst people I do not understand, unable to live the life I choose."

"That will happen no matter who you marry. Unless you marry someone who lives in the village and how likely is that with such limited available men worthy of you?" He took a deep breath. This conversation had become more heated than he had intended. If he was going to continue to talk to her, and he wanted to, he would need to find common ground.

Saga's head was bent low. Christ's teeth he had not meant to make her feel ashamed. He could kick himself for doing so. This was all wrong—and all his fault.

"Do you like music?" he asked her, tilting his head in an attempt to make eye contact with her.

"I do not know," she said, looking up at him with a genuinely curious expression. "We tell stories for entertainment."

"Well then let us find out," he said.

"Gunnar, gracious host," Giric said over the din in the room. Conversations ceased and heads turned to him. "Would you permit me to share some music in your hall?"

"If it will make my guests happy, by all means."

Giric turned to his crewman, Lachlan, who nodded. He pulled out a long thin pipe from his tunic and stood. As he played the first few haunting notes, Giric watched the Norsemen in the room, but he was more curious about Saga's reaction.

Her wide-eyed, open-mouthed expression told him she had never heard anything like it before. As Lachlan played, he increased the tempo, playing an old tune he'd learned long ago that had been handed down from father to son from the time the original Gael's had sailed forth from Ireland. Before long, his own men clapped along and nudged the man beside him. Giric joined in and smiled as Saga turned toward him with brows raised, watching him clap a beat in time with the music Lachlan played.

"You should try it," he said to her, adoring her look of surprise at his suggestion.

"I do not know how," she said.

"Watch my hands and follow with yours," he said.

She tried and failed a few times, her frustration apparent

at every attempt. Giric placed his hands on hers and held them still. Would she let him show her how? The heat from her hands sent a jolt through him the likes of which he had never felt before. She must have felt it too for she gasped and pulled her hands back.

"Is this magic?" she asked.

"Not the kind you are thinking of, but it is a version. Let me take your hands and guide you," he said.

Saga offered her hands again. When he touched them this time, the same feeling was there, but this time it made her smile. He liked that very much.

Giric listened to the music to find the beat. He clapped both their hands together. She watched their every movement and before long he could feel her hands moving of their own accord. He slowly lifted his hands away from hers and watched her efforts improve.

"I'm doing it," she said.

"You are," he said, laughing.

Giric sat back and watched as she turned to Lachlan, concentrating on his actions with her hands clapping in time. A part of him wanted to point out that this moment proved the benefit of two cultures learning more about one another, but he would rather hear that from her tongue.

He glanced over her head to see Gunnar grinning at him. He looked down at her and winked at Giric before tilting his head back and letting out a mighty laugh.

"Stop it, brother. You're breaking my concentration," Saga said, prompting Gunnar to laugh even louder.

When the song ended, loud cheers resounded through the hall. Could that have been the turning point in some kind of acceptance between them? Could a simple tune have been the one thing to make a firm crack in the wall?

Saga turned to him with a beaming smile. "I love this music of yours. Can your man teach us to play?"

"Aye, that he can, and he would be happy to do so."

She sat back and took a deep breath. "Thank you Giric of Alba. You have given me a gift and I shall never forget it."

"You are most welcome, Shield-Maiden. Your smile is all the thanks I require."

With that her cheeks pinked again, and she turned back to Lachlan who had been convinced to play some more.

CHAPTER FIVE

*P*ulling the furs up over her head, Saga tried to block out the images of Giric flooding her mind. Though their chamber was well secured beside Gunnar's, she could still hear the festivities continuing in the hall. No doubt they would see the sun rise on the morrow. Gunnar had always been careful with them when he felt the men had gotten too full of drink to be trusted.

"You cannot ignore my question all night," Vigdis said, peering under the furs to make eye contact with her.

"I do not know what question you mean. I believe tomorrow's feast shall top tonight's. Wouldn't you agree?" Saga asked, trying desperately to change the subject.

"Since you've never taken any interest in what was served at these feasts as long as your kill was the central display, I cannot imagine you are doing anything now but trying to avoid talking about the Scots. Very well. I shall not ask again. But know this, I am interested in learning more about their culture."

"You are interested in learning more about Osgar MacAlpin," Saga said.

"Perhaps, I am. Is that such a bad thing?"

"Nay. I do not suppose it is."

Vigdis sat up and pulled the furs back from them both. "Did I hear you correctly? Are you saying you think an alliance by marriage is now acceptable?"

"I am saying he seems an honourable man and you appear interested in his world. I am not opposed to you learning more about one another if it pleases you."

"You surprise me, sister."

"How so? My only complaint in all of this is that women on both sides of the alliance would be forced into a life they do not want. That is not our way, Vigdis. Have you known any woman who was forced into a marriage against her will?"

"No I have not."

"But the Scots arrange their marriages all the time. I have only ever said I will not be forced."

"And if you developed feelings for a Scot, perhaps a tall dark-eyed one, you would have no objection?"

"I cannot marry a Scot, Vigdis. You know this. I imagine they expect their women to be ladies who abide by the rules set out by men. Can you really see me in that world? Not allowed to hunt? Not allowed to fight? Forced to wear gowns even more restrictive than those we wore tonight?"

"Our mother did not mind. I do not mind."

"I believe you would do well in that world, sister. Perhaps better than in this one."

"What are you saying? You think I should approach Gunnar about Osgar?"

"I have a strong feeling your Osgar will beat you to it."

"And what about you? What about MacDomnail?"

"There is no future for us." As she said the words a dull ache settled in her belly. Her mind told her there was no way forward for such a match. That she would be forced to leave the land and way of life she loved so dearly and that she would bring nothing but misery upon herself and him. It did not matter that he was strong and handsome and worthy. It simply could never work.

"How can you say that? I see the way he looks at you. And I've seen you look at him too."

"He is pleasing to look at—"

"And I am certain he is as pleasing in other ways," Vigdis said with a grin.

Saga smiled at the thought. It would not take much to envision the man's arms around her, his lips brushing across hers.

"Why do your cheeks flush when I talk of him in such a way?"

"If you want me to admit that I like him, here it is. I like him. But that does not mean there is any future available to us. He did not come here to ask if he could move in. He wants to take his wife away. I simply cannot reconcile that thought, Vigdis. You know me well enough to believe that to be true."

"I supposed I do. I want to see you happy."

"I will be happy," she said. She was sure she could settle down at some point when the right man came along. Why the gods had forced her attention toward a foreigner she did not know. "I just need to be patient."

"Perhaps Freydis could consult the runes and see what is in store for you."

"And what exactly do you think I should ask her? Whether or not I will find love? Or whether or not this stranger is a man I can trust with my heart? Do you not think Freydis will find it all far too amusing?"

"I think that you are used to getting your own way by brute force and now you are faced with a problem you cannot fight your way out of. You must accept there are other ways of solving problems."

Saga sat up. "Our brother placed a sword in my hand when I was but five summers. And while you were being fitted for gowns, I was building muscle and scars. I do not criticize you for the things you like, and I think it unfair of you and unkind to do so to me."

Saga threw the furs back and flicked her fancy shift over her head and onto the floor. She donned her leather trews and tunic, fastening them at her waist with her belt.

"I know you are angry with me, but you cannot go out there among the men while they are in their cups. It is not safe."

"Do you really think me so weak that I cannot best a man when he is drunk? You continue to insult me sister. And do not worry, I will ask Bjorn to guard your door, so no one disturbs your slumber."

"There is no need. I shall bolt the door," she said in utter defiance.

With that Saga left the chamber. Did Vigdis really think she could throw insults and she would just stay and take it? Not in this life.

Not wanting to draw any attention to herself, Saga slipped out through a side door in Gunnar's chamber. She turned the corner of the hall to see two men silhouetted against the inky sky. She stopped and waited for them to finish relieving themselves before moving forward toward the path leading to Freydis' hut. The woman had long admitted she but rarely slept and so perhaps she could ask the gods for clarity surrounding Saga's feelings at the very least.

Though it was dark, Saga knew exactly where she was going. She'd walked these paths her entire life and could do so with her eyes closed. Though, it was close to that this night with no moon and a thick cover of cloud.

As she drew nearer to Freydis' hut, she caught a low mournful sound coming from the opposite direction. It was not an animal, most likely a man who'd had too much to drink at the feast. Still she would not leave him there to suffer alone so she turned right toward his quiet plea.

His figure grew in size as she drew nearer. He was a big man and only as she bent down to speak to him, recognized his scruffy blonde hair. Bjorn was one of few men in the village who cut his hair short.

"Odin's blood! Bjorn is that you?"

"Ja. Saga? You need to get out of here. It is not safe."

"Bjorn what happened? Come let me help you to Freydis' hut. She will tend to you."

"Please," he said. "It is not safe." As he said those words, his head fell back.

Saga listened for his breathing. It was very faint. She felt around his body until she found a sticky wet mass below his breastbone. It did not appear to be near his heart, but from what she touched, he'd already lost a lot of blood.

"Bjorn, I am going to get help. I will be back shortly, I promise."

Saga ran to Freydis' hut. A small light shone through the window, so she did not wait for her to answer the door, merely knocked and entered.

Inside, were two men who looked like they had been weeping although upon closer inspection it was clear they were raving drunk.

"Saga, what is it?"

"It's Bjorn. He's been stabbed. He is too heavy for me to carry here. You, and you. Come with me now!"

She did not wait to see if they followed as she ran back to

where she'd left Bjorn. Once back to him, she lifted his head and held it in her lap.

"Hold on, Bjorn. Help is on the way. Listen to my voice and do not even think about feasting with Odin in Valhalla this night!"

She continued to whisper to him and the two men and Freydis came to help bring him back to her hut. It was a struggle even for the four of them, but before long they managed to secure him on a cot.

The sight that met her eyes when Freydis removed his tunic made her want to retch. Multiple stab marks spread across his gut.

"What do you need?" Saga asked.

"I need alcohol. Bring your brother's ale. And I need someone to heat strips of cloth for me. Send me three men from the hall."

"Done."

Saga left her hut and in a full-on run, headed toward the hall. By Odin's breath, someone would answer for this crime.

~

Giric listened as Gunnar detailed the exact dimensions of the hall in which they sat. The man had surely consumed his bodyweight in ale, yet his mind remained sharp even if his words slurred. Giric had given up on the drink long ago. Besides being bitter, it was far too strong and made his head spin. Not a desired effect when a guest at another man's table.

From time to time, he glanced back at the door through which Saga and Vigdis had retreated hours ago. He let his mind drift to images of her laying naked across the furs on her bed. He longed to explore her curves as much as he longed to feel her muscular arms wrapped tightly around him as they shared their pleasure. He had no doubt in his mind she would be as free with her pleasure as she was with her opinions. Everything about her drew him in and held him there. From her strength, to her wit, to her beauty, she was what he craved.

"Are you listening to me, Giric?" Gunnar asked. "I'm telling you that I oversaw the building of every part of this hall."

Giric turned back to agree with his host as the object of his distraction threw open the main hall door and rushed up to her brother's side. She wore her warrior's clothes and a wild look about her face.

"Bjorn has been stabbed," she said to Gunnar.

Several Vikings, who formerly looked like they'd had enough to drink, stood and unsheathed their swords.

Gunnar was on his feet in an instant.

"What? How? Where is Einar?"

"I do not know," she said. "I found Bjorn on my way to Freydis' hut."

What was she doing out late at night with so many strangers around? Giric didn't like it. He also didn't like the logical conclusion to which Gunnar would arrive.

Gunnar turned to Giric. "Shut the doors, Saga. We will take account of every man in this hall."

Giric nodded and looked at Osgar. "Count each man. Twice. Make sure everyone is accounted for."

The process took but a few minutes. Giric and Osgar counted their twenty-four sailors twice to be sure.

"We are all accounted for, Gunnar."

He nodded then turned to the two guards he had originally left to stand watch at the ship. "Did you do a headcount earlier today, when I asked?"

"Ja, Gunnar. We counted six and twenty men plus the lords."

Both guards looked at one another and nodded their heads.

"You are sure you counted six and twenty sailors plus these two men?" Gunnar waved his hand toward Giric and Osgar.

Bile rose in Giric's throat. Would Gunnar trust the men who were clearly lying? Who were either too uneducated to count or too stupid to realize a galley only had seats for twenty-four rowers? And what about the earl Bjorn was supposed to guard?

If Gunnar decided to trust them, there was little Giric could do but fight. Much was at stake and the next few moments were tense while the large man beside him contemplated his next move.

Giric glanced over at Saga. Instead of seeing an accusatory glare, she too, wore a knit brow as though she was trying to sort something out.

"They couldn't have done it," she said to Gunnar.

He turned to her. "I know that. But I would like to hear your reasoning for it."

Giric tried not to make too much noise as he released some of the breath he'd been holding.

"Their ship has twelve oars, six per side. Four and twenty men are needed to sail it. Not six and twenty."

"Very clever, sister."

"There's more," she said. "Bjorn was stabbed many times in his belly. That is not what one man would do if he were to engage in a drunken battle. It looks like—" she stopped and swallowed hard. "—like he was held down and stabbed."

"And you do not think these men are capable of that?"

She looked directly at Giric. "I have seen no dishonour in these men. I do not think they are responsible for this crime. And besides, Einar is the obvious culprit."

Gunnar nodded and placed his hand on Saga's shoulder.

He leaned in toward her and spoke something in her ear inaudible to Giric.

"This is a dangerous business to which we aspire," Osgar said.

"Aye, but they came to the correct conclusion," Giric said quietly.

"This time."

Gunnar turned back toward them. "I trust you do not take offence of my need to eliminate you?"

"Not at all. I would have done the same. Can we offer any service to you in helping flush out the man responsible?"

"Nay. You and your men will stay here along with my sisters." To Saga, he said, "I will find the earl and secure him. He can't have gone far." Then to Giric he said, "I have naught but the benches and chairs to offer you for your slumber, but I trust you will make the best of it."

"Do not worry about us, Gunnar. Find the man."

Gunnar nodded. "Oh and Giric?"

"Aye?"

"Keep an eye on the door leading to my sister's chamber."

Giric grinned. He'd known all along. "Aye, Gunnar. I will do that."

Saga nodded to her brother as she made her way to the back of the hall and toward her chamber door. Giric caught up with her just before she opened it.

"Might I have a quick word with you, before you retire?" he asked.

When she turned he caught the full sense of the impact the night's events had on her.

"You are close to Bjorn," he said.

She met his gaze. "We have trained together since we were but six summers."

Giric reached out to touch her shoulder. "I will help your brother find the man responsible. You have my word."

"That is twice this night you have given me your word," she said. "I hope it is as worthy as it appears to be."

"I know of none more reliable," he said. And he meant it. He would do everything he could to help sort the mess out, for her sake.

"Then I bid you a good night and good dreams, Giric of Alba."

Giric grinned at her but said nothing. Her gaze dropped to his mouth for a moment then back to his eyes, having taken on a softer look.

Giric leaned forward slightly to see what she would do. To his delight she leaned toward him as well, their mouths only inches apart. His back shielded her from the rest of the hall so there was no chance anyone would see if he simply closed the distance and kissed her.

Giric leaned closer. She did too, her breath now fanning his face.

"I want to kiss you," he whispered. "Will you let me?" His heart threatened to pound out of his chest. Their proximity made his loins tighten.

His words appeared to bring her back to the present. She shook her head and pushed him back slightly with her hands. Not in a rough way, but making her point, nonetheless.

He was glad for the reprieve. He wanted to be sure there would be no regret when they did kiss. "Until the morrow, Shield-Maiden."

The address brought a small smile to her lips. He knew at that moment, he would be kissing them and soon. And by the pink of her cheeks, he was certain she knew it too.

"Until the morrow, Giric of Alba," she said and lifted the latch of the chamber door. She swung it wide and stood behind it, locking gazes with him while she closed it. With a deep breath she shut the door and latched it.

Giric stood there for long moments waiting to hear her

footfalls indicate that she had moved away. When they didn't he leaned close to the door and said, "I will have my kiss soon, Shield-Maiden. And you will enjoy it as much as me. Tonight I will dream of you."

The soft gasp he heard on the other side of the door further heated his blood. With that he turned back to the hall, grateful that no one appeared concerned about him or his actions. He located a heavy fur and settled back into a chair to try to find a comfortable spot to encourage slumber. After rooting around for a few minutes, and realizing it was not possible, he reached for the horn of ale and downed it. Perhaps that would help the dreams of his shield-maiden emerge.

CHAPTER SIX

Her sister's soft snores pulled Saga from her slumber. Since their chamber lacked a window, she could not discern the time, though it felt like morning. She dressed as quickly as she could and entered the hall hoping to make as little noise as possible in case the men still slept. She wanted to see how Bjorn had fared through the night and did not want anything or anyone to delay her. The fact that Gunnar was not in his bed was not a good sign.

Creeping through the chamber door and out into the main hall, she took in the scene. The stench of last night's ale and drink as expelled by the men hung heavy in the air. If only she could lift the roof off the place sometimes.

As she turned the corner of the head table she spied a red robe covering a pair of long legs. The poor man was far too big to sleep in a chair.

Saga could not help but admire his features as he slumbered. His thick, straight brows and long, dark hair framed a strong face. There was no denying he was an attractive man. Her gaze fell to the hand that had fallen open and hovered above the floor. It was curled slightly as if he held a sword.

Her gaze drifted down the length of him. A part of her, the honest part, wanted to know what his long, hard body would feel like pressed against hers. The thought warmed her body. Were it a quick tumble with him she wanted, she could have had that last eve. But she sensed he wanted far more from her and was cautious as to how far in she should let him. Her body was interested—her heart was not.

"Is aught wrong?" he asked softly.

Her gaze shot up to meet his. She cursed herself for getting caught staring at him. How mortifying.

He smiled at her as he sat up and rubbed his neck. "How long have you been up?"

"Just now. I was about to go see how Bjorn fares. Would you like to join me?" Where that had come from she could not say.

He scraped his hand down across his beard. "Aye. I would like that."

As he drew nearer she noticed the dark circles under his eyes. "I do not think you slept very well, Giric of Alba."

Shaking his head, he said, "I managed a little. Better than most, I expect," he said, nodding toward the rest of his men who lay in various positions of slumber either on or near the tables. "Has Gunnar returned?"

"Nay," she said. "Come let us make our way. I believe we both could use some cleaner air."

"Aye, that we could," he said with a grin.

As they were about to open the door to the hall, several servants arrived and propped them open wide. They entered with buckets of water and kindling to start the fire for cooking. It would be an hour or more before the first meal was ready and she chuckled when Giric's stomach rumbled.

"Let us go see Bjorn then we can break our fast."

"Aye, I think I can last that long."

They walked in silence to Freydis' hut. Smoke plumed

from her chimney indicating someone was up and about. Saga knocked softly on the door and opened it slowly. She did not want to disturb them if they were in fact sleeping.

Freydis snoozed in a chair as Gunnar sat near Bjorn. He put his finger to his lips, but it made no difference. Freydis stirred as soon as Saga and Giric stepped inside the hut. While it was not very large, with the three big men inside, the space now felt quite cramped.

"How is he?" Saga asked.

"He will live," Freydis said. "But he will be weak for a while. I can only imagine how irritated he will be too, when I tell him to stay abed for a sennight."

To this, Gunnar scoffed. "You may as well tell him to don a woman's clothing and take up weaving."

The sound of Freydis clicking her tongue at Gunnar roused Bjorn. His eyes fluttered open.

"Where am I?" he asked quietly.

"Here," Freydis said, going to him with a cup. "Drink this."

Bjorn tried to sit up, but fell back down onto the bunk. He took the cup and lifted his head to drink, downing the fluid in one gulp.

"Thor's breath woman, what was that?" he asked after the liquid made him cough.

"That will help you heal and hopefully keep you on your back where you belong for at least the next day and night."

"Did you see who did this to you, Bjorn?" Gunnar asked.

He brushed his hand over his belly as his brow knit.

"I found you," Saga said, coming forward.

"I remember leaving my hut to relieve myself," he said. "Where did you find me?"

"But a few paces from Freydis' hut."

"That's a fair way to go for privacy, Bjorn," Gunnar said. "I never took you for modest."

"I am not," he said with a grin and sobered when Saga

frowned at him. "Einar was tied to a post behind my hut and I remember hearing raised voices up the path so I went to see what was going on."

"You wanted to see if there was a row you could join in on," Freydis said. "I've stitched you up more times than I can count."

"Ja, you have, and I am grateful for it."

"What happened then?" Saga asked.

"I came through the trees and into the clearing and saw two men arguing. It was dark last night, and I couldn't make out who it was, so I called out to them. When I got closer I felt something pinch my guts a few times and they ran off. I remember feeling something sticky on my hands and I woke up here."

"Do you have any idea who it was, Bjorn?" Gunnar asked.

"No. I didn't recognize the voices at all and after I called out to them they didn't speak again."

Saga reached out and took Bjorn's hand. "You were unconscious when I found you. I had to get some men and Freydis to help me carry you here."

"Do you remember anything they said?" Gunnar asked. "Anything that might help me confirm who they are."

"I—nay, Gunnar. I heard their voices raised, but do not know what they were arguing about, except—"

"What? Do you remember something?"

"One of the voices was higher. Ja, one of the voices was female. I have no doubt about it. It was a woman and a man arguing."

Saga sat back. It didn't make sense. Why would they stab Bjorn if he simply happened upon an argument?

"Do you think the man, or the woman stabbed you?" Giric asked, stepping forward.

Saga looked up just as his gaze fell to her hand holding Bjorn's. He looked at her for a second and back to Bjorn.

"I could not tell. Most of the women here are as tall as the men. But maybe the person who stabbed me was shorter than me? Maybe?"

"Give it some time," Freydis said. "You need your rest and so I want you and you and you out," she said pointing to them each in turn.

Saga leaned down and kissed Bjorn on the forehead. "Get well," she said and squeezed his hand before releasing it and moving away.

At the door she looked back at Freydis and said, "Thank you. Please make him well."

Outside the hut she drew a deep breath. Thank the gods he would recover. She did not know what she would do without him. And as Giric walked up and stood beside her the thought occurred to her that if she were to have a future with this or any man, she would have to leave Bjorn and this place behind. She did not know if she was prepared to do that and the thought made her heart ache.

~

Giric noted the change in her almost immediately. Tears pooled in her eyes.

"Your friend will be well. That is something to celebrate," he said, trying to break the silence and get her talking again.

She looked up at him with what looked like a forced smile. "I am very pleased Bjorn will recover. He and I have known one another our whole lives and I do not know what I would do without him."

Her words gave him pause. It had not occurred to him that she might have a husband in mind. And there was nothing wrong with Bjorn, but he did not want to picture her with another man. The thought surprised him. How had she made such an impact on him in such a short time?

"I understand," he said and walked quietly beside her.

After a few paces she turned. "You think Bjorn and I are lovers."

He didn't know how to respond to her statement. That was what he thought, but having to have a conversation with her about it might prove a bit too much.

"I see it in your eyes," she said. "Well I can correct you on that count. Bjorn and I have been close friends since we were very young, and though he has asked me many times, I am not interested in him in that way."

"And is there anyone you are interested in, in that way?" Giric could not help but ask.

She frowned. "I am unattached, Giric of Alba." And she squared her shoulders and looked directly at him. "And if you intend to speak to my brother about me, know this. I cannot leave my home and live elsewhere. I would never survive." With that she turned on her heel and walked on ahead of him toward the hall.

Giric turned to the sound of Gunnar chuckling behind him. "I guess we should talk about my sister, then," he said. "Do you intend to ask for her?"

He did, but God's breath, it really was all a bit sudden. There was nothing subtle about these people in the least. He'd not known her for a full day yet. Was he really prepared to ask for her? By contrast was he really prepared for someone else to do so instead?

"You look like you've been clobbered over the head. Come, I must send a party to search for Einar and we will break our fast and speak. Do you plan to stay another night?"

"That depends on my host."

"Then it's settled. You *will* stay another night and we will talk more of this alliance of yours. Sometimes knowing something is right does not require days, weeks, or months to process. Sometimes you just know."

Giric knew something, but putting a label on it or defining it was the problem. Lust? Infatuation? Love? He surely did not know the answer to the questions. All he could say for certain was that there was a definite connection between himself and Saga that was inherent and understood and perhaps beyond the rudimentary confines of the spoken word. He tried to shake his muddled head as he followed Gunnar to the hall.

Once there, Osgar stepped out. He looked like death warmed over. Clearly his constitution was not meant for Norse ale either.

"I think I will offer you mead instead of ale from now on," Gunnar said as he clapped Osgar on the back. "Come let's eat!"

Osgar looked like he was about to lose his belly and instead of joining them inside, walked toward the beach and sat staring out at the sea.

"I will join you in a moment," Giric said to Gunnar.

He walked over to Osgar and sat beside him. "Too much ale, my friend?"

"Aye. Too much ale and not enough sleep. How does their man fare?"

"He will recover. The mystery behind his stabbing is unresolved and is concerning to us all. He is sending his men to locate the missing earl."

"You like it here, don't you?"

"Aye, I admit, I am impressed with this place and how organized they are. I mean, just look at that hall. What a great feat of design," Giric said.

Osgar nodded. "I will give you that. They are not like I expected."

"You thought them mindless barbarians."

"Aye, you know I did. I admit, I thought you mad to consider asking a Viking for anything."

"At least you are a big enough man to admit when you're wrong."

"I was very wrong. There is much about these people I admire."

"Mayhap one in particular?"

Osgar smiled. "Mayhap. And what about you? Are you prepared to ask for the shield-maiden's hand?"

"It would do me no good. She has said she will refuse to come to my home with me."

"And so you will walk away from her? That's not like you Giric. You either realize you do not want her, or you are formulating another plan. You have never given up on anything you wanted until you held it in your grasp."

"I have to make a decision soon. Gunnar said he will engage in alliance talks with us today. We need to be clear about what we are willing to commit. We came here thinking it might be a fruitless endeavour and we'd be fortunate to return home with our lives. I had no idea we would be so welcome. It is a good exercise for me to consider my own self in the negotiations for it was wrong of me to have ever considered pushing someone else in my family to do something if I had not been prepared to do it myself."

"It will be a good alliance as long as we can trust that they will not go back on their word."

Osgar's comment was somewhat surprising. While strategic, the man had not yet displayed any cynicism.

"Have you seen anything to give you cause to think they are not honourable?" Giric asked.

"No, I have not."

"Then we must enter into these arrangements in good faith. We will stay tonight and on the morrow sail home. I will need to get word to the king to request assistance in

Gunnar's fight against Short-Beard's war band. I do not think the king will hesitate."

"I agree," Osgar said. "You are following suit with the same idea he started. I think he will be pleased to hear it and pleased to be a part of anything that will bring about peace."

"I am concerned the earl tried to convince Gunnar that Olaf was involved. I plan to remind him that an alliance with us extends to both King Constantine and King Olaf."

What would Saga think, considering those circumstances? Would she feel further coerced or volunteer freely to protect her clan? It all made his head pound a little harder and he couldn't entirely blame the ale.

"Why don't you go sleep in the galley for a few hours," Giric said. "No one will bother you there. I hope to have Gunnar and Saga show me around the village more this morning and I'll come find you when we are ready to talk."

"Aye, I will do exactly that," he said as he got up too quickly and almost fell over.

"Steady man," Giric said. "You're no good to anyone if you're broken."

Osgar chuckled as he staggered down the dock toward the moored galley.

Giric turned back to the hall and noticed someone at the far end ducking in behind as he turned. Were they watching him and Osgar? Instead of walking into the hall, he walked around the other side in case the person thought to slip back inside unnoticed.

When he got to the other side there was no one there. Whoever it was must have gone up the path behind. And perhaps with everything going on and his own head aching from too much ale, his mind was playing tricks on him.

Giric entered the hall and was pleased to see his men there, all eating. He passed by the hearth and was given a trencher of meat and bread, his belly rumbling its approval.

The air was thick with the irresistible aroma of roasted boar, making his mouth water in anticipation.

He sat in the same chair he had the night before beside Saga and smiled at her. She said nothing so he would not push her. Gunnar passed him a steaming cup and he smelled it first. Mead. This was a drink he enjoyed much more than ale. He sipped and swallowed, enjoying the sweet beverage as it warmed his throat, the silky honey flavour soothing as it filled his gullet.

They ate in silence and when he had consumed his full, he leaned back and stretched his legs out in front of him.

"You look like you could use a bed," Gunnar said. "You are welcome to take mine if you like. I have some things to attend to this morning, but I will have someone wake you later."

As tired as he was, Giric could not imagine sleeping when there was so much to do and see. "I thank you, but I was going to ask you if you could give me a tour of the village."

"I would like to, but I have to see to the ship's repairs. I am sure Saga would be pleased to show you whatever you wish to see."

Giric could not see her expression as she turned to her brother, but watched as his eyes crinkled at the sides.

"I do not wish to inconvenience you, Saga, but I would very much like it if you would."

She turned to him masking any disinterest if she felt any, wearing a shy smile. "I will happily show you my village, Giric of Alba. You may discover all the reasons I believe this to be the best place in the world."

"I very well may," he said, enjoying the look of surprise on her face and the smile that now played on her lips.

"Are you telling me you would consider living in a small Viking village?"

"I am not saying anything at the moment, merely asking a beautiful woman to show me her world."

She scanned his features as if examining him for sincerity. After a few moments she nodded.

"Very well, then. Let us get started. We have a lot to cover today if you want to learn all there is to know about Viking life."

"I very much do, thank you."

Giric stood and pulled back her chair. At first she appeared startled but then she stood and composed herself. With her height and build, she possessed grace and great balance.

He stepped back, allowing her to walk on ahead only partly because it was the polite thing to do. The other reason had everything to do with him wanting to watch her bottom in those leather trews of hers. The sight of it made his cock ache. Could he manage a morning with her without wanting to bend her over the nearest fallen tree? He had no choice. He would treat her no differently than any other lady he knew, despite how much he was growing to want her under him, atop him, beside him, or in any other position she'd allow. Christ help him. When she was near all reason appeared to fly away like pigeons that had been caged up too long.

CHAPTER SEVEN

Saga led Giric along the path away from the longhouse toward the main part of the village. She was ever aware of his nearness.

As they approached the first turf houses she noticed him touching the peat bricks.

"What is used to support the structure?" he asked. His wide eyes gave him a look of boyish wonder.

She liked seeing this side of him.

"The frame of the house is built with tinder and the peat bricks are packed all in around. This helps with the wind and the rain, but does not always smell so nice. That's why air flow is important. You will see holes in the roofs to let out the smoke, but also some in the sides to help create a draft. Do you not use peat bricks where you come from?"

He shook his head. "Not like this. Most of our dwellings are built with wood and stone."

"Does that not make for a cold place to live?"

"Aye, that is why we have hearths in most rooms and tapestries on the walls."

Saga showed him how some of the homes were built with

tinder and peat, but others were built strictly from tinder with two or three stories.

"These are for larger families," she said. "Most of the residences are close to one another and belong to those who support the chieftain. I assume it is the same for you?"

"Aye, there is usually a village close to a castle made up of the people who work there."

She led him toward the central part of the village which was already bustling with activity.

"I understand you have already seen the forge."

"Aye, and the armoury. It's quite impressive."

She liked that he seemed genuinely impressed. "And here is the tannery and the weaver, though during the colder months, the weavers are invited to the hall where it's warmer for their hands."

She showed him the pottery and the trading tables at the market.

"How many people live here?" he asked after touching nearly every item on a jewellery and pottery table.

"I do not know exactly, but I believe it to be several hundred. But if you count the farms and all their hands, all collected I would say there are more than five hundred of us. Gunnar could tell you specifically."

They walked to the end of the village boundaries and onward to the cattle holding and leaned against the fencing.

"You said last night you'd never heard music, but you were singing yesterday. Where did you learn it?"

"That was not music," she said. "Not like your piper."

"It sounded like it to me."

"My grandmother taught my sister and I when we were little. What you call a song, I call a kulning. It's only meant to call them home."

"But how do they know which one to go to?"

"Because each one is different. They are taught our kulning from the time they are calves, and they remember."

He smiled at her and brushed a piece of hair from her face that had drifted across her mouth with the breeze. Drawing a deep breath he looked out over the pasture.

"Your brother and I are to speak of alliances when I return to the hall."

Saga held her breath. Would he ask for her? Did she even want that? Well, she might, but would he want her to leave with him now? The thought of it made her head hurt.

"I know you feel an alliance would be good for us both," she said.

"And you do not?"

"I didn't at all before yesterday. When my brother told me of this first, I was quite vexed. I felt like he was giving up everything we have worked for."

"And now?" he asked.

"Now I see that we are not so different, you and I. We both want to protect those we love and preserve our way of life."

"And would it be so bad to live somewhere else?"

"I believe it would," she said and locked eyes with him. "I am as much a part of this place as it is of me."

"Then you can take it everywhere in your heart."

Saga tilted her head back to consider his words. Her belly tightened at his nearness. His scent was that of leather and wood and fresh air. Giric placed his hands on either side of her face and leaned down. Brushing his soft lips across hers sent a thrill through her body.

She placed her hands on his chest. The hard muscles there excited and tormented her; she wanted more of him, on her, over her, in her. She was not unaware of the ways between men and women, but for the first time, she wanted to experience it.

Giric claimed her mouth, his lips sweeping across hers, his tongue probing, coaxing hers to dance with his. As the kiss deepened, her hands found their way to the back of his neck, drawing him closer. There was too much clothing between them. She groaned as one hand held the back of her head and the other reached down to cup her bottom to pull her closer to him, his hard erection evident against her thigh.

Odin's blood she did not want this to end. Thrilling sensations raced through her veins as he laid claim to her mouth and her body. Surely there was no other man who could stir her in this way. She was certain it was the same way for him. Wanting to drive him to a similar madness, she reached around to cup his hard bottom as well, mirroring his movement. The resulting growl from his throat set a thousand butterflies loose in her belly.

Breaking the kiss, he whispered, "I want you."

Saga smiled and gazed at his mouth. She wanted to taste him again, so she reached around to the back of his neck and pulled him down toward her.

"Kiss me again," she said.

Another growl. He kissed her with greater need this time, almost bending her backward with the power of his passion. Saga felt completely dominated by someone for the first time in her life and she liked it. She liked that he wanted her so fiercely he could barely control himself. Finally she'd encountered a man strong enough to match her strength. And so, if that was the case, there would be no other man to compare for her either.

Giric broke the kiss and brushed his lips along her jaw and to her neck. Thor's breath, his mouth was surely akin to something magical. Her sex pulsed with a need she barely understood. When Giric pulled her tunic down and grasped one breast she arched toward him, wanting that mouth on her flesh. As if reading her thoughts, he found her nipple and sucked hard. Saga's head fell back, and she gasped.

"Oh!" she said.

In the next moment, she was on her back with Giric grinding into her. Pressure and pleasure built within her. She did not know what the end result would be, but she did not have the strength to stop no matter the consequences. She had to know what it felt like to find that release and she was desperate to know how he felt inside her.

"I want you so much," he said as he pressed his thick erection against her, holding himself there.

Saga opened her eyes and nearly jumped out of her skin when she saw not just Giric above her, but the brown furry face of a cow who had come to inspect what was happening. She had stuck her head in between the fence posts and was sniffing Giric's robe.

Saga started to laugh and Giric's confused look only made her laugh harder. He turned to the side and realized the cow was there. The look of curiosity on the cow's face, coupled with Giric's startled expression sent her into fits of laughter as Giric rolled off her and lay flat on the grass. Before long he joined in with her, his deep chuckle dancing in the air.

Saga held her belly and tried to catch her breath, noticing that Giric now lay on his side with his hand propping his head up, watching her. She enjoyed the smile playing on the lips she had just tasted. Freya help her!

~

Lying on the ground and watching her, in a heartbeat everything in Giric's world clicked into place. Aye, he'd been with other women, but not many, and none like her. Had they not been interrupted, he was not certain either would have wanted to stop. And whatever the issue with where they would live, they would have to figure that out because the option of him leaving without her as his betrothed was now gone. He would run any man through who ever dared lay a finger on her.

Between her passion, her intelligence, and her strength, he was unable to consider any other alternative but ask or even beg for her.

A light rain fell on them as her laughter died down. Giric's pulse took a while to slow but by the time it did the rain was falling harder. He jumped up and held out a hand to her. Taking it and standing, she did not let go as they walked away from the pasture and toward the village. Giric linked their fingers together and squeezed her hand as the hall came into view.

"Oh I did not show you the shipping shed," she said, and released his hand and pulled him toward the other side of the hall, through some trees, and to another large structure.

Inside was the largest ship Giric had ever seen. The prow extended far above the height of the shed and there was little room left between the width of the ship and the doorway. Gunnar was inside yelling instructions at a man hammering pegs into the ship's side.

When he noticed them, his gaze darted between them, and he grinned. "I take it your tour was pleasing?"

"Aye," Giric said, glancing at a rosy-cheeked Saga. "Very pleasing."

Gunnar approached them. "I am done here if you would like to have our discussion now."

"I would like that very much," Giric said. He could not read Saga, but hoped she would at least hear him out. His mind buzzed with the possibility of making her his.

"Will you join us, sister?" he asked.

She nodded and walked ahead of them.

They walked back to the hall in silence. When they entered, Giric noticed a large iron pot hanging from the ceiling posts by thick iron chains and Osgar drinking from a bowl. Whatever was in the pot smelled delicious. An older woman smiled at him and handed him a wooden bowl full of the broth and a piece of crusty bread. He sat at a nearby table and sipped the liquid. His stomach rumbled in approval as Gunnar and Saga followed suit and the older woman refilled his bowl twice more.

Without asking, they were brought a trencher of meat and horns of ale. This time when Giric drank, the liquid seemed more palatable and was not at all like the brew from the night before. Gunnar laughed as Giric looked at the liquid in the horn.

"You are not losing your mind. I gave you and your men an older, more bitter brew the first time. A kind of jest I suppose," he said.

Giric admired that and the man. While he had been convinced there was more to these people than met the eye, nothing could have prepared him for his experience so far.

"Shall we get down to business then?" Gunnar asked.

"Aye."

"What do you propose?"

"I wish to ally your family with mine so that we may set about a new era of peace between our people. I am a wealthy landowner and the chief of my clan. I offer dowries for any woman in my clan who wishes to marry someone in yours and will carve out property and farming land for any men who wish to resettle on our lands."

Gunnar stroked his beard. "And my threat in the west?"

"Between MacAlpin and me, we can amass enough men, coupled with the king's army to secure these lands for you. Any alliance with the king further solidifies your connection to Olaf of Dublin. I also do not believe Einar when he says Olaf plots against you."

"You are saying the king will not try to run us off this land even though we took it long ago from his own kind?"

"I am saying the king wants peace. I believe he will not take issue with you staying here as long as you bring no harm to any Scot."

"I can agree to those terms," Gunnar said. "Sister, do you have anything to add?"

"I do. No woman or man shall be forced into these arranged marriages. I would like your word from all three of you on that."

They all nodded in agreement. "And now to more specifics," he said looking directly at Saga. "I wish to ask for your sister's hand."

Gunnar sat back and folded his arms across his chest. "You spoke of dowries. We call it a bride price. What do you offer?"

"I believe you should ask me if I agree first, brother," Saga said.

Giric held his breath. Would she refuse him? Or insist they live here instead of on his lands?

"Very well, sister," Gunnar said. "Will you accept this man's proposal of marriage? Before you answer, I want you to consider the value this alliance brings and the security you will provide to our family and our clansmen. You are a warrior in your heart, and this is a different sort of negotiation than anything you've endured in battle. The choice is yours, Saga. You will be looked at with no less admiration from me or this clan should you refuse. This decision is entirely yours."

Saga stood and walked toward the wall behind Gunnar's chair. Her fingers traced the serpent on the shield. Giric's guts coiled into a knot while he waited for her to contemplate her brother's words. He would accept her decision whatever it was and as Gunnar pointed out, he would admire her no less. But the longer she took to respond, the more doubt crept into his heart that he would have her as his wife.

Saga returned to her seat and met Giric's gaze then Gunnar's. Her face was expressionless. "I will consider his proposal."

Giric took a deep breath and smiled at her. "Thank you," he said.

"On one condition," she said.

His guts lurched.

"And what is that?" Gunnar asked.

"That we live here for one year. After that we can live wherever you want. But I want my first year here."

Giric would have to think about that. She could not imagine the responsibility of running a castle from so far away. His steward was reliable, but that was a lot to put on him.

"I would have to travel back and forth regularly to see to my responsibilities. Will you join me any time I return home?"

Her brows knit as if she had not anticipated such a scenario. After a long agonizing few minutes, she nodded and said, "I will."

"Gunnar, I will give you lands plus one thousand marks."

Gunnar's brow shot up and he cleared his throat. He took both their hands and placed his over theirs. "It is done," he said as a looming shadow blocked the light from the door-way. He turned as a large axe came down and split the table inches away from their hands.

CHAPTER EIGHT

*W*as it really him? How long had it been? Two summers? Three? Magnus Haraldson was one year in age between her and Gunnar and had always been an advocate of violence before questioning anyone left standing.

"Welcome home, brother," Gunnar said, standing. "How do you fare?"

"I am well, but I have received some disturbing news," he said pointedly, looking at Giric and Osgar.

"Of what nature?" Gunnar asked.

"Have you welcomed Scots into our village? And have an inclination to betroth our sister to one of them?"

"I have on the first part, ja," Gunnar said. "But you are mistaken on the second part."

"Thank Odin for that," Magnus said. "No sister of mine will marry a Scot."

With that Saga and Giric stood at the same time. "It is already done," Saga said.

"You lied to me, brother?" Magnus asked Gunnar.

"No, I did not lie. You asked if my intention was to betroth our sister to this Scot, and it cannot be my intention when it is a done thing," he said, grinning. "This is Giric MacDomnail and this is Osgar MacAlpin. They honour us with their proposal."

"You make light of such a serious matter," Magnus said. "You have grown soft in the head since I have been away."

Gunnar grabbed Magnus by the throat and pushed him against a post. "You do not speak to your chieftain that way. You, who have been away these two summers, would know nothing of the challenges we face here every day."

With that Gunnar released Magnus and walked away from them to take his chair at the head of the hall.

"You may come forth and report on your journey, brother," Gunnar said to Magnus. "Leave out no detail."

Magnus looked at Saga and frowned. She could not bear the disappointment resting in his eyes. They had always been close, and it had taken her a long time to accept that he would go raiding without her. From time to time a ship would arrive to trade goods and there would be some trinket for her from him. Most of her was glad to see him, but a part of her still reeled from his arrogance in forbidding her to go with him.

Still, he was her brother and most like her of all of them. "It is good to see you, Magnus," she said. "Will you not greet me properly?"

He stopped and turned to her. She held her breath as he approached and kissed both cheeks and pulled her into an embrace. "You have grown much," he said. "And I have missed you."

Tears welled in her eyes, but she would never permit them to fall in front of him. Magnus valued strength more than anything.

"And you look worried when you need not be," she said, offering a smile to show him her confidence in the situation.

He searched her face for a moment, nodded and stepped forward to stand in front of Gunnar.

"I have seen much these past months, Brother. Some that concerns me, and some that gives me hope."

Saga did not want to miss one moment of his tale and so took a chair near Gunnar, leaning forward.

Magnus turned and watched as Giric and Osgar also came forward to sit near them. "Do we share everything with these Scots now?" he asked.

"There is much you do not know, Magnus. And if you will share your tales I will share mine."

Magnus looked at Saga again. She nodded and smiled at him in encouragement. He was an act first sort of man, but he was intelligent and would see that aligning with the Scots was a logical and sensible solution to their plight.

"Very well. I have spent much time in Iceland. It is exciting there now and much has been established to make the villages viable places to live and prosper. They have a council gathering to air grievances called an allthing and it is quite effective."

"How does that work?" Gunnar asked him.

"The chief oversees the proceedings. Each person who has a grievance has the opportunity to speak their piece and call witnesses. The accused may do the same and between the chieftain, council members, and those villagers in attendance, they pass judgement, which is final.

Saga sat back and thought about that. Including the villagers in decisions on grievances not only made them a part of it and therefore more likely to accept the judgement, but also took the pressure off the chieftain. She liked it.

"And what is the success of these proceedings?" Giric asked.

Saga noticed that he was leaning forward, practically hanging off Magnus' every word.

"Much success in the villages employing it."

"Do they not value the word of their chieftain alone?" Gunnar asked.

"They do, but these villages are new and so therefore the chieftains are not as established as they are here."

"Where else did you travel?" Saga asked.

"I traveled to Lewis and Orkney. I wanted to see for myself how the villages were managing."

"Lewis has tried and succeeded with marriages between our cultures, Magnus. Yet you oppose that happening here. Why?" Giric asked.

"Because it is a way of diluting out culture. We risk losing some of ourselves by absorbing others into our villages and homes."

"I felt the same way at first," Saga said. "But I believe the benefits outweigh the negative possibilities."

"And do you think you are being influenced by this man because you want to take him into your bed?" Magnus asked.

She stood, her cheeks burning. Magnus had never spoken to her like that before. He essentially insinuated she would give up everything she cared about in order to bed a man. He went too far!

"How dare you say such a thing to me," she said. "I am and always have been loyal to my family and my people."

Magnus frowned. "I am sorry, sister. I did not mean that kind of offence."

"What exactly did you mean?" Giric asked, also standing. "Your sister and I are betrothed. We have entered into the agreement freely and have the blessing of your chief. You are entitled to your opinions, but you do not get to insult my future wife without answering to me."

While it was kind of Giric to speak on her behalf, it was not Saga's way. She could defend herself and did not need his interference in order to put Magnus in his place.

"But you do not have my blessing. Nor will you get it," he said. "I do not recognize this betrothal."

"You are not chief here, brother," Gunnar said. "I am and I have given blessing over this union. It is good for our sister, and it is good for this village. You do not know what we face here."

Magnus folded his arms across his chest. "Nevertheless, I cannot condone a marriage between one of my family members and a Scot. You do not know of the things I have seen."

His words were daggers in her heart. Would he really make her choose between the brother she adored and the man to whom she was betrothed?

"Then I have nothing more to say to you," Saga said with a heavy heart.

With that she left the hall. She had no intention of a particular direction and so went where her feet led her. Magnus was wrong, just like she'd been wrong at first. Giric had said from the beginning that the less they understood one another, the more likely they were to never settle their differences.

One thing was for sure. Gunnar was the kind of man to whom a peaceful, settled life was appealing. Magnus, on the other hand, was like their father had been. A conqueror. Thank the gods Gunnar had been born first. And thank the gods Giric of Alba was like Gunnar.

~

Giric watched Magnus as Saga left the hall. He wanted to go after her, but he needed to have a better understanding of Magnus' reasoning. If he thought there was a problem on Lewis with the intermarriages, Giric would rather know why now in order to make their efforts a success.

"You said we do not know of the things you have seen in reference to alliances between our people," he said to Magnus. "What kind of things? You do recognize that your people came here and took that which was not yours."

If that offended either Magnus or Gunnar, Giric did not care. He could not accept this entitled attitude Magnus displayed.

"I have been to Lewis," Magnus said. "There is much dilution of cultures on both sides. I do not think it is good."

"What kind of dilution?"

"Well, many villages have constructed churches and our people do not even pray to our own gods anymore."

"Some have converted to Christianity?" Gunnar asked.

"Ja, and the same has been happening in Ireland and in England," Magnus said. "Who are we without our gods?"

"No one will be forced to enter into an agreement with us if they do not wish it," Giric said.

"No, but if a man here takes a Scot for a wife will he be expected to build a chapel for her to pray? Will she be willing to follow our ways? I would not take a Scot for a wife if that was what she expected," he said.

"Magnus, you raise a good point. But what about our threats? We cannot keep Short-Beard at bay forever. Giric and Osgar have offered their armies and can secure the Scots King's army as well. That will secure these lands for us."

"We do not have to stay here," Magnus said.

Gunnar sat forward. "And where would we go? Iceland? How long before all the land there is taken up and the same squabbles over land begin anew—then what? Move again? I tell you brother, Giric of Alba's proposal is a good one. And the best way for our clan to continue to prosper."

"There is talk of more land to the west. We can go wherever we want."

Gunnar shook his head. "No, Magnus. We will stay here, and we will make peace with the Scots and build our markets."

Magnus clenched his fists. "It is a mistake, brother."

"It is my will," Gunnar said. "Now bring your spoils so they may be divided up among your crew and me."

Giric watched as Magnus' jaw ticked. Giric suspected this was the usual way of things, but that Magnus was reluctant to share his wealth. Would he be allowed to take his belongings and leave again? Having no experience in how a raid worked when the men of the clan returned, he was curious to see what would happen. And just as curious to see what they considered spoils.

Monasteries all along the coast of Britain and well into the mainland had been raided for decades by these men. Precious treasures symbolizing the glory of God. And these men had used brute force to destroy places of sanctuary. The thought made Giric's guts churn, but also strengthened his resolve to solidify these alliances and the resulting peace he was certain would follow.

Magnus nodded once at Gunnar and with barely a glance in his and Osgar's direction, left the hall only to return with six men all carrying heavy chests, overflowing with shiny objects.

The volume even made Gunnar lean forward.

"You've been busy," Gunnar said.

"That is not all of it," he said.

The men placed the chests before Gunnar and left the hall.

"There is four times that to be brought from the ship," Magnus said.

"From where did these spoils originate?" Giric could not

help but ask.

"We raided some chapels on Lewis and on Skye. We figured Iona was pretty much stripped by now, so we focused on some smaller islands."

"Smaller chapels and islands. There's far more here than that," Gunnar said.

Magnus smiled. "Ja, brother. You are as shrewd as you have always been."

"Where did this come from?" Gunnar asked again.

"You may not like the answer," he said.

"Where?"

"From Snorri Short-Beard."

Gunnar's eyes grew wide for a moment. "Do you know what you have done?" he asked in a quiet voice.

"Ja, I do. I have prevented him from attacking us and claiming these lands, and I did not need to marry off my family to foreigners to do it."

"You have brought war upon us," Gunnar said.

"When did you take these things," Giric asked.

"Last summer."

"And does he know it was you?"

"Of course he knows it was me. I walked into his hall and told him what I was about to do."

Giric shook his head and looked at Gunnar who appeared just as incredulous.

"Magnus, this is why Short-Beard plans to attack us."

"You are a fool if you think his plans for attack began a year ago. I have been telling you for a long time that Short-Beard had his sights set on our village," Magnus said.

"You have, but your actions have brought about more trouble than solution," Giric said. To Gunnar, he added, "I fear if I ask my king to get involved now we risk full on war between our people instead of peace."

"You will go back on your word?" Gunnar asked, his fists clenching.

"We need to keep our heads calm, Gunnar," Giric said. "What Einar said now must be true, that your king supports Short-Beard's claim to these lands, and it is because he thinks you have stolen from the man," he said pointing at the chest. "Because you *have* stolen from him."

Gunnar turned back to Magnus. "You have brought a lot of trouble to my hall, brother."

"Then let it come. Short-Beard has been plotting to destroy you and I prevented that from happening. Without his gold he cannot pay his men to cross Islay and attack which gives us time to form a plan."

"So you're telling me that you decided to rob from him, and you didn't think of the full consequences, but you criticize me when I am left to clean up the mess you have made."

To Giric, Gunnar said, "Our betrothal stands. You will follow through with your agreement of extra men, when and if Short-Beard manages to amass enough men. Magnus, you will take some men and bury all of this and create stake out points along the border farms. I want reports back every day."

He stroked his beard and stared hard into the chests of treasures. "I have not received any word from King Harald concerning this matter and so will not make contact with Short-Beard."

"And what about Saga?" Giric asked. "Should she not come with us when we leave on the morrow?"

"Nay!" Magnus said. "My sister will stay here where she belongs."

Gunnar stroked his beard again, still staring into the chests. "She will go with you, and you will keep her safe until you return here to fulfill Saga's requirement. Nothing in that has changed. If Vigdis wishes to go with her sister, I will support it as long as Saga is married before she leaves here. Tomorrow is Friday, a good day for a wedding feast. You will have to delay your return journey by another day."

"I cannot believe you are letting them take our sisters," Magnus said. "Saga will not leave here if she knows we are under threat."

"Then she will not know," Gunnar said.

Unease settled into Giric's heart. While he agreed he wanted to keep her safe, she was a warrior like the rest of them and believed that it was her place to protect her people. He was not comfortable beginning their marriage by lying to her. He would not do it.

"She will be told, or I will not allow her aboard my ship," he said.

Both Gunnar and Magnus turned their heads quickly to him. "You will break our agreement?"

"No. But I will not risk her finding out about the threat while we are at sea and attempting to return. Your sister is headstrong. You know I speak the truth."

Gunnar nodded. "She is headstrong. I will tell her myself," he said.

The two brothers left the hall leaving Giric and Osgar and the cooking women alone.

"This business will end badly," Osgar said. "The king will never get involved now."

"I believe he will, but it will take more effort than before."

"We did not come here to make enemies, rather forge alliances. Now by allying with Gunnar, we make an enemy of Short-Beard."

"Aye, but as Magnus pointed out, Short-Beard does not have the means to pay his men to attack. And if there's one thing I have learned about these people, they do little without a well-formed plan."

"But Magnus did not have a plan."

"No, he does not appear to. But I believe there is more than meets the eye with that man. I think he knows more about Short-Beard's plot than he is letting on. Did you notice he did not elaborate on how he acquired the treasures? Are we really to believe he walked into the hall and said I'm taking everything, and they said here you go?"

Osgar shook his head. "There is much here we do not understand."

Very much indeed. And Giric would find out as much as he could before he left. The last thing he would do is bring a Viking war band back to the mainland on his heels. Agreement or no, he would be certain of the situation here before leaving. Something in the pit of his stomach told him he would not be leaving with Saga either way.

CHAPTER NINE

Freydis' opened her door and quickly pulled Saga inside before she had a chance to knock. Bjorn lay sleeping on the cot and so Freydis placed her finger to her lips.

"Your brother has returned," she said. "And you are now betrothed."

How Freydis knew so much so quickly in this village would never cease to amaze her.

"He has and will not give his blessing for my betrothal."

Freydis shook her head. "Do not mind him. He has always been stubborn. He will come around."

"I hope you are right."

"You are worried. I have seen it, that is why I was expecting you," she said. "You must let me read the runes."

Saga had only allowed Freydis to read them once before, believing that the gods had a will that was not meant to be meddled with even in knowing what that was.

"I will permit you," she said. "There is too much here that I cannot foresee. What if Magnus convinces Gunnar to break the betrothal? What if Giric changes his mind?"

"The gods will tell us what we need to know. But I must ask you to answer truthfully, do you want to marry this man Giric?"

Saga looked over to where Bjorn slept. She supposed he was the only man who had ever mentioned marriage to her and so was the only man to whom she could compare Giric. And in her heart there was no comparison. There was something about them together that made sense. She recognized great honour in him despite the differences in their ways. She was certain. She wanted him and him alone.

"I want to marry him," she said, nodding.

"Very well, I shall summon Freya for our casting."

Freydis spread a white cloth on the table and untied a small leather sack from her apron, the stones inside rattling. Shaking the pouch, she opened it and offered it to Saga.

"Extract three stones only and place them in front of you left to right."

As Saga pulled out the stones, Freydis said, "Hail to thee, Freya, Queen of the Aesir, Mistress of Magic, Mother of Midgard. By the sovereign power of Seithr and the strength of Brfsingamen lend me your insight in this my rite. Come Queen of all, into this circle and bless the casting that is to be performed."

Saga considered the three stones as Freydis straightened them. She had always been a little in awe of them, if also a little afraid at the same time. To think that Freydis could interpret messages from the gods from these tiny stones was rather incredible.

Freydis pointed to the first rune. "Laguz," she said. "This stone represents your past and signifies a journey over water. Since you have not been on a ship in many years, I believe it to mean our people's journey in coming here."

That made sense, they did not originate on Islay and in fact her grandfather had arrived here by ship decades ago.

"How far into the past does this usually go?"

Freydis nodded. "I see your meaning. It is usually more recent than this."

"Then could it mean Giric's journey over water to land here?"

Freydis cocked her head to the side. "It may be possible for his path to be linked with yours, but he is not here, nor does he believe in our gods."

"But if his path is linked with mine than his journey is my journey too, is it not?"

Freydis considered her for a moment and nodded. "Ja, it would be as you say. Perhaps the remaining runes will give us more insight."

Bjorn grunted and snorted behind them causing Freydis to stop with her hand hovering over the stones. Once he had turned on his side she continued, pointing to the second stone.

"Inguz represents the present and this stone signifies the god Ing and the literal representation of male sexuality and fertility. This is where you are right now."

Saga's cheeks warmed, thinking of the encounter she'd had with Giric a few short hours ago.

"Considering the look on your face at the moment, I think it likely you have an understanding of this stone. But this may not only represent the relationship you have started with the Scot. Rather it may represent releasing potential stored energy and the change within you that will put you on your future path."

Saga pondered that for a moment. While the literal meaning was true and there was a definite heat between them, something had been welling within her for a time. As though she'd been preparing for something her whole life and it was on the horizon.

"And what is the last stone?" she asked.

Freydis smiled. "This is a good stone, my friend. This last one represents your future. Othala represents property."

"You mean I will remain here and inherit our lands? But how is that possible when I have two older brothers?"

"It also represents a new beginning and perhaps that is more likely in your case. I see change for you, Saga."

"Ja, change, but here or in the land of Scots?"

"That, the runes did not tell us."

"Then I am no further ahead," she said with a sigh.

"You may consult the runes to seek guidance, Saga. But they will not tell you what to do. For that you must seek your own conscience. The gods may lay a path for you, but it is you who must walk that path of your own will."

"I do not know what to do."

"You must follow your conscience. If you think you can love this man in time, you must go with him."

"But I do not wish to leave my home, and I do not wish to fall out with Magnus."

"Do not worry about Magnus. As I said before, he is stubborn, and pig-headed sometimes. Gunnar is far more sensible, and he has given you his blessing. Does that not speak louder to you?"

It should, but in her heart, she still believed partly as Magnus did, that they should find a way to preserve their way of life.

"Have we not been acquiring items from other cultures for generations and incorporating them into our everyday life?"

"What do you mean?"

"Ever since we started trading, we have brought home things like new spices for our food, new fabrics for our clothes," she said as she tugged on a piece of gold stitched edging from Saga's tunic. "That gold thread was not made in this village or by our weaver. How can you criticize diluting our culture when we've been doing just that our entire lives?"

Saga looked down at her own garments. She had not considered that other cultures had been seeping into their own for a very long time and no harm had befallen them. Well none from that form of trade anyway.

"You always find clarity for me, Freydis. If I was to leave here, what would I do without you?"

"You'd take me with you is what you'd do. I for one would love to see more of the world and learn of other healing ways outside of our own."

"Do you speak true? You will come with me if I have to leave here."

"I speak the truth. There are plenty of others in the village who know enough of the healing ways to protect the villagers."

Suddenly the thought of travelling to Alba with Giric did not sound so unappealing now if both Vigdis and Freydis were with her.

"Giric leaves here on the morrow. I will speak to my brother. I had not intended to go with him this time, but you and your runes have awoken a curiosity in me about his land and his people."

"I am very glad to hear it," Freydis said. "For we are all better off if there is tolerance in our hearts."

"How wise you are for one so young, Freydis."

"I am not so very young," she said.

"You are but two summers older than me."

"Ja, and at twenty-one summers, I am already an old maid."

"That is not true. You are young and beautiful. I remember the way my brother used to stare at you."

"That was years ago. He is a man now and no doubt has no interest in an old maid in a tiny village."

"I think you still have feelings for him," Saga said. When Freydis turned her head away, Saga thought she may have hit her mark. Disliking the frown upon her friend's face, she kissed her on the forehead, thanked her and left. She would ask Gunnar if Freydis could accompany them to Alba.

The setting sun cast a red hue over the horizon as Giric left the hall to check on the galley. They would have had a good sea on the morrow, but now he must wait another day and he hoped the good weather held out. Not that he was complaining. The cause for the delay would be worth it if she agreed.

As he approached the dock, he caught full sight of a ship that had not been in the harbour when they arrived. It was as large or larger than the ship that was being constructed in the shed. With a long prow that curled outward into a spindle and a massive sail tied to the mast, he wondered if there was any sea this ship could not tackle.

"Do you think my ship is pretty?" Magnus asked from behind him.

"Aye, that I do."

"Yours is well built, but your shipbuilders do not seem to possess the craft for making yours quite wide enough. That aspect really aids a rocky sea."

Giric nodded. Magnus pointed out the positioning of the wood on the hull.

"But I suspect you get more sea spray on your face," Giric said with a grin.

"That keeps us from falling asleep," Magnus said and crossed his arms over his chest. "You want to know how I really acquired Short-Beard's treasure, don't you?"

"Aye, the thought had crossed my mind."

"Well perhaps I will tell you at the feast later."

"Why not now?"

"Because although you have convinced my brother you are here with genuine intentions, I am not so easily convinced or swayed."

"Well then we shall have to talk later," Giric said and walked away from the man.

He was curious, but there was something about Magnus that was more than a suspicious nature. There was no doubt in Giric's mind that he was fishing for information. Two years was a long time to be away and to return with such a loot of treasure begged a question. Just what in heaven's name had he been up to?

If Short-Beard's treasure was that great, how was that relative to Gunnar's?

Saga had said their lands were about the same in size and so if that was the case, why not just come to an agreement on the border and be done with it. No, there was much more going on here than met the eye.

Giric jumped onto the ship and watched as the men unravelled and ravelled the rigging to ensure it was secure and easily loosed while at sea. Should they have a good western wind they would be home by dusk on their sailing day. Otherwise they may have to dock part ways across, though Giric did not think so. The storm on the way over had gotten them there in record time. Perhaps he would ask the healer to send up a favourable wind with some incantation for he was certain that was also a speciality of hers.

And it was no different in any of the villages near his lands. There were still plenty of pagans who practiced their ways, and he took no contest with it.

As he jumped back on the dock he noticed Saga walking toward him. Her beauty struck him again. She walked with such pride in every step. Her long golden hair flicked behind her, and her hand was ever on the hilt of her sword. Only in his dreams had he ever beheld such a vision.

Beauty and strength. Surely she was an angel cast in human form.

"I have come to talk with you, Giric of Alba," she said.

"I am all yours," he said in a low voice so the other men could not hear.

"Is this your ship?" she asked.

"It is one of my ships," he said.

"And how long is the journey to your lands?" she asked.

"We can do it in a day with a favourable wind and calm waters."

"Then I shall travel with you to your lands and see your castle."

His heart caught in his throat. Gunnar must have spoken to her, and she'd agreed. His pulse picked up a notch. He had anticipated an argument, but this was a great surprise.

"Should I ask what brought about your change of mind? Earlier you had insisted on my return as well as the wedding here plus the year. Have you changed your mind?"

"Nay, I still wish to be married here. But I just spoke to my brother, and he does not wish me to be here until he is certain the village is safe. While I can wield a sword as good as most men here, he wishes me to get to know your people better so that we may call on your men as our alliance states should we need them."

"Ahh, so it is a military strategist I return with to my home, not a warrior then?" he asked, teasing.

Frowning, she said, "I am not trying to deceive you," she said.

Giric shook his head, "Saga that is not what I meant. I am sorry, I should not have teased you. The truth is I am delighted you will be returning with me." He reached for her hand. "I did not know exactly how I would be able to sail away from you."

His words brought a devilish smile to her face. She threw her arms around his neck and kissed him soundly. Her full breasts pressed against his chest making his loins tighten and his breath catch in his throat. God's teeth, but she would drive him mad with need.

Giric pulled back and studied her face. She gave so freely of herself with no pretence. He'd never known any woman like her. Most of those he knew were quiet with a polite demeanour and a masked expression, making a man wonder what they might be thinking pretty much all of the time. But not Saga. She wore her feelings out there for the world to see and did not make any excuses for them.

He took her hands and walked back toward the hall, noticing Magnus glaring at them along the way. If Saga noticed she did not say anything.

"My brother says if I am to leave here with you, we must marry here tomorrow," she said.

Giric stopped abruptly and regarded her. "Do you speak true? You would marry me here tomorrow though you barely know me?"

"I know you enough to know the kind of man you are, Giric of Alba. My brother's reason for me to accompany you is sound and I respect his request. Will you marry me by my laws?"

"Aye, if you will marry me by mine."

"What do you mean?"

"We will be married by a priest in a chapel at my home."

Her brows knit. "You mean the kind of chapel Magnus has stolen from?"

"Aye, the very same."

"But why do you need gold in a chapel in order to pray to your god?"

"We bring gifts to the church to honour him."

"And we steal these gifts," she said.

"Aye, many have been stolen."

"Will I not be shunned by your priest because I am Norse?"

"Have *you* ever raided a chapel and stolen that which was not yours?"

"Nay. I have never stolen anything."

"Then you do not need to worry about my priest," Giric said. "There are many Norsemen and Swedes and Danes who have decided to take up Christianity and recognize Christ as their saviour."

"Is that what you expect of me?" she asked.

Giric cupped her face with his hands. "I will never force you to believe in anything if you do not wish it. I would like to show you the scriptures and tell you the stories though. In the same way I would like to know more about your gods."

"You would?" she asked.

"Aye, I would like to know everything about you."

"Then it is settled. We shall be married twice, by my gods and yours, for surely being blessed twice will bring about good fortune."

Giric squeezed her hand and entered the hall to find Gunnar seated near the hearth. Saga kissed his cheek, joined her sister, and disappeared into their chambers. He would not see her until she was to be his.

Gunnar passed him a horn and patted the seat beside him. "It will be less enjoyable here without those two. You must promise me you will return with them often."

"We are but a short boat-ride away, Gunnar. I would like you to visit us too."

Gunnar downed the drink in his horn and reached his hand out for Aslaug to fill it again.

"Tonight you will see a true Norse celebration. It is not

every day one of our best women marries." Then clapping him on the back and rising, Gunnar said, "Get some sleep for you will get none this night."

Giric looked out at the sky. It was close to twilight. Exactly when was he supposed to sleep? Shaking his head he headed back to the ship and to collect Osgar. Forget sleep, he could rest when he was home. He did not want to miss one moment of this evening.

CHAPTER TEN

*P*icking at an unravelling thread on her tunic, Saga sat on a chair while Vigdis untied and removed the leather-braided kransen from around her head. Vigdis passed it to Saga and brushed her hair. Saga held it and smiled. This tiny piece of leather signified all her maidenly years up to now. Tomorrow she would don the wedding crown Freydis now fashioned in the corner of the room near the best light.

The ceremony was to take place the next day and she was not permitted to see Giric anymore until then. Tonight the men would feast in the hall, and she was unlikely to get much sleep from the noise, not that she was likely to get any regardless. Thoughts of Giric becoming her husband the following day filled her with an excitement she'd never felt before.

"Must you keep grinning like that," Vigdis said. "You look like you've gone mad in the head."

"I cannot help it," Saga said.

"I think it is wonderful," Freydis said. "You have found

someone you can learn to love in time and that's rare under any circumstances, much less with a stranger."

"Love may be a little premature, but I do like him."

"I cannot wait to see his castle," Vigdis said. "The MacAlpin told me all about it and I cannot imagine a structure so high above the ground."

"You have become quite interested in the things *the MacAlpin* has to say, sister. I believe you like him."

Vigdis blushed bright pink and lowered her gaze. She appeared rather uncomfortable and so Saga did not press the subject.

"Come let us get you to bed," Freydis said after a time. They had been talking for hours now whilst the din in the hall had grown louder.

Freydis removed her trews and tunic. Tomorrow morning she would take the cleansing bath but for tonight she must remove her warrior's clothing and don a shift that had belonged to her mother. She had not discussed her status in Giric's household and suddenly realized as she folded her clothes, that he may take issue with them.

"What if I am not permitted to wear these in Giric's castle?" she asked.

The two other women shared a glance with raised eyebrows.

"He seems to be agreeable where you are concerned, Saga. I do not believe he will set out to change you entirely," Freydis said.

Vigdis giggled. "As if he could. Really, sister. You are the strongest-willed woman I have ever known. I cannot imagine what it would take for anyone to change you."

She supposed that was true. She'd never been good at listening to what someone else wanted, especially if it conflicted with what she wanted. Having said that, she had always been disciplined when it came to training. A part of her was disappointed that Gunnar wanted her to leave when the village was under possible threat, but she understood the value in this alliance. They simply did not have the numbers to fight Short-Beard on their own regardless of their collective courage.

A soft knock on the door drew their attention.

"Who could that possibly be?" Freydis asked.

"It's her lover come to beg for a kiss goodnight," Vigdis said.

Saga crossed the chamber and opened the door to find a wide-eyed and shaking Aslaug.

Drawing her inside, Saga said, "Aslaug, what has happened?"

"Someone has set fire to one of the market huts. The men have gone to douse it, but it looks like there will be damage to the tannery and possibly the pottery."

Saga's heartbeat picked up. "Are we under attack or does Gunnar think it is one of our own?"

Aslaug wrung her hands and shook her head.

"Well, tell me," Saga said, grasping the woman by the shoulders.

"Saga, give her a chance to answer you," Freydis said.

Drawing a shaky breath, Aslaug said, "Magnus thinks it is mischief made by one of the Scots."

Cold needles of dread seeped into Saga's belly. It was no small crime to damage the property and livelihood of another. If it could be proved there would be a hefty fine.

"The chief has locked everyone in the hall under guard until he and Magnus can find out who did this."

"Thor's breath, this will end badly," Vigdis said.

"There's more," Aslaug said. "Magnus insists that your marriage cannot go forth on the morrow as planned and that the Scots must leave at daybreak."

"And what does Gunnar say?" Saga asked.

"He does not contradict Magnus," Aslaug said.

Saga closed the door and pulled her shift up and over her head and tossed it on the floor. She grabbed her clothes and put them on as quickly as she could. If a Scot was responsible for this they would be punished, on that she did not disagree. But to cancel her wedding because of it was ridiculous. And if it took her finding out what had happened, so be it. But she could not sit idly by while Magnus filled Gunnar's head with his own biased theories.

"Where do you think you're going?" Freydis asked. "You cannot go out there."

"I am not going out there," she said. "I'm going out through Gunnar's side door and I plan to sneak over to the village and see what I can learn."

"You cannot do that, Saga," Freydis said. "You must stay here where it is safe. What if this person is lurking about?"

Saga nearly laughed at her. "Do you think I am afraid of a couple of men?"

Freydis shook her head. "No I do not, but if they are wretched enough to cause this kind of harm, they will not hesitate to attack you."

"I will take an extra axe from the armoury."

Freydis shook her head. "This is Loki's work," she said in a mutter under her breath.

"Loki or not, I go to see what I can discover." To Aslaug she said, "How does everyone fare in the hall? Is anyone bothering you?"

"No, the men are kind, especially the Scots."

"Exactly my point," Saga said. "They have no reason to engage in this crime."

With that she left the chamber and snuck out through the door in Gunnar's chamber. As she inched the door closed to make no sound, she stopped and listened to ensure there was no one around. The smell of burning wood met her the second she was outside, and smoke filled the air.

Creeping along the path behind the hall she made no noise. She and Bjorn used to play a game as children to determine how close they could get to one another before being detected. She always won.

Near the village where hours earlier Giric had been fascinated by the turf houses, Saga crept behind the buildings until she was close enough to see exactly who had gone to help douse the fire.

She had no trouble making out Gunnar and Magnus. Under normal circumstances Bjorn would be there too and she suspected Giric was having a difficult time being prohibited from lending aid.

Eight other men, all her clansmen, and all reliable helped get the fire under control. Luckily it was contained to three market huts. They could be easily rebuilt in a few days.

As she watched she wondered if Bjorn's stabbing and this fire were connected. While the two events had occurred while the Scots were here, she was not convinced they were responsible.

Saga stepped back to draw a breath of clean air since the smoke billowed thicker once the water doused the flames. She accidentally stepped on a branch which drew Gunnar's attention. He came bounding for her as she stepped into view with her hands raised.

While Gunnar ran toward her, she noticed something moving in trees off to the side. Magnus' head turned in the same direction as well and they both started toward it. By the time Gunnar caught up to her all three were chasing what looked like a slight man running several paces ahead of them. He was fast, and Saga's lungs already burned from the smoke. Running made it worse.

Magnus' stride was longer than hers and he passed her

and within a short time, she heard a thunk and *'oof'* coming from up ahead.

By the time she got to where they were and bent over to catch her breath, Magnus had the man's arms pinned behind his back and his hood pulled back.

Aslaug. Saga could not have been more shocked if she'd been punched in the gut.

~

Giric leaned forward watching every man's face in the hall. He'd already scrutinized each of his own men thrice over and had whispered to Osgar to do the same. After all he'd been the one to hand pick these men. If there was a criminal among them, Gunnar would have to stand in line to punish him.

So much could be lost and at a time they were so close to forging a mutually beneficial and permanent alliance. All they had worked for may have just gone up in flames.

While he understood that Gunnar had to make decisions based primarily on what was best for his people, Giric would not give up on the alliance or having Saga for his wife without a fight.

"I see no sign of guilt in any man here, Giric, much less our own," Osgar said.

"Aye, nor do I. I have done everything I can to detect any hint of deceit and unless the man is good at deceiving, the one responsible is not here."

"Which is good because now the wedding can proceed."

"Aye," Giric said. "Providing half the village does not burn to the ground. I do not know why Gunnar did not take more men. I saw how close those buildings were together. If one catches they are all gone."

Osgar leaned back and looked around. "Where is that maid gone with the ale?" he asked.

Giric too looked around. She was nowhere in sight. "Mayhap she is seeing to Saga and her sister," he said. It was odd that she was gone since she'd been present and attending ever since their arrival.

The door swung wide and Gunnar entered followed by Magnus holding a frightened looking Aslaug, the server in question, and finally, Saga.

Giric was confused. How exactly had his future wife been able to leave her chamber without him seeing her? He had no idea there was a different way out of her chamber. Something was wrong.

He stood up as they approached. Giric searched Saga's expression for any clue as to what was going on, but she was stoic and would not meet his eye.

"Go to your chamber, sister," Gunnar said.

Saga nodded and proceeded to the chamber door without one glance in Giric's direction, in fact her head was bowed low the entire time which was not like her at all. If there was one thing he had gleaned about her in the times since they'd met it was that she was proud. At that moment the only essence about her was shame.

Once she'd disappeared into the chamber, Gunnar turned to address the hall.

"We have uncovered the person responsible for setting the fire and for stabbing Bjorn," he said. "This woman, Aslaug."

"What?"

Several men in the hall, including Giric, said this in unison. She looked too small and too timid to be capable of either act. Giric shook his head. There was no way he would be convinced she acted of her own accord.

"Gunnar, surely you cannot believe this woman committed these acts alone," Giric said.

Gunnar turned to him with a frown. "She has already admitted Einar put her to these tasks, though he had been secured." He looked pointedly to his men. "He has managed to escape. No doubt with Aslaug's aid. I will send more men in search of him in the morning, but for tonight she will remain in shackles and upon the morrow she will receive judgement for her crimes."

"And what is the punishment for such crimes?" Giric asked. He was not sure he could watch a young woman suffer through a flogging. Under his laws, she would be flogged and imprisoned.

"Punishment for attempted murder and a fire set with the intention to destroy a village is death."

Giric shook his head. "But she was put up to it as you said."

Gunnar approached Giric and stood toe to toe with him. "This is my hall, and these are the laws by which we abide. You may be more lenient in Alba, but here we deliver our justice swiftly and decidedly. The woman may have been led to the crimes, but they were done by her hands, and she must pay the price for them."

"And what of Einar? Will his life be taken too?"

"It will."

"Your punishment fits the intent and not the actual crime, Gunnar," Giric said. "No one died."

Gunnar's jaw clenched. "I have tolerated your inquiries up to now, Giric, but if you continue to question me, I will have you removed from my hall."

Giric stood his ground. Something had shifted between them. While he understood the inherent differences between their cultures and the necessity for them; Giric lived on a much bigger island than Gunnar and so the need for swift justice was greater. But it seemed an extreme punishment to take a life when none had been taken.

But what could he do? Should he fight for the life of a servant who had actually committed the crimes? Or accept the judgement of the man who had up to now impressed him with his intellect and patience when it came to decision making.

Giric stepped back and bowed in concession. A part of him wondered if he would look back on this moment in the future and wish he had made a different decision.

"You are a smart man, Giric of Alba," Gunnar said. To Magnus he said, "Secure her in irons and post two men."

The maid's head was bent low as Magnus pushed her ahead of him. Her body was limp as though she had given up interest in fighting for her life. Giric had seen enough punishment in his day to know when 'twas necessary and when the lines blurred between the right and wrong way to account for a crime.

"Sit with me and share my mead," Gunnar said quietly behind him.

Giric did as he was asked, accepting the horn Gunnar offered.

After a time, he said, "This punishment worries you, greatly."

"The whole business worries me," Giric said. "It is clear to me Einar is working against you and has plotted to bring harm to you which benefits Short-Beard more than anyone else. By what means Einar coerced this young woman to do his bidding I know not, but I tell you that she does not carry the look of a criminal. For her to pay the ultimate price for the devious workings of another man feels wrong," Giric said. "I know you do not agree, and I respect that your word is law here. But you asked, and I am telling you, the punishment of death feels wrong considering the circumstance."

Gunnar downed his horn and poured another as Saga entered the hall, her head still bent low.

"Brother I wish to speak to you," she said still not meeting Giric's eyes.

Gunnar looked over his shoulder and stood. "I will come to you," he said.

Giric drank from his horn. The ale was cool and soothed the dryness in this throat. He needed to know if Gunnar had changed his mind about the wedding. He did not know what he would do if he was asked to leave without Saga.

When he came back he was chuckling. Filling their horns again he said, "It seems you and my sister are well matched."

"How is that?" Giric asked.

"Because she just said pretty much the same thing you did and begged me to spare Aslaug's life."

Giric smiled. "And how was it that she came to be outside of the hall without walking through it."

"A good warrior never reveals his secrets, Giric," Gunnar said with a grin. "You know this."

Giric took a deep breath. "And the wedding? Will it proceed on the morrow? I cannot imagine an execution and a wedding on the same day would be something your gods would smile upon."

Shaking his head, he said, "I hope I do not live to regret this, Giric."

Giric grinned. He knew what was coming and was pleased the man could be reasoned with.

"You will find another fitting punishment for the maid?" Giric asked.

"I will. My sister suggested she be banished from our village. Saga will take responsibility for her until she reaches Alba, but as for this village, she will never be permitted to return."

"So it is a wedding on the morrow only," Giric said. "But

why would Saga not look at me earlier when you returned and then when she asked to speak with you?"

"The wedding will proceed as planned and my sister is not permitted to lay eyes upon her future husband the night before the wedding. The goddess Freya forbids it. Now I must go speak to my brother. He will be vexed with the change in punishment, but Aslaug need not spend the night thinking it will be her last."

Giric was surprised once again at the compassion the man displayed in contrast to the fierceness he could convey when needed.

CHAPTER ELEVEN

Two maids sloshed cold water over Saga's body. In Gunnar's chamber, she'd been scrubbed from head to toe in a wooden tub lined with cloth with the hottest water she could tolerate. Freydis explained that each steam particle took with it one more piece of her maidenhood. Now being doused with cold water, they sealed in her true self which she would take into womanhood.

They wrapped her in cloths and patted her skin dry then walked with her back to her and Vigdis' chamber to dry and braid her hair. She was to marry Giric MacDomnail of Alba this day and every fibre in her body told her it was the right and proper thing.

The night before she had prayed to the goddess Freya for clarity. When she awoke in the morning there was absolutely no doubt in her mind that he was entwined in her life's journey.

Saga wore a long green gown that was tied at the waist by a gold stitched belt and fastened at the shoulders by two gold brooches embedded with rubies her brother had put away for her after their mother entered the realm of the dead. On her arms, she wore coiled gold bands also studded with rubies.

Once she was dressed, Freydis brought her to sit by the fire so they could work on her hair. They braided it away from her face and adorned the braids with tiny bands of gold and placed the elaborate wedding crown upon her head. Freydis had spent countless hours modifying it the night before. The piece was heavier than Saga had originally thought but it fit comfortably on her head because of the padding Freydis had fastened to the inside of the crown. This one had belonged to her mother as well and was made of silver and contained green and clear crystals that resembled the branches of the tree Yggdrasil, a symbol of extended life.

When they were done she stood and faced them. "Well?" she asked.

Vigdis put her hands to her mouth.

"You are the most beautiful sight I have ever seen," Freydis said with wet eyes. "Truly, Freya smiles down on you today, Saga. You are the vision of a true goddess.

Saga was afraid to look down, lest the crown fall off her head so she would have to take them at their word.

"I have never seen you look more powerful," Vigdis said. "Even though I have seen you every day of my life, I have never seen you looking so much like a goddess yourself."

Saga smiled at them both and walked toward the door. Lifting the latch she pulled it open to a waiting Gunnar. His eyes grew wide, and his jaw slacked

"Close your mouth, Gunnar," Saga said. "You look like a fish gulping for air."

Freydis came up to him and pushed his chin up. Saga noticed the look that passed between them. She had suspected the attraction between them had never really expired, but had pushed those thoughts out of the way considering it none of her business. Perhaps her own nuptials had opened her eyes to such things at which she would otherwise scoff. She smiled to herself; she didn't mind that at all.

"Are you ready?" Saga asked him.

"Ja," he said in a rough voice and offered his arm.

Saga had seen enough marriages over the years to know hers would be a quick ceremony, including a sacrifice to the gods, laying on of hands, followed by the feast. Since Giric wanted to return so quickly, he promised a full day of feasting there and another full three days once they had gone through the ceremony at his home. Married twice and by all their collective gods. Surely their marriage would be blessed and fruitful. A small tinge entered her belly at the thought of bedding him later. The brief tryst they'd had in the field was enough to show her they were compatible in that way—more than compatible. She longed to feel his hard body pressed against hers again.

As they walked to the great hall and to her future she could not help but wonder how so much had changed in the past few days. She'd been vehemently opposed to any possibility of an alliance with the Scots. But now she felt differently, and it wasn't because of her yearning for the irresistible Giric MacDomnail.

She'd learned that seeing only the boundaries of one's own borders was the first step in one's downfall. Her people had taken this land from others and claimed it for their own. What right had they to do so except that they had been stronger and more determined?

And what of Giric's family and the people who fell under his protection? Did they share his vision for an aligned future with the Vikings, or were they as skeptical as she had been?

Giric had siblings, but she did not know how many yet and wondered how they would receive her. It was clear his friend, MacAlpin was in favour, else he would not have come. Or so she supposed. He may have intended to talk Giric out of the plot for all Saga knew.

An inkling of doubt slithered its way into her heart. What if she'd allowed herself to be caught up in the fantastical imaginings of a mad man? She shook her head.

"This is right," Gunnar said, as though he could read her thoughts. His reassurance would have to be enough to quell her nerves.

As they approached the hall, she caught the first sight of him. Adorned again in his crimson, fur-trimmed robe. The intensity in his eyes was almost more than she could bear. His gaze swept the length of her sending thrills up and down her spine. Blessed Freya, what that man could do to her with just a look!

As she drew closer he held out his hand. She took it and Gunnar placed his own hand atop them both.

"I ask thee, Odin and thee, Freya, to bless this union. May it bear the fruit of many sons."

Saga searched Giric's expression. This man held her future in his hand. Though she had insisted upon her own conditions of the marriage, in truth, he could discard them once Gunnar said the final words. But she saw nothing in the man before her to suggest he would be anything but agreeable to those and any other demands.

His warm brown eyes drew her in and held her captivated. She noted his straight nose and sensual mouth that curled slightly at the corners. How she wanted to taste him, all of him.

"She is yours, and you are hers," Gunnar said as he lifted his hand from theirs.

Saga smiled at Giric. He leaned down and brushed his lips across hers. "Mine," he whispered.

"And now we feast!"

Gunnar's booming voice was followed by a cheer from those attending, which by Saga's estimation was the entire village.

As they walked outside for the ceremonial sacrifice to the gods, she noted Giric had taken her hand and linked his and her fingers together. From time to time whilst Gunnar performed the ritual, Giric's hand squeezed hers and at others his thumb caressed her hand. The sensation of only one part of him touching her roused her desires.

Once the ritual was complete, they returned to the great hall to where the servants had lined the tables with several platters of bread and meat. A boar turned on a spit in the centre of the hall and bundles of burning sage hung over the fire to ward off evil spirits and further bless the union. Saga drank in the aroma. When would she see her home again? Her mind once again flooded with questions about her husband's home which she would see soon enough. Would she be happy there? Would his people embrace her, or would she stand out amongst the women of his world? And worse, would he insist she become like them? Like her sister?

Giric dipped his head and caught her eye, his brow furrowing. "What is it?" he asked. "Does something displease you?"

Shaking her head, she said, "Nay. All is well, I assure you."

How could she confess her insecurities to him? She had not even given his home a chance and yet here she was already dooming it. She drew in a deep breath and offered him a bright smile. She would try her best to fit in wherever they lived. He had certainly done his best in her home. She could afford him the same courtesy at the very least.

~

*B*rushing his lips across the sensitive flesh at the base of her neck, he asked, "You will tell me if anything troubles you, aye?"

She smiled at him, her eyes lighting up. "I will."

"Good, mayhap we should excuse ourselves so I may discover every way I can please you."

His body hummed with anticipation of having her as his own. How could he possibly have become so enthralled with her in such a short time? Only God knew the answer to that question and at this point he didn't care. He wanted her in every way she could take him.

Her lips parted as she gazed at his mouth. Giric leaned down and stopped himself before kissing her. "Would it be considered inappropriate to leave right now?"

"Nay," she said. "You are mine and I am yours now. We may do as we wish."

That was enough for him. Giric stood, taking her hand in his and bowed low to Gunnar who raised his horn in salute.

He marvelled at the difference between their cultures. If they were at his home right now, the ladies would whisk the bride away to change her and place her in the bed. The husband in turn would be carried to the chamber, stripped bare and placed in the bed with her. In some cases, the lords and ladies present would remain in the chamber but off to the side until the deed was done. Giric had never cared for that tradition and much preferred this way, which was that the bride and her husband simply left the feast without a fuss and went on their merry way.

Once inside her chamber he turned her around and pulled her close. He softly brushed his lips across hers while caressing her breast. She surprised him by pushing him back and tugging and unpinning until her garment was loose.

Once she pulled it from her body, she threw it at him and dashed to the bed, piled high with furs.

Giric disrobed in record time and crawled on top of her, pinning her underneath the furs.

"My beautiful Viking wife. What shall I do with you?"

"Anything you want," she said and lifted her head to take his bottom lip into her mouth.

She sucked hard, sending a jolt to his cock. Christ's breath, would he survive this night? Her?

He pulled the fur down beneath her breasts and tucked it around her arms and shifted his body so that she could not move her arms.

He loved the way she tried to buck him off but couldn't. Close. But he was stronger and wanted to drive her as mad with need as he was at the moment.

Giric leaned down and took one hard nipple into his mouth and sucked hard. She arched against him and groaned. He released it and blew on it lightly making the wet skin cool. He moved to the other breast and while sucking on this one, pinched the other nipple making her cry out.

"Giric please."

"Oh love, you are not getting away that easily. I plan to learn your limits tonight and hope to learn some of my own in the process."

He inflicted his sweet torture back and forth between her breasts until her breathing came in shallow pants and her body squirmed beneath him.

Pulling the fur down, he released her hands and hooked her legs over his shoulders so before she could respond, he'd wedged himself between her legs. Giric found her hardened bud and flicked it with his tongue as he slipped two fingers into her slick opening. Her flesh quivered around him. He found a rhythm between sucking and pumping his fingers into her, marvelling at the way her body arched against him.

He reached up and pinched her nipple as he sucked deeply, bringing about her first climax. God but she was glorious in her passion with her head thrown back and her body bucking off the bed.

Before she fully came down from her orgasm, Giric shifted his body and stroked the head of his cock across her heat. He was so rigid and desperate for release he had to clench his jaw to keep from slamming into her too quickly.

Slowly he stroked in and out of her a little bit at a time watching the desire rekindle in her eyes.

"Please, more Giric," she said and grabbed his ass with her hands while wrapping her legs around his waist drawing him into her.

They both gasped as he penetrated past her maidenhead, taking her fully. His entire body was poised and ready to take her with the full fury of his passion, but he waited for her to adjust to his size.

"Do not stop," she said. "I want this, all of this."

Giric pulled out of her and when she whimpered he thrust hard and deep within her. Her head was tossed back, and her mouth was open wide. "Yes!" She said as she slapped his ass.

He needed no further encouragement. Giric grabbed her hips and thrust forcefully in and out in a pounding rhythm. God this woman was built for passion. She pulled at his shoulders, his hair, and his hips while her own rose to meet him in the same passionate dance.

Harder and harder he pushed into her body until a familiar tingling started at the base of his spine thickening and hardening his already stiff cock.

Just as her body tightened around him he felt the pull of his entire body before emptying his seed into her. Her legs were wrapped so tightly around him he couldn't pull away from her which tipped him over the edge.

Never had he been so swept away by desire's release. His head grew light as wave after wave washed over his body.

When he came back to his senses his mouth was on hers and he was being properly devoured by her. She had yet to release her legs from his waist and she still pulsed around him giving his body little jolts.

Saga placed her hands on his face and stared into his eyes. The look of wonder on her face was worth a king's ransom.

"I did not know it could be like this," she said, breathlessly. "I mean I know men always liked it, but I did not know I would like it so much too."

"I have never known anyone quite like you, wife."

"Have you done this with a lot of women?"

Among the women of his acquaintance, he would have been wary of answering that question. But he had no problem answering it for her. She did not possess the manipulative nature of a lot of the women he'd encountered in his life.

"I have been with three women in my life," he said.

"And was your sex with them like this?"

He knew she was asking out of genuine curiosity. "No, wife, it was nothing like this. I have never felt such desire and such a release in my life like I have with you. What we have is more than I could have ever hoped for in this life. It is a true gift."

She smiled at him. "I am glad to hear it. And if you ever want to have this sex with another woman," she said and kissed the tip of his nose, "I will cut your member from your body." With that she released her legs from his waist.

He slid out of her and moved to her side to stroke her hair. Kissing the base of her neck he grinned for he did not know if she was serious or not. And it didn't matter—there would never be a need to find out.

CHAPTER TWELVE

The galley rocked in a maddening pattern of bow to stern then port to starboard. Saga leaned over the side of the galley and let her guts spill once more. She'd been to sea before, but had never gotten sick like this. Giric had been gracious and offered her a blanket, but all she really wanted at that moment was to slip into the sea and perish for surely that would be better than this misery.

Freydis wiped her brow with a damp cloth. She didn't know where Vigdis and Aslaug had managed to sit, and at this point, she hardly could bring herself to worry about them.

"We will dock soon," he said whilst wrapping the blanket around her anyway. "Only another hour or so."

"I have never felt like this before," she said. "Why am I so ill?"

"The sea swell was heavier than normal today. Do not worry, love. We will make landfall soon and you will feel better."

She prayed to Odin it would be so. Curling into a ball, she lay down close to the prow of the ship ignoring the staring eyes of her husband's crew and the concerned look on Freydis' face. The woman had insisted she wear a gown for the voyage and her first introduction to the people of this castle. Now the damned thing kept tangling around her legs as she tried to find some reprieve.

They'd left at daybreak and her stomach protested almost immediately. She'd been uneasy about the trip to begin with, and her illness had taken a toll on her courage, something on which she could always rely. Saga closed her eyes and visualized herself back in the fields of home practicing her bow and arrow and axe throwing skills. She'd give anything to be back there right now.

Her thoughts turned to her husband. They'd shared a glorious night in each other's arms. Perhaps the lack of sleep was a factor in her reaction to the sea today. She hoped it was that simple. A hot meal and a good rest would restore her strength. It had to. Weakness was not something she'd ever experienced, and these past few hours had proved to her that she did not like it in the least.

"We're here, love," Giric said, gently shaking her shoulder.

Saga emerged from underneath the blanket and struggled to stand. As Giric aided her, she gripped the railing and peered out toward the mainland of Scotland, her new home.

The first thing that struck her was the mountains in the distance to the north and the lush woodland. While the island had plenty of wood to sustain them, there was no abundance like this. Saga wiped her face and blinked as the landscape widened before her.

"It is beautiful is it not?"

"Ja, like nothing I've seen."

"But you said you'd been to sea before."

"Not to the Scots-land. I've been to Iona and Skye, but not the mainland."

Giric wrapped his arms around her waist and placed his

chin on her shoulder. Her courage surfaced when in his arms like this. She was sure she could face even the trickster Loki with Giric by her side. The thought made her smile.

"You're feeling better," he said.

"I am."

"Good, because I want you to love your new home as much as I do."

Saga turned her head to look up onto his face. The strength there awed her. She'd spent her entire life around strong men, but Giric was different. His power came from his mind and body, and he seemed to know her to her core on instinct. Freya had smiled down upon her the day he'd sailed across the Clyde.

Crossing the gangway, she noted the differences immediately. No war party waited to demand identification. Then again, this was Giric's home and so they would recognize his sail's colours, but the hustle and bustle of the area around the docks was quite different than she'd expected.

Aslaug stood beside Saga with a forlorn look on her face. She regarded the woman and considered her plight.

"You had a choice, Aslaug."

"I had no choice," she said. "The earl threatened to kill my mother."

"And had you brought that news to Gunnar, he would have protected you and your mother and justly punished the earl. Now you must suffer the consequences of your lack of faith."

"But where will I go?"

"I will approach a tavern owner on your behalf," Giric said, though Saga hadn't realized he'd been standing so close. She would not stop him, but she could not bring herself to help the woman for the permanent damage she nearly caused.

"Stay here for a moment," he said to Saga and moved off

with Aslaug to enter a wooden structure nearby. A short while later he returned alone.

"She has employment and lodging."

"You are kinder to her than I can be."

"Aye, mayhap." He looked in the direction she stared. "You are taking it all in."

Men moved sacks of Odin only knew what from one side of the docking area to the other. Several ships were either being loaded or unloaded, and Saga could not help but stop and stare. Gunnar owned three ships. She'd never seen this many before.

"Are you impressed?" Giric asked.

"You do much trading here."

"Aye, we do. Crofters from my lands and many others provide goods for trade coming out of this port. You can imagine how devastating it would be for us if Gunnar attacked here."

Something niggled at her. While she had agreed to this union to prevent such attacks, surely there was more than that binding them now as husband and wife. Or was that just how *she* felt?

She looked at Giric and watched as he nodded to the men as he passed. Many even bowed to him. They appeared to respect him, but it seemed no different to how men and women regarded Gunnar in their village. What she did note was the stench. Fish rotted in a barrel along the harbour and flies buzzed round something a filthy wretch pushed in a cart.

He'd talked at length about ensuring men were free to choose for whom they worked. But by her estimation for the small amount of coin that passed between hands, these men were dirty and scrawny and little better off than those in her village. At least her people were clean.

They came to a structure with a short door, or at least one under which Saga would have to duck.

Once inside, the aroma of cooking food hit her, and she realized that her earlier sickness had fully passed. She and Giric, together with Vigdis, Freydis, and Osgar, sat at a large wooden table while a woman with a hefty bosom fussed over the men.

"We have to wait for my men to return with enough horses so we may as well eat," Giric said.

The bowl put before her contained chunks of meat and broth; she was also given crusty bread. Saga glanced over to see what Giric did with his and followed his lead by dunking the bread in the stew and lifting the bowl to his lips when all the meat was gone.

She recalled the feast and how he had tried to feed her. Was that the way of it at his castle? Would he insist upon it at their next meal and in front of everyone?

Once they were all finished, Giric ordered a tankard of ale and engaged Freydis in conversation about her healing techniques and particularly the herbs she would need.

"We are always in need of a good healer. If you wish to settle at Castle Domnail, I will secure lodgings for you in the village. I believe you will find the people to be accepting in time."

"Thank-you," Freydis said. "It is my wish to see Saga settled before I make any decisions as to my future. I would very much like to see this Edinburgh Vigdis has been talking about."

"Then once we are settled in, we shall go," Saga said.

She hadn't had much interest up until now, but the scene at the dock had intrigued her. According to Vigdis, Edinburgh was a large city. Saga was curious to learn exactly what that meant.

Giric gave her a curious glance and said, "We should go. The horses will have been here by now."

As they left the tavern, Saga noticed the streets had become much busier than when they'd entered. She looked around to take it all in.

Giric touched her arm and said, "Come let us get to our horses before we are set upon."

"Set upon by whom?"

Before she had the words out of her mouth, a dozen or more young children surrounded her with their hands outstretched. They gazed up at her with wide eyes, their mouths agape. She looked at Giric and lifted her hands in the air. "What do they want?"

"Coin," he said as he reached into his purse and grabbed a small handful of coin and placed one in each hand.

Saga did not understand. Why would children come to this place to receive payment? How had they earned it?

"Come," he said and guided her by her elbow. "I will explain once we are on the road to home."

Once mounted, they trotted out of the centre of the town and onto a well-worn road. The trees rustled and creaked around them drawing her attention time and again. There was comfort in the sound and smell of the vegetation all around. Living on a small island, things like wood and wild herbs for medicine could be in short supply if one were not prudent in their use. Here, that did not seem to be as much of a concern. Even in her homeland, they were cautious overusing the woodlands. Land was in such short supply that was why they had set out to find new places to settle in the first place.

"Do you like what you have seen so far?"

The comment drew her out of her musings. "I was thinking how fortunate you are to have such a bountiful place to live. And yet I do not understand why those men back there have so little. And what sort of employment do the children have to earn your coin?"

Giric's brow knit. "They have no employment. They beg for money to help their families who are struggling to make ends meet."

"And are you not responsible for everyone in your village?"

He shook his head. "The people of this town engage in free commerce. They buy and sell and barter from one another. I do not provide for them." He pulled back on the horse's reins. "You do not approve?"

"At my home, you said your people were better off because they had the right to choose. But I do not see that. I see people who are hungry. My people are not fat, but they are fed and no children in my village have to beg for food."

"It is not that simple here," he said. "Your village holds a few hundred. The cities here on the mainland hold thousands. It is not possible for one laird to feed so many."

She shook her head. "Your people are not better off than mine." She turned her head away from him and trotted on ahead to ride with Freydis and Vigdis. Without knowing the way to his castle, she had to wait for him to catch up and was grateful that he remained silent for the next few miles. His description of his home thus far was not what she expected. She now wondered what awaited her at the castle.

~

Giric could not put his finger on the moment Saga's mood soured, but considering how sick she'd been on the crossing, he figured she would prefer silence during their travels. Once at the castle, he'd have a bath carried to their chamber and ensure her every comfort. He hoped she would see that people were better off having a choice for how they wanted to live versus having that taken from them. But that was a debate they need not have this day, or at all if she did not wish it. He would not impose his values upon her, rather he hoped she would understand in time once she lived among his people longer.

"Have you sent word ahead of your arrival?" Osgar asked from beside him. He'd been hanging back whilst Giric rode with Saga, but now that she had moved away, Osgar joined him.

"Aye. I sent word to my sister, Aislin. She has far more sense than my brother, Donnan. He had ranted and raved about me taking this journey. That lad needs a broader view of the world. I hope to keep him far away from my wife at least until she settles."

"I agree with you there, my friend. I have wondered how your wife will fit in."

"Is that a comment about her height?"

"No, merely an observation about the differences in how we see one another. You realize that most of the people living in your castle and surrounding village fear the Vikings. And now you bring one into their homes and expect them to love her outright. I am saying be patient with them and with her in the coming days."

Giric shrugged and watched Saga as she trotted ahead of them. Her back was straight as she sat tall on the horse. He was well aware of the danger of the situation, but the effort was well worth the risk if the final outcome resulted in peace among his people and hers.

After a couple hours, they finally reached the roadway leading to the castle. Giric rode up alongside Saga and offered her a smile.

"Would you prefer to ride with me as we cross over the drawbridge, or ride yourself?"

Her quizzical expression nearly made him burst out

laughing. "Why would I ride with you? I am perfectly able to ride by myself."

"Some women prefer the protection of their husbands upon arriving at her new home for the first time."

Shaking her head and laughing, she said, "Why would I need your protection?" She looked ahead of them and back to him again. "Am I in danger here?"

"No—I—never mind. You will soon see that you are unlike most of the women here."

"Your women are weak and need a man's protection in their own home?"

When she put it like that, it sounded deplorable. But that was not what he meant. "Our women are not weak, not at all, but it is our job to protect those under our care."

Saga shifted in her seat, so her body was turned to face him. "Your words do not make sense to me. I will see how your women are treated and if I do not like it I will tell you so."

Of that he had no doubt. Something told him there would be much upheaval in his world henceforth. Giric smiled to himself. He had to remember that she was a warrior first and weakness was not in her vocabulary. He'd offered her the same courtesy he'd offer any woman entering his domain. The danger to any woman was from men who assumed they could take liberties even when told outright they were not welcome. Giric did not tolerate such behaviour, but acknowledged some men simply took what they wanted. He'd run off more than one guard for such behaviour.

As they approached the castle he said, "Here we are. Do you like it?"

He watched as she took in the view of the guard towers as they passed through the outer wall of the bailey. She stopped and stared as they entered the main courtyard and watched the men spar with wooden swords and the kitchen lads wheeled carts of vegetables. She placed her hand on her forehead and looked up at the tall round towers that flanked the drawbridge leading into the inner courtyard of the castle.

"I did not expect to see such a large house. Do you have so much family that you need such a large dwelling?"

Giric laughed. "No, lass. Those two towers offer a vantage point to allow the guards to see anyone approaching. Would you like to see?"

"I would like to see that very much."

Once dismounted, he took her hand and led her to the winding staircase leading to the east tower. From up there they would be able to view the Firth of Clyde and beyond to the Isle of Arran.

At the top she placed her hands on the stone ledge and gasped. She looked down to the ground and gripped the ledge tighter. "You can see so much up here." When she looked back at him, light danced in her eyes. "You would know when ships are entering the port and when riders are approaching your lands."

"Aye, that's exactly the purpose. Not everyone who passes this way wants to share in a goblet of ale."

She turned to him, concern filling her eyes. "This castle was built to keep my people out."

"Aye. But others as well. I have enemies enough both here and across the sea."

"Am I still your enemy?" she asked with an impish grin.

Giric shook his head. "You are not, and neither are your kin. Our marriage will bring peace to our people. I know it in my heart." He paused and drew a breath before letting it out slowly. "But we must be patient."

"I can be patient, husband," she said.

"Are you out of your mind?" a stern voice asked from behind them.

A small knot formed in his guts. Placing his hand at the

small of his wife's back, he turned and said, "Sister. How do you fare?"

"How do *I* fare?" she asked with her hands on her hips. "Some word would have been helpful, brother. Half the castle is in uproar at your display and the other half is in shock."

"Saga, this is my sister, Aislin. And sister, this is my wife, Saga. Mayhap we can sit by the fire in the great hall and discuss this matter."

"You are quite welcome at Castle Domnail, my lady," she said. "To speak true, it is not I who have any issue with you or any of your people so long as you do not invade our lands. But there are many here who are not so open-minded as my brother."

"You did not tell anyone you were bringing me here?" Saga asked.

Giric put his hands up. "I sent a rider ahead of us once we reached Prestwick. Now, can we please continue this in the hall so we may eat and celebrate my nuptials and I can properly introduce my wife."

Giric watched Aislin's expression soften. She regarded Saga for a moment and smiled. "My dear it is a good thing you appear strong. I fear you may need to draw from that strength it in the days ahead. Lord help us when Donnan finds out." As she said this she touched Saga's arm and the fabric of her gown, her gaze resting on the sword strapped to her side.

Saga stepped back. "My brother will adjust, like everyone else." Giric squeezed Saga's elbow; she regarded it with a quizzical expression. "What are you doing to my arm?" she asked in a low voice.

"'Tis a way to offer comfort."

Shaking her head, Saga said, "You people have strange ways."

"I'm beginning to see that," he said.

As they followed Aislin to the great hall, Giric took note of those they passed along the way. She was right. He'd been somewhat blinded to the shock of what the sight of Saga and her sister might evoke in his people. He'd have to tread carefully and with clarity if this was going to work. Of one thing he was certain, ignorant people conjured strange ideas especially when fear was added into the mixture.

CHAPTER THIRTEEN

The great hall was nothing like the hall from her village. Large woven images adorned the stone walls depicting various scenes though the colours were not overly bright, they were fascinating stories told through the weaver's talent. Some were images of fields and flowers, whilst others appeared to tell the story of these people in battle. Upon closer inspection, she noted the conquered warriors of one tapestry wore furs and wielded axes. The Scots were the clear victors in this scene. Vikings lay scattered about the beach in pools of pink or red oozing from their bodies and in the distance the unmistakable sail of her grandfather's longship.

"'Tis a story told through fabric," Giric said from behind her.

"It is meant to send a message to your people. And not one of peace. This tapestry of yours does not depict us sharing a horn or shaking hands. This is about conquering us."

Her body recoiled from the sight of it. If that was the

mentality promoted here, she would never have a chance to fit in.

"Saga, look at all the tapestries in order," he said and pointed at the others adjacent to this one.

She didn't want to look any further but did so now out of morbid curiosity. There were additional tapestries woven in the same artistic style as the one before her. The second depicted priests holding crosses over the dead Vikings. The third were Scots with their heads bowed surrounding burial fires. And the final one made her breath catch in her throat. this one was prominently visible above the hearth. In it, a Scot who could have been Giric, grasped arms with a Viking who could have been Gunnar. All those surrounding them cheered.

"These were woven in my father's time," Giric said.

"I do not know what to say."

"You do not need to say anything, but I urge you to enjoy this hall. You may examine any and every thing here. This is my gift to you."

"You wish to give me everything in this hall?'

"Because you are the lady of this castle."

"You have strange ways, husband," she said and shook her head. She did not have a need for so many things, and would not accept them but wanted to explore more of this hall of his.

Saga had never seen such a sight in her life. In between the images was an array of weapons including swords, shields, axes she definitely wanted to view closer, and something with a long handle and chain protruding out of the top fastened to a metal ball with spikes surrounding it.

In the centre of the hall was a long, wooden table, surrounded by heavy looking intricately carved chairs. She was certain it could seat nearly as many as Gunnar's hall could contain. Giric motioned for her and her sister and

Freydis to be seated to the right of the head seat. Osgar and Aislin sat at the left and Giric sat at the head.

Giric had asked his steward to summon everyone in the castle for the announcement of their marriage and for the first time in her life, Saga felt an odd sensation creep into her belly.

Looking around the hall at those gathered thus far, one thing rested most commonly on their faces—fear. She compared the gowns she and Vigdis wore to Aislin's. Where hers was sleeveless and fastened at the shoulders with heavy brooches, Aislin's had a fully stitched upper bodice with long sleeves and ties at the sides. Saga couldn't imagine how restrictive that must be on the woman's arms. Could she even raise them over her head?

Just then a man entered who had the look of Giric, but was far shorter and wore a scowl and pout that was almost humorous. He reminded her of Earl Einar. The man did not hang back with everyone else in the hall, rather he strode with purpose directly to her and Giric.

"You have brought the enemy into our home," he said to Giric, as he flicked his head in her direction.

Giric stood so suddenly, his chair teetered before resting upright. "You will take a seat and show fealty to me, brother, or you will leave this hall."

"I have a right to speak my mind and I will do so." Pointing to Saga he said, "She and her kin will destroy our homes and glory in our suffering."

"I said be quiet, brother!" Giric's fists clenched at his sides.

Saga watched the two men glare at one another. While she understood why Giric wanted to speak to everyone at once, surely silencing a voice of concern was not the answer to anyone's fear. She had to admit, she was in uncharted territory. At home if there was word of an attack or an actual attack, they would prepare and fight and the gods would decide who lived and who died.

Here the people seemed to thrive on their fear instead of face it and deal with it. Thor's teeth, no wonder her people had been raiding here for so many years. Their indecisiveness made them easy prey.

Saga wanted what Giric wanted, but realized acceptance could not be forced upon people. The tension in the room was thick when she stood. Whether from fear or submission, Giric's brother took a step back and returned to the others along the hall's periphery.

Giric stood beside her and smiled. Not really knowing what else to do, she squeezed his arm. He glanced at it quickly then winked, sending an odd flutter in her belly.

"Thank you for attending, everyone," he said. His voice carried well in the large room. "As you know by now, I have taken a wife. Her name is Saga Haraldson and she is the sister of Chieftain Gunnar Haraldson of Lagavulin."

A low murmur grew in the hall. No need to worry yet. No one questioned or outright jeered at Giric. But the dissent was apparent from the frowns many wore.

"Our people have been attacked by my wife's people for decades. This union will put an end to all of that. Gunnar and I have struck an accord and we will both honour it. Saga, her sister, Vigdis, and their healer, Freydis are our guests. You will treat them no differently than you would any other guest in this castle."

"How do we know she won't slay you in your sleep?" someone asked from the back.

Saga scanned the hall, but could not tell who it was. Mayhap the brother, stirring trouble, but it really could have been any one of them.

"Because he has my word too," she said before Giric could answer. Her comment drew audible gasps.

"Aye, she speaks our tongue. So if you think to trick her, you will be disappointed. You should also know, Lady MacDomnail is a shield-maiden, which, as some of you may know, is a warrior and I will add that her skills in battle can rival many of the men I've seen fight over the years. So do not think to challenge her either. She is your new lady, and I expect her to be treated with the same respect you show me. If that is a problem with anyone, the door is there and you may leave at any time."

More rumblings erupted among the servants and those gathered. It didn't take long for the din in the hall to rise enough for Giric to raise his hands to settle them.

"I know this may not be what you expected, but this is the best way forward. And now you may all return to your duties. I wish to feast this eve with my new wife."

As the crowd disbursed, one man wearing long black robes came forward. He bowed to Giric and held out his hand to him, who promptly took it and kissed the ring on the man's little finger.

"Father Gilwin, this is my wife, Lady MacDomnail. My lady, this is Father Gilwin who serves the congregation of this castle and the surrounding villages."

"It is my great pleasure to meet you, Lady MacDomnail. You are most welcome here and if there is anything you wish to have explained as you receive your first sacrament, I will aid in any way I can."

Shaking her head, she looked at Giric and asked, "What is a sacrament?"

"My wife will not be converting, Father."

Some of the colour drained from his face. "But how can that be? Your children will be heathens, her soul will not be saved," he said as he produced a small white cloth and dabbed at his eyes and his forehead.

It all sounded ominous to Saga and the Father did seem

quite upset about it. But she didn't understand what they meant by converting.

"And your marriage," he said while wringing his hands, "it has not been blessed by God. It is not recognized by the church which means any children she bears will be bastards."

Giric put his hands up. "We have already agreed to marry in the chapel as we have married before her gods as well."

"Blasphemy!"

"No. Practical," Giric said, placing his hand on the man's shoulder. "You may prepare yourself in any way you require to make this happen, but we will be married in the chapel today, and our future children will be baptised as well. Are we understood, Father?"

Once Giric dropped his hand, the man stepped back and straightened his robes, and his shoulders. "Aye, my lord. I understand fully. However, I will need to send a letter of this most unusual occasion to the bishop."

"You should do that and while you're writing letters, please send one to the king. I am certain he will approve of my following in his footsteps in ensuring the future peace of this country."

This time all the colour did drain from the man's face. Saga almost laughed. What strange ways these people had. They oft battled with words instead of weapons, whereas she would have lifted him by the scruff of the neck and shook him until he complied.

"I will do as you say, my lord. With haste, I must return to the chapel and make ready." He skittered away from them and left the hall.

Finally alone, Giric turned to her. "How do you fare?"

"I am well," she said. Though her belly flip flopped when he looked at her like that.

"Do you wish for privacy before we go to the chapel?"

"Privacy? For what purpose?"

He laughed, sending a delicious caress of sensation across her flesh. "To mayhap change into your wedding clothes or anything else ladies do when preparing for their wedding day."

She had not thought of that. As far as she was concerned, they were already married and so she did not look at this ceremony in the same way as the one on Islay.

"If it is your wish for me to dress as a bride like I have already done, I would do that for you." She smiled at him hoping he would understand her meaning.

He placed his hand on her arm and rubbed. The sensation was warm and added to her growing desire for him. "Aye, I would like to see you dressed as the lady you now are and walking toward me to be mine forever."

It occurred to her only in that moment, that he did not consider them married either. She would see it done. In her eyes they would never be parted and if going through this with him would seal that fate for him as well, so be it.

~

The chapel was not overly large, but the aisle seemed a mile long whilst he watched the door for her to enter. He'd left her with his sister and hers an hour ago and couldn't imagine what took that long since she had not even considered changing until he brought up the subject.

"You have developed feelings for her already," Osgar said. "I can see it in your eyes. This woman you've known for only a few days has stolen your heart."

Giric looked over at Osgar and frowned. It was not exactly like that. Aye, she had captured his attention, and she was more than a match for him in their bedchamber, but as far as love went, it was far too soon for any of that and it was irrelevant for what their union represented. The fact that they got along and were compatible for procreating, was a blessing in itself. He did not require anything more for this union to be considered a success—or so he kept telling himself.

"I wish this part of the union to be complete so we can move forward with everyone accepting it and for Saga to take her place in this castle."

Osgar crossed his arms across his chest and lifted one eyebrow. "Aye indeed. You are practically sweating like a lad about to lay with a woman for the first time. I admit I did not notice your countenance on Islay because I was too busy trying to keep us both from being killed."

"You mean you were too busy trying to catch the eye of my wife's sister."

Shaking his head he said, "That is not true. Though she is a lovely woman in every sense, you did not notice how many of Gunnar's warriors glared at you the entire time you were there. The only two people you noticed were Gunnar and his sister. Truly, I was not certain with whom you wished a union."

Just as Giric took a step toward Osgar to put the man in his place, a silhouette crossed the doorway drawing his attention. Moving back into place he watched Saga as she made her way slowly toward him. Once inside the chapel, the light from the side windows illuminated her and the sight caught his breath.

Instead of the long green gown she'd worn on the crossing, she now wore a flowing crimson gown similar to those his sister wore, with a wreath of the same colour flowers in her hair. She carried a handful of wildflowers in front of her which caressed the top of her breasts as she walked. With a square neckline, her breasts appeared firm and heavy. Giric looked into her eyes and was transfixed. Clear blue like the sea on a calm, clear day, her countenance was that of wonder and the pink in her cheeks showed a tiny amount of shyness he'd never witnessed in her before and he suspected was not an emotion she often encountered within herself.

Once she was before him, he smiled. God's breath, she was something to behold in all of her honesty and purity of heart. It did not matter to him if she was raised by Vikings or toads. This stunning woman had more honour and intelligence than most men he knew. Aye, he was a lucky man to have gained her acceptance.

"You are enchanting," he whispered and gloried when she smiled.

"Thank you husband," she said. His cock engorged as her gaze drifted down across his body and he was glad he'd taken the time to don his fur trimmed cloak and chest plate. He hoped she would approve of how he appeared as well.

Once she stood in front of him he took her hands in his, Father Gilwin recited the scriptures and had them repeat many vows. It was as if he was trying to ensure the ceremony did more than secure marriage. Eventually, Father Gilwin pronounced them husband and wife.

"We are joined before your gods and mine," he said. "Nothing can separate us now."

Her brow knit for a moment. "Unless we stop liking each other and then we can divorce."

Her words took him back. How could she possibly think about divorce the moment after they were wed? Never mind the fact that he couldn't divorce.

"Our lord does not allow divorce," Father Gilwin said.

"What do you mean, 'does not allow'?" Saga asked. "If we wish to divorce we can."

Giric took her by the hand and walked away from the Father. This conversation was not going down a path with which he was comfortable. "We need not discuss this right now," he said. "It is our wedding day and I for one am anxious for you to enjoy our feasting and hospitality as I have enjoyed yours."

Nodding, she said, "I will allow that. But we will return to this conversation on the morrow when I am rested. And I will not be addressing you as 'my lord'."

Of that he had no doubt. His new wife was intelligent and used to exercising her free will. It would be an adjustment for her here and he would do all in his power to allow her as much freedom as security would allow. But he would never risk her safety no matter if he had to keep her locked in the tower. Then again, he would simply lock himself in there with her. His cock lurched as he envisioned her naked body writhing beneath him day and night forever.

"Come let us feast," he said. He took her by the elbow and led her back to the great hall. He was proud of his castle and pointed out various extensions that had been built in his father's and grand-father's time. All detailing a need for added security from Viking raids or attacks from other clans trying to expand their region. Only once or twice did she stop and regard him with a sad expression. There was no point in sugar coating any aspect of how things had been. She knew he sought peace and she agreed to be a part of it. Understanding the full extent of how the raids had affected him and his people was important for her to grasp if she was going to be able to settle here.

"Your people must despise me," she said.

"Nay. But some fear you. I only want you to understand why that is. Many here have lost family members to your raids. That is not something easily forgotten."

"So you expect me to apologize to everyone on behalf of my brother?"

He could see she was getting upset. How could his words be twisted so, he was not sure? "Nay, wife. I am trying to help you see why some here may need extra time to adjust to our union."

"I may also need extra time."

"Aye, I see that too and I will do everything I can to aid your adjustment."

Giric and Saga walked the rest of the way to the great hall in silence. Though he held her hand and squeezed it a couple of times to try to urge a smile from her, she continued her pensive stare forward.

He took it as a small victory that she made no attempt to retrieve her hand.

Once inside the hall, Giric smiled at the efforts of all his servants. The tables had already been adorned with flowers and wreaths and garland. Pitchers of mead and ale were surrounded by goblets, and platters of bread and cheese had already been laid out.

"Come, my Viking wife. Let me show you how we feast here."

He brought her to the head of the table and pulled out a chair to the right side of his. He motioned to the lute and whistle players to come forward and begin their tunes. Saga perked up immediately and gave them all her attention. Before long she was clapping along with them and Giric's heart soared. She'd remembered how to keep the tempo and it was clear she enjoyed the music. He'd be sure to hire as many musicians as the castle could employ to keep her happy.

"They are wonderful," she said as the tune ended.

"Not nearly as wonderful as you," he said and kissed her hand. She squeezed his and somehow he was sure it would all work out in time.

CHAPTER FOURTEEN

*B*etween the mead and the music, Saga fell into a comfortable ease during the evening. The platters of rabbit and deer were among the best she'd ever eaten and she was sure there was enough food to feed the entire castle for a sennight. Her husband watched her closely. She appreciated his efforts, but the truth of the matter was she was not so sure she could fit in here. For starters, when would she hunt? Glancing around the table it was easy to discern that none of these delicate ladies had probably ever lifted a broadsword, axe, or bow.

But she would try. For her brother's sake and for her husband's sake. He was clearly well respected among his clansmen. And more than one lady cast her eye longingly in his direction only to glare at her. Saga understood that. She'd seen the ways of relationships over the years and was not ignorant to attraction and lust. She'd seen its fury as it waxed and the disappointment as it waned. Which was why divorce happened. She simply could not wrap her mind around why a couple would be forced to stay together if they made one another miserable.

"You seem lost in your thoughts, wife," Giric said, pulling her from her musings.

"I am taking all of this in."

"And what are your conclusions?"

"I do like your castle. And this is some of the finest food I have ever eaten."

"But?"

"But I am different than any other lady at this table."

"I do not have a problem with that."

"You cannot turn me into one of them."

She loved the sound of laughter that erupted from him. "I would never dream of it. I do not wish to change one thing about you, wife."

"But you expect me to be understanding to them."

"Aye, and I expect them to be understanding to you." He cast a glance around the room. Her belly fluttered when his gaze drifted across her breasts and up again to lock with hers. "I will help you adjust, wife. I promise you that."

"Very well," she said. "When do we get to go to bed and mate?"

Half choking on the ale he'd just swallowed, he said, "We must stay here for a while yet so that everyone may have an opportunity to offer their congratulations." He reached behind her hair and stroked the delicate skin there. He leaned in close to her ear. "But when I get you alone, I plan to remove your clothing slowly and taste each and every inch of you."

Her body shivered in response. By Freya, this man could make her legs wobble with just a few words. In her hall, she would grab him by the tunic and drag him to the nearest corner to have her way with him. But here they had to wait and be polite and she already knew that was going to take a lot of patience.

"I must say, I do like the disappointment in your eyes

right now," he said. "It makes me think you want me as much as I want you."

"The truth is, if I had my way, we would slip into a dark chamber, bolt the door and pleasure one another then return to the feast. Do you think we would be missed?" she asked as she slid her hand up his thigh and grasped hard.

His resulting gasp made her grin. She could affect him in the same way he could affect her. She too could not wait to strip him and explore his muscular frame.

"Christ's teeth I do believe you're going to be the death of me," he said as he pulled her close and brushed his lips across hers.

At that moment a high-pitched voice cleared her throat. "Cousin, I do believe you are rude to keep your wife all to yourself and not let her mingle with everyone else."

Saga could feel the shift in him. His whole body stiffened as he leaned back. A brief flash of apology appeared in his gaze and was masked with emptiness. She'd never seen him like this before.

"Cousin Naywin. How do you fare?"

"I am well, my lord as you can see," she said as she smoothed her breasts and the bodice of her gown. She moved over to Saga and stretched out her hand. "I am Giric's cousin. We were betrothed at one point. But he would not have me." Her gaze flicked over Saga's hair and breasts.

"Now, cousin. You know that is not how it happened."

"My reputation was at stake—"

"I am so sorry, Giric," a man said from behind Naywin, grabbing her by the arm. "I promised to keep an eye on her."

Giric stood and motioned for Saga to stand as well. "Norfolk," Giric said, "I did not know you had returned to Prestwick. How fares your father?"

"My father is not well," he said. "The physic says he does not have much time."

"Then why are you here?"

"To witness the dawn of a new age," he said and grasped Giric's shoulder. "Your marriage is the talk of Prestwick so I came as soon as I heard. Your father and mine would be proud of this moment."

"I believe you are right. My father talked to me on many occasions about the best way to bring peace to this situation."

"You are all fools," Naywin said. "She will slay all of us in our sleep."

"Perhaps some, but surely not all," Saga said in an attempt to lighten the mood and put the woman in her place.

Giric turned to look at her. She shrugged and smiled and he burst into gales of laughter. Leaning in close and whispering in her ear, he said, "I believe I shall enjoy having you protect me."

"I will see my sister safely to her chamber for the evening now, Giric," Norfolk said. "She will bother you no longer this night."

After they retreated, Giric turned to her. "Would you like to mingle with the lords and ladies now so I may introduce you? I believe a lot of uncertainty can be dispelled once they meet you and realize you are not a big scary Viking."

"But I like being a big scary Viking."

"Aye, but there are no enemies on the drawbridge to slay at the moment."

"No, they are much closer," she said. This was a different kind of warfare—one of deceit and cunning. She would be mindful and watchful of all those she met.

For the next couple of hours Saga was introduced to several people. She noted the wide-eyed appreciative glances she received from the men in contrast to the frightened looks of the women. Oh she was going to definitely have to do something about that. Both Freydis and Vigdis were deeply engrossed in conversation with MacAlpin and Aislin so she did not mind leaving them to meet some of the other guests.

From time to time she noticed a woman staring at her from the periphery of the crowd. She offered a smile each time their eyes met, but never approached her. At a moment when Giric was engaged with Norfolk again about how wonderful their union was and the change it would bring, Saga made her way to the hall's entrance way to where the woman stood watching her.

"I wondered when you would come to me," she said. Offering a deep curtsy, she said, "I am Eloisa, the village healer."

"I am Saga of Islay. Can you tell me why you stare at me so?"

"Aye, lass. I can."

Saga waited. Nothing. "Will you tell me?"

The woman laughed. "There is an aura around you. One that speaks of power and of great strength. But there is also danger surrounding you."

"Do you profess to be a seer?"

"A seer?" The woman scratched her chin. "Aye, I suppose I am a seer as well as a healer."

"And you see that I am in danger."

"Aye, grave danger."

"Then your powers are merely the result of good observance. There isn't a person here who actually wants me here. Except for my husband."

"Aye, but the danger runs far deeper than the fear instilled in the hearts of those present. You must come to my cottage and let me cast the bones for you."

"Ahhh there you are," Giric said from behind her.

Saga turned at the sound of his voice but when she turned back, Eloisa was gone.

"Who was that woman?" she asked him.

"What woman?"

"The one who was just standing here."

"I saw no other woman but you, wife. I thought you were standing at the door to indicate to me you wanted to retire for the evening so I said our farewells. MacAlpin will see that your sister and Freydis are shown to their chambers."

Giric placed his arm around her waist and led her out of the hall and toward the stairs. She looked back over her shoulder once and thought she saw the sash of the woman's gown disappearing around the corner. Perhaps she was tired from her travels and the activity of the day. She was grateful for the escape from the crowd and the full impact of where her husband led her, hit home.

~

Giric bent low and hoisted her over his shoulder, entered his chamber, and kicked the door closed. He loved the way she pounded on his back and was quite certain she would never give him the chance to catch her by surprise again.

He dropped her onto the bed and laughed as she immediately barrelled into his guts and landed him on his arse, with her on top. She pinned both hands above his head. Christ's teeth he'd yield to her any day of the week if she would sit atop him like this with her golden tresses surrounding them both and her breasts begging for his touch. The glint in her eye told him she liked this game.

"Do you submit?"

"Aye, I am yours in any way you want me." As he spoke the words, he pulled out of her grasp, grabbed her waist and flipped her, pinning her with his body.

"You will do as I say," she said with a grin.

"Anything you desire," he said and brushed a kiss along

the base of her neck. Her scent of lavender and wildflowers enveloped him.

Her breath came in shallow pants and he kissed her neck, her ear, and nipped her flesh with his teeth.

"I want to explore you."

"Aye, you may do anything you like to me," he said as he pulled her gown low to reveal one taut nipple. He sucked hard until it was firm and her body arched.

"I cannot do anything while you inflict your torture."

With one last, light nip, Giric stood and pulled her to her feet. She scrambled to the bed and sat on the edge.

He turned to face her and waited. Giving up all control was not something he'd ever done before, but the reward would be worth it.

"Remove your belt."

Giric brushed his hands over the knot and pulled the leather strap slowly upward. Once it was loose he slipped it from his waist and approached her. He slid the material across her breasts and her bottom lip. She gasped, her eyes locked with his. This would be fun.

Offering her the belt, he stepped back and waited for her instruction.

Smiling, she said, "I see you are obedient and that will earn you rewards. You may request that I remove one piece of clothing."

"Well then it seems only fitting that you give me your girdle."

Saga kneeled up on the bed and unbuckled the gold clasp. It clinked against itself as she removed it and tucked one edge into the neckline of her gown. She stuck out her chest in offering.

Giric stepped toward her and brushed the back of his fingers from her neck down to the tops of her breasts. He tugged the girdle from her gown and kissed the place where metal had met flesh. He stepped back again.

"Now your tunic," she said.

Ignoring that it was covered by his breastplate, Giric tugged the garment upward, removed the breastplate letting it fall to the floor and slipped the tunic over his head. Once done he tossed it at her. Not surprisingly, she caught it. Her eyes travelled the length of him. Standing in only his boots he watched as her eyes swept across his chest, down his torso, before resting on his growing cock. The more her gaze lingered there, the harder he became.

"Am I being obedient?" he asked in a raspy voice.

Her eyes locked again with his. "You are."

"May I have your gown, please?"

Grinning, she pulled it from under her knees and then lifted her arms so he could untie her bodice. Giric took his time as he untied the leather straps under her arms. Once they were loose again he waited for instruction. But she had started stroking his chest and his need was growing. Grabbing fistfuls of her gown, he pulled it upward. She lifted her arms and allowed him to pull it over her head and dropped it to the floor.

The only garment remaining was her shift and he wanted her out of it. Now.

"I'll trade you my boots for your shift."

"I will accept that bargain," she said, "but I want you to remove them slowly."

Giric stepped back and looked around the chamber, and located a chair. He pulled it over to the bed and sat. Saga scooted to the edge of the bed again and watched as he hooked his fingers into each bootlace and tugged them free. He lifted his leg and offered his foot to her. She pulled them off quickly and straddled him on the chair.

"I thought you wanted me to do that slowly."

"Enough with slowly," she said. "I want to explore you."

"Not yet. You have not kept up your end of the bargain."

She pulled the shift up far enough to reveal her legs and brushed her lips across his. "If you want the shift, take it."

He needed no more encouragement than that. Giric grabbed the bunched fabric and pulled it up over her head. Her breasts were at perfect sampling height and he could not resist taking one taut nipple into his mouth and sucking while shifting her body closer to his now throbbing cock.

"Not yet," she said.

Saga stood and spread his legs wide. Kneeling in front of him, she wore a particularly impish expression. She leaned up for a deep kiss taking his tongue into her mouth in an erotic dance. She broke the kiss and with her hands and hot tongue, trailed her way down his body. He was not sure he could make it when she grasped his cock in her hands and stroked.

"Ahhh, love, I do not think I can handle it if you do that for very long."

"We have all night," she said before taking the tip of him into her mouth. A jolt of sensation shot through to the base of his spine. She sucked and stroked at the same time taking him higher and higher until he reached the cusp.

"I am going to explode," he said.

His words seemed to fuel her efforts. She took more of him into her mouth until he was sure he hit the back of her throat and that was his undoing. With one more squeeze at the base of him she sucked long and hard and his body began the familiar quaking as his seed shot hot and hard down her throat. By God he'd never felt anything quite like this in his life. She slowed her motions, but did not stop until the last wave of his passion waned.

Leaning back in the chair he watched as she sat back with a satisfied look on her face. "Christ's teeth, woman, what you do to me!"

"I have been wanting to do that all day," she said.

"I will keep that in mind the next time you want to find a secluded place to hide."

"You should."

Saga took his hand and led him to the bed. He placed his hand on her face and kissed her long and slow. He had every intention of returning the favour and he had every intention of having her many times before they slept that night. But for the moment, he revelled in his great fortune.

CHAPTER FIFTEEN

Heaving a deep sigh of contentment, Saga turned over to face her husband, careful not to disturb the heavy arm slung across her waist. He snored lightly and his expression was completely relaxed in his slumber. She noted his thick straight brows, his straight jaw and firm lips. He was an attractive man but so much more than that. His body was firm and toned and muscular, and she'd never imagined the things he could do to her body. He was intelligent and sensual and honourable.

She pressed her body closer to his and watched as a smile tugged at the corners of his mouth. They'd loved long into the night and the soreness between her legs was proof of it, but she didn't care. She would have him anywhere, anyhow. The man knew his way around a woman's body and knew how to use his own. Never had she imagined she would be so perfectly matched in that regard.

Scooching a little closer, she reached down to see if he'd stirred in his sleep. He had. Saga took her time and caressed his backside and his thighs before taking his erection into her hands and slowly stroking him awake. Soon one eye opened and the grin on his face spread wider.

"Good morn, my insatiable wife."

"Good morn, husband. Do you object?"

His answer was to flip her onto her back, spread her legs wide and plunge deep within her. The sensation took her breath away.

"I will never object to my vixen wife waking me with her passionate need." As he spoke he thrust harder and faster. Her breath came in short pants as he pounded within her carrying her higher and higher and closer to her climax.

She gripped his shoulders and matched his rhythm so close to the brink she could almost reach out and touch it.

"Please," she said. "Harder, Giric, harder!"

Before she knew it he withdrew and flipped her over so that she was on her hands and knees. He placed a hand on her hip then entered her completely again. Oh sweet Freya! She'd never survive this. With both hands on her hips he slammed into her over and over, their flesh slapping out their time. Liquid ecstasy flooded her veins and he grunted and growled behind her. Their lovemaking was purely animalistic and she could not get enough. Harder and harder Giric thrust into her and as quickly as her first orgasm waned, a second waxed.

Surely this could not be possible.

She flicked her head back and turned to see him. The power exuding from him as he stared hard at her and drove himself into her was an image she would never forget. As his orgasm began and he thickened inside her, another wave washed over her forcing her body to arch and quake. No pleasure she'd known before could compare to this intense, almost crazed feeling between them.

Giric gave one final thrust and grunt behind her and collapsed onto her back before slipping out of her and rolling to his side. Saga merely let her body drop to the bed, trying to steady her breath, her blood pounding in her ears. That was almost panicked. She wondered if it would always be like that with them—frenzied and demanding.

After a few moments, he placed his arm around her waist again.

"You can wake me like that any morning you like, wife."

"And you may do that to me anytime, anywhere."

"Really? Like at our morning meal? Just bend you over the table whilst our guests are stuffing their gullets with my food and ale?"

"Exactly like that. Then maybe they would look at me with less than fear."

"Aye, but they would regard you with something else and I will not tolerate disrespect against you."

She turned toward him and placed her hand on his face. "You are a good man, Giric MacDomnail. I am glad you sailed to Islay."

"As am I," he said. "I do believe we are crafting peace, you and I. There will be challenges, but as long as we work together, I have faith this can work."

"As do I."

The morning meal was pretty much a continuation of the previous evening's feast. Platters of bread and meats and cheese accompanied pitchers of ale and mead. Saga was famished and did not even try to hide her appetite. After her second helping she noticed some of the ladies staring at her. Annoyed with the implication of disapproval, she gathered up her trencher, filled it and left her husband's side to go sit with them. Letting opinions stew made no sense to her. If they had something to say to her, she would give them the opportunity and correct where necessary. She hoped today's gown of sky blue but similar style as theirs would put them further at ease. Aislin had managed to find six gowns for her to wear that were barely long enough until she could have more made.

"Do you live near here?" Saga asked.

Both ladies looked like she'd appeared out of thin air. "I—well—I live close, but my cousin is here visiting me from Edinburgh."

"And your names?"

"You met us last night, Lady MacDomnail."

"As I met dozens more. Surely you do not expect me to remember all the names of all the people here upon first meeting."

"As lady of this castle you will be expected to do just that," the cousin from Edinburgh said. "Let's face it. You do not fit in here and you never will."

Saga did not stop eating, though she wanted to throw her trencher at the nasty little woman. She wondered at the woman's motives, too. If she lived in Edinburgh as a lady, chances were any Viking raids never touched the fancy hem of her gown.

"Speaking of fitting in, do you both know my husband well? Has he always been such a buck?"

The Edinburgh lady turned as many shades of red as Saga had ever seen. An inkling of understanding dawned on her. Mayhap some of the animosity the woman had displayed was similar to the cousin, Naywin last eve.

Thankfully the woman's companion found humour in Saga's question. "I am Elora MacAlpin. My brother is your husband's friend. I believe you have met him already."

"I have. He appears to be a sensible man, strong and wise in the head."

"He is that and values your husband. Is it true he is taken with a woman from your village?"

"That woman would be my sister and, ja, I believe they have made a connection."

"You are all filthy heathens," the other one said. "You should go back to your own land and leave us alone."

"And what would you know of it, Ada?" Elora asked. "The king himself has pledged his daughter to a Viking warlord. Giric is merely following in his footsteps and doing his part to ensure peace."

"We would not need peace if they had stayed where they belong. You are all filthy, rotten animals who take what is not yours."

Saga drew a deep breath. She would not cause a scene here, and physically harming this woman would only prove her point. She was trying to provoke and doing a good job, but a shield-maiden possessed strength of mind as well as body.

"That's enough, Ada," Osgar said from behind her. "You will leave this hall at once. Sister, take our cousin back to the castle and confine her to her chamber until I can make arrangements for her return to Edinburgh."

Saga nodded at Osgar in thanks. She supposed she should have expected that and by all accounts the woman's words were none she hadn't heard before. One thing was for certain, when Giric said they had their work cut out for them, he had not exaggerated.

"What passes here?" Giric asked.

"Nothing we cannot handle," Saga said. "Elora, I have enjoyed meeting you and I hope we can converse more at another time. Ada, it has been quite enlightening meeting you. I do hope your journey to Edinburgh is free from danger."

The colour drained from the woman's face. Did she only now realize the gravity of her words and the impact they could have by threatening her—a Viking? Safe to say when surrounded by Scots, but once on the road, anyone could overtake a carriage and inflict harm.

She watched as they retreated from the hall. Turning to her husband, she said, "I wish to explore the village. Will you accompany me?"

"Aye, wife, I shall. I look forward to repaying the tour you provided me on Islay."

Saga smiled at him and squeezed his hand. She wished more of the people here were like him. All in time, he'd said. Patience was not something to which she was accustomed, but she would do her best to learn it. And mayhap she would encounter the strange woman from last eve as well. Something about her was a little off and Saga was determined to find out what that was.

~

Choosing a horse for Saga was no small task. She'd said she could ride, but living on an island, there was no real need and so despite her lifted chin, he was certain she was not skilled enough to handle a larger destrier. He chose a white mare he'd recently acquired that had not yet been named. Graceful and even-tempered, it would suit his wife perfectly. As he drew the horse nearer to her, he thought again to their lovemaking the previous night and again in the morning. He'd never imagined in all his days that he would have found a woman like her, and especially not when he'd set off for Islay mere days ago.

But here she was and he could not remember what his life had been like without her.

"She's for you," he said as he handed her the reins.

Her eyes grew wide as she stared back and forth between him and the animal. She reached forward and stroked the horse's snout and rested her forehead on its neck. The horse's eyes closed a little and opened again. That was a good sign.

"She does not yet have a name. What would you like to call her?"

Saga stroked the mare's neck and cooed in her own tongue. "You are a beautiful goddess. The only name I can give you is Sif. Thank you, Giric. She is beautiful."

"Would you like to mount her now?"

He loved the slight grin playing at the corners of her lips. He was not the only one remembering their passions from earlier. Giric moved toward her and pulled her into his arms. She slipped her hands around his neck and drew him down into a deep kiss.

"Thank you for this gift," she said. "I love her already. She has a special spirit."

"I am glad to hear it. Let's make her ready for you."

Giric motioned for the stable hand to place blankets on the horse and offered his clasped hands for Saga to use for leverage to mount the horse.

Once up, she trotted outside the stable and urged the horse into a full on gallop. A moment's panic swept over him until he heard her laugh. He quickly mounted his destrier and followed at a gallop.

They raced across the countryside together and he was captivated by the sight of her bright eyes, huge smile, and flaxen hair flowing in the wind. The image of her like this would be emblazoned on his mind forever.

After about an hour's ride, they stopped by a stream for the horses to catch their breath and have a drink. Giric dismounted and moved to her side to assist her. On the ground she flung herself into his arms and hugged him tight, laughing freely.

"I have never felt so free," she said as she pulled back from the embrace.

"I do not imagine you can ride like that on Islay."

"I can, but to what end? We have horseflesh aplenty, but

they're workhorses and not used for transportation. And we do not have this much country to cover should we wish to ride."

"We can ride every day 'tis fine, if you like. But I will need to teach you how to properly care for your horse. We have stable hands, but you are ultimately responsible to make sure she is brushed and covered after every ride so she does not fall ill."

"I will care for her," she said as she drew the horse to the stream to drink then stroked her neck.

"And I will care for you," he said. "Come let me show you something."

He led her through a small opening at the edge of the clearing and down a narrow path with dense evergreens. The running sap weighed heavily on the air. It was intoxicating. He noticed how she stopped a couple of times to sniff the branches.

At the end of the path was a crag and beyond, the village. He stopped her before they reached it and covered her eyes with his hands.

"Do not open your eyes until I tell you. Do you agree?"

"Ja."

Giric took his hands away and moved to stand in front of her so he could see her expression. "Now open them."

Saga slowly opened her eyes and gazed at the sight. The village of Prestwick was really a township and a busy place by any standard. Inhabiting close to 1000 souls, it was a gateway to the inner countryside and the last main point of rest for travellers to Glasgow.

"It is much larger than I expected."

"Aye, it is no small village. Many of the people who work here have some affiliation with the castle, but it is also on a well travelled road which is why you will see taverns and other shops you wouldn't normally see in a village that only supports a castle."

"Can we go down there now?"

"Aye, in a few minutes. The horses need another little while to rest. We rode them hard to get here, though there is a shorter way."

"Why did we not take it?"

"Because you were in the lead and I could not catch up."

Slipping her arm around his waist, she leaned into him and said, "It is beautiful here."

"Aye, that it is. Do you think you can be happy here?"

She lowered her head for a moment, and looked up. "That will depend on how I am received. It is clear that some will not accept me, now or ever. But there may be some who can see me for who I am and not judge me for what my people have done here."

He did not want to respond. She understood the gravity of the situation and there was no point in adding to that. The fact that she was here and interested in peace was enough. Everyone else would understand in time.

She heard the bushes rattle to her left. Giric put his finger to his lips as an enormous feline emerged. It sniffed the air and gave them a curious glance and retreated through the trees.

"Highland wildcats are clever, stealthy, and deadly. The smartest thing to do when you encounter one is to ignore it. Even if it comes up to sniff you."

Saga thought the creature beautiful, but realized the gravity of what a spooked wild animal could wreak.

Once the horses were rested, Giric and Saga rode to the village. They tied up the horses at a local tavern and entered. Of course everyone in the village knew Giric, but the slack- jawed expressions that Saga received might prove taxing if they continued. He was sure news had spread like wildfire of his taking a Viking wife. Hopefully he could keep this visit peaceful and not have her lose all faith in these people. They were inherently good, but superstitious and tended to believe all rumours. Giric opened the tavern door and they went inside.

CHAPTER SIXTEEN

The tavern was dark and smelled of peat. A fire crackled in the hearth and something bubbled in a pot above. At mid afternoon, there were surprisingly few people in the establishment, all men except for one woman who wore her shift and gown so low Saga wondered how her breasts remained within the garment. Was that the usual dress for serving maids here, then?

All din ceased as soon as they were noticed. The barkeep, and older man with wild grey hair and cunning eyes motioned them forward. "What can I get for you, m'lord?"

"Ale, Ronwald."

"Aye, m'lord. Choose a table and I will bring it to you."

As they sat, she took in those gathered. Some kept to themselves after they sat, but others continued to stare openly. One in particular wore a hooded cape hiding the features of their face, though intense eyes glared at her.

"Who is that?" she asked Giric.

Giric turned to see who she meant and turned back quickly. "He is no one with whom I wish you to acquaint.

Stay away from anyone who looks like that, do you understand?"

"I do, but I will keep asking you questions, even if you do not wish to answer."

"He is a member of the king's private guard and often when you see one of them around, something bad is about to happen. Come, let's forget the ale and continue on our tour of the town."

With that Giric stood, reached for her elbow and lifted until she had no choice but to stand. He walked with her over to the counter, dropped some coin on the counter and left.

"Giric, what was that all about?

"There are more dangers about than potential raids from your people," he said.

That comment was a little irritating considering the vows they had both taken and the peace accord struck.

"At some point, you have to stop referencing me as the enemy," she said.

He turned quickly to her and grasped her shoulders. "You are quite right, wife. I sincerely apologize."

"This man has rattled you. I have never seen you like this."

"Aye, mayhap we will cut today's tour short and return to the castle."

"If you wish," she said. "But I am armed."

Kissing her forehead, he said, "I never doubted it for a minute. We shall ride back swiftly. Keep your eyes and ears sharp."

Saga and he mounted and headed toward the castle at a hard gallop. He'd spoken true in that they had taken the long way to the village for the ride home was complete in less than half that time.

As soon as they reached the outer bailey and guard house, Giric dismounted and motioned for the guards.

"Get everyone inside and seal these gates. No one comes in or leaves without my permission, is that clear?"

"Aye, m'lord. Are we under attack, m'lord?"

"Of sorts," he said. "Someone has sent an assassin."

"For whom?" Saga asked.

"I do not know, but if he was staring at you, I can make an educated guess." Then to the guard he said, "Has anyone come through here today you did not know? Anyone? A messenger or someone selling goods."

"No one, m'lord."

"That may only mean they didn't come through the front gates. Someone could still be in the castle. Gather twenty men. Everyone inside must be accounted for and the entire castle must be searched."

If he'd punched her in the guts, she couldn't have been more surprised. She did not know this place like he did and so could not do anything but agree to his demand that she enter the castle and go straight to their chamber.

Giric wrapped his arm around her waist. "I will meet you back here as soon as I have my wife and my family secure."

They entered the castle and she couldn't help but notice how calm everyone seemed until they spied their lord. All stopped in their tracks at the sight of him.

"Gather everyone in the great hall," he said. "Now!"

Once all were gathered and accounted for, Giric raised his hands and the hall fell silent. "I have reason to believe we may be under siege. The source may be a single person and so I want each and every one of you to take stock of every person you have seen here in the last two days. If you have any suspicions about anyone you must come to me immediately. Is that clear?"

A few murmurings could be discerned around the hall and it fell silent again. "Anyone here now must stay here until this danger has passed. If we are not already infiltrated no harm will come to anyone. But for now, unless you have a specific duty to attend, you must return to your chambers and stay there until the evening meal. I will have my house-keeper gather servants as necessary."

"And do we know why we are under attack?" Giric's brother asked, looking directly at Saga.

"We do not, and we will not make assumptions."

But she knew. And she hated the look on some of the faces as they regarded her. She'd brought this upon them. It would be so easy to extend this danger from how they must have felt each and every time a Viking raid party was in the area, but she was certain no party ever attacked this castle. They'd need an army.

"May I take the women aside, husband?"

He turned to her, "For what purpose?"

"To teach them some basic skills," she said flatly.

"Christ's teeth, aye. And now I feel like a fool for never having thought to do that myself."

To the crowd, he said. "The men will come with me and help prepare for what may come. The women will stay in the hall with my wife."

"She will kill them all," his brother shouted.

Saga laughed and walked to the wall, selecting a sleek axe and attempted to swirl it over her head. The stitching on the bodice of her gown was so tight that she could only raise it halfway.

Pointing at one of the few women who did not look terri-fied, she said, "I need you to remove these sleeves." The woman's brows raised. "Ja. You," she said and motioned her forward. The woman did as she was bid and with one rough tug, removed one sleeve and the other. Saga threw the sleeves on the table and picked up the axe again.

She turned toward the table and heaved it through the air before it landed deep into the table with a loud crack. A couple of the women screamed and more started crying. She walked over to Giric's brother and stood toe to toe. He was no more than an inch or two taller than her.

"If you had taken the time to teach these women how to defend themselves instead of stirring dung, brother, they would know they do not need to fear me. For they could have taken me down at any point."

She noted how he quickly masked the fear her actions had urged to the surface. "You mean to train them? Our chambermaids and servant girls learning how to throw an axe like a Viking?"

"Nay, my brother." With one flick of her hand, she released the dagger she had strapped to the inside of her girdle and held it at his throat. "I intend to teach them to be stealthy like a Highland wildcat."

Laughter erupted behind her. "It would appear, brother," Giric said, "that having a Viking warrior in our midst, might be the one added defence this castle has been missing." To the women, he said, "My wife will show you ways you can defend yourself at least enough so that if you are ever attacked by anyone, you can buy yourself some time to find somewhere safe to hide. Do you understand?"

Several wide-eyed women nodded, still a couple more cried, but that was understandable. They were used to having no control over their safety, but by Thor, not if she had any say over it.

After Giric and the men left she told the women to find a partner. To the woman who had helped remove her sleeves, she asked, "What is your name?"

"Anna," she said.

"Does the castle have enough wooden spoons for each person here?"

The woman's brow knit. "Aye, we have more than double that."

"Very well, take someone with you for safety and bring them back here. Until I can secure daggers for you all, you will practice with spoons."

"Everyone else," she said to the crowd as Anna left to do as she was bid, "I want you to know that it is my intention to train you so that any man or woman who ever comes at you will regret it. In my village we women do not wait for the men to save us. We save ourselves."

Audible gasps could be heard around the hall. While she was certain she could convince most of them to go along with her plan, others may simply be too afraid, and though that was a foreign concept to her, she remembered her own training and how her sister had acted at first, too scared to even lift a blade. So she would be patient, but by the time she was finished, each woman here would be more skilled than when they had walked into this hall.

~

Giric met with the men outside in the bailey. The guards had already gathered with the swords from the guard house and four men instead of two were now split between the guard houses on either side of the gate.

"Will you tell us what is going on?" his brother asked. "You've caused quite a stir today, brother."

"Aye, and with good reason."

"And what is that?"

"I spied a manslayer at the tavern."

"What?"

Giric wished he never had to speak the word. They were the most dangerous and elite of the king's guard. He was certain of the king's support in his marriage because he'd secured it before travelling to Islay. No, this was something else and something far more dangerous.

"You heard me."

"But you have the king's blessing for this insane marriage of yours."

"Aye, I do." He paused and drew a deep breath. "I do not believe the king sent the assassin. Which can only mean—"

"That the castle has been infiltrated at the highest level. The king is in danger too."

"Aye, I believe that is the case. Which means if they are here for my wife and me, we will not see them coming. I want this castle scoured top to bottom, twice."

"Aye, m'lord," the main guard said.

His brother said, "We can fight an army much easier than one assassin."

"That is exactly why Saga is teaching the women to defend themselves. Not only so they know how, but also it will become apparent quickly if the assassin is a woman."

His brother scoffed, "Surely you do not think there are women among the elite."

"Aye, I do and you clearly did not pay close enough attention to what my wife can do with an axe. I have seen her wield a broadsword as well as any man here. You must release your prejudice and accept her."

"I will not jump into bed so quickly with our enemy," he said and spat on the ground. "And the day will come soon when you realize your mistake."

"Are you threatening me, brother?"

"I would not dream of it. But you need to keep your eyes wide open. There was no need for an attack on us until you brought that heathen into our midst."

Giric grabbed him by the neck and squeezed. "You will hold your tongue or you will lose it. I have tried to involve and include you in this process, but you refuse to see a path forward where there is peace. All you can see is the past and you will bury yourself there."

"She would have been my wife!" His brother said and jerked away from Giric. "You do not know what it was like to lose her at the hands of those barbarians."

"They were not Saga's kin and you know that; we do not even know if they were Vikings."

"I know it in my heart. They are all alike and the sooner you accept that, the sooner we can get back to normal. She must be sent away or else we will all be slain in our beds."

Giric shook his head as his brother strode away to the armoury. He understood his brother's pain, but the only way to prevent the same thing happening again and again was the peace treaty he and Gunnar had struck. He was on the right path forward, every fibre of his being screamed it.

Just then a lone woman approached the gates, she was dressed head to toe in a green and blue flowing gown and held a basket full of flowers. The wolf in sheep's clothing, mayhap? He was about to find out.

Walking to the gate, he noticed her bright green eyes and beaming smile. She was beautiful whoever she was.

"Who are you?" he asked as he approached the gate.

"I am Eloisa, and I have been drawn to your wife in my dreams. I believe I am to assist her on her journey."

"I see," he was not letting this woman near his wife. For both their sakes. "And what do you carry in the basket?"

"Herbs for my healing potions, my lord."

She did not carry herself as a servant woman, rather she carried the air of a noblewoman.

"Well, Eloisa, we are not accepting any visitors today. Mayhap come back in a fortnight and we can receive you."

She grabbed the gate posts. "But you must let me in," she said. "I know about the assassin."

Giric turned and stared hard into her eyes. How in God's

name would she know that? "Mayhap you are part of the scheme."

"Nay, my lord. But I know about the scheme and I am come to assist." Then looking over her shoulder, she said, "But the danger is closer than you think. Please let me in and I will reveal all that I know."

He considered her for a moment and reached out to lift the heavy wooden post barring the gates. Two other guards assisted him in his endeavour. When Eloisa slipped through, they replaced the post and he turned to her.

"Know this, woman. I will tear you limb from limb if you bring harm to anyone within these walls, do you understand?"

"Aye, my lord," she said. "You have nothing to fear from me."

Giric was not so sure, but he would keep her in a guarded chamber during her stay. He did not trust one hair on her head.

CHAPTER SEVENTEEN

For some of the women, learning how to conceal the weapon was easy; they chose to hide it up their sleeve, in their apron, pocket, or in some cases the bodice of their shift. For a precious few, their fear prevented them from understanding the lessons Saga offered. She'd have to find a different way to teach them.

"Remember to distract your attacker's attention away from where you will strike. The goal is to keep them from seeing it coming. The likelihood that you will be in armed combat is minimal and so this is about the man who decides he's having you tonight whether you like it or not. Or if the castle is ever attacked. You have the advantage of knowing every dark corner and can use that to your advantage."

Most of them had not asked many questions and some giggled whilst Saga placed their hands into position as to how to defend themselves and when to strike.

"You cannot hide your weapon so well that it cannot be easily attained when needed," she said. "Up your sleeve is ideal, or on a strap on your leg. But the most important piece of information I can give you is this, be fully sure the person is an enemy before you attack. It is easy to be spooked and you do not want to stick your blade into one another when getting a start in the kitchens."

The women continued to work on the defensive and offensive moves Saga showed them. She moved about the hall to raise an elbow here, position hips there, lift a chin and such.

Her back was to the door when gooseflesh formed on the back of her neck. Without turning she sensed a shift in the air. Tension spread amongst the women and a few dropped their arms and stared.

Somehow, Saga knew who she'd find standing there when she turned.

She didn't expect to see her husband standing with the woman from the night before, however.

"Wife. I would have a word."

To the women, she said, "You will continue to work on your lessons. I shall return, and I will show you how to trip a man. Even a tall one," she said with a grin.

Giric met her halfway between the women and the seer. "How goes the training?"

"Very well, husband. Most of these women have been fighting off the guards and other men of the castle for years. I will say this much. Some of your men will find a different result the next time they try to take one of these women without her permission."

He smiled. She was pleased he approved for had he not, they would have had a real problem on their hands.

"I will enjoy their discomfort," he said.

"Where did you find the woman?" she asked.

"Find her?"

"That is the woman with whom I spoke last evening," she said, motioning to Eloisa.

"I did not realize that. She was at the gates asking to come in to speak with you. She says she is here to help you on your journey."

"I am going somewhere?"

"I believe she means a spiritual journey."

"She said last night that she was here to help me. I do not understand. Do you trust her?"

"I was hoping to ask you the same thing. Between us both, I believe we are a good judge of character, but I cannot gauge this woman at all."

"Very well, let us interview her together," Saga suggested.

"My lady, it is good to see you looking so well," Eloisa said as they approached.

"You disappeared last night," Saga said. "Where did you go?"

"Upon meeting you, I realized why I needed to be by your side and needed to travel to my home to gather some things."

"I do not understand," she said.

"I have had visions of your coming for many months," she said with a smile. "I'd heard talk of the king marrying his daughter to a Viking warlord, and started having visions of you shortly after. I knew you would come here."

"Are you a witch?" Giric asked, crossing his arms over his chest.

"Some may call me that, but what I am is a healer," she said to him. "Your wife will need my aid in the coming months and I am here to answer that call."

"And what do you get in return?"

"The work you do here, my lord, is important for us and for Scotland. She cannot continue as she is, peace must be found or I fear we will never find a way forward."

"Insightful words for a peasant."

"Who said I'm a peasant?"

Saga regarded her garments closer. There was no doubt the woman had money coming from some source. Her gown's fabric looked new and she wore gold rings adorned with various stones. She either had a wealthy benefactor, or worse—a husband. Saga would not want to get in the middle of a domestic squabble."

"My money is my own. I was married, but my husband passed away last year. My uncle is now my steward, but he is often in his cups and so I am left to my own devices. It was not long after my husband's passing that I began to have visions. They frightened me at first, but they started providing more clarity. It was not long before I started seeing you."

"Who was your husband?

"Fraser."

"*The* Fraser?" Giric asked, his whole demeanour changing to stand a little taller.

"Aye, the very one."

"Lady Fraser, I apologize to you. You should have said that from the beginning."

"I am Lady Fraser no longer. I have given my home to the church and kept back enough for my comfort. Minding my finances gives my uncle something to do."

"Lady Fraser, I would like to formally introduce you to my wife, Lady MacDomnail, lately Saga Haraldson, sister to Chieftain, Gunnar Haraldson."

"It is my great pleasure to see you and to formally address you, Lady MacDomnail," she said as she grasped Saga's hands.

"I will have a chamber prepared for you, Lady Fraser. You will remain with us for as long as you wish. I am afraid we've reason to believe there is an assassin sent for either myself or my wife. Or both."

"I thank you for your kindness, Lord MacDomnail. My husband always spoke well of you. I shall tell you what I know when we have more time to talk of it—and in private. You both need to hear what I have to share."

Giric went to fetch a couple of the maids who'd been training. Pointing to one, he said, "Lady Fraser shall be given my mother's chamber during her stay."

"Yes m'lord," she said and scurried away.

"I must return to the men," he said, placing his hand on the back of Saga's head and kissing her forehead. "I will leave Lady Fraser with you and see you both at the evening meal."

After he left, Lady Fraser linked arms with Saga. "We have much work to do, my lady."

"I am preparing the women for possible attack. Can you believe they have never received any defensive training?"

"Aye, my lady, I can indeed. Your people have no barriers to women defending themselves. Such is not the case here. Men like to be in charge and the best way to keep a woman under your thumb is to keep her depending on you."

"You are a wise woman, Lady Fraser."

"Some have said I am too clever for my own good."

"I have been accused of that myself. So tell me, Lady Fraser, why do I need your help?"

"It is Eloisa, and in my visions I see you abed and me tending to you."

An eerie feeling crept into her belly. "And my husband? Do you see him in your vision?"

"I do not."

Some part of Saga told her to keep her wits about her with this woman regardless of the respect she evoked from Giric. But she would play along regardless, if for no other reason than to glean what the woman knew or wanted to impart, for often what people did not say spoke loudest.

~

Sparring with Osgar always proved a thorough and entertaining workout. Being a couple inches taller than his friend afforded Giric an advantage every time. He knew every weak point on the man's body and how to use it to his disadvantage.

He swung his sword sideways forcing Osgar to jump back and rammed him with his right shoulder as his arms were stretched wide. Osgar went flying to the ground. A heartbeat later, Giric's blade tip touched the sensitive skin of Osgar's throat. Blood pounding through his main artery was clearly visible.

"Do you yield?"

Osgar glared at him like so many times before. "Never," he said, swatting Giric's blade away as he tripped him and twisted his body hard, forcing Giric to fall onto his stomach. "You always let your guard down too soon."

Laughing as Osgar pulled him up to standing, Giric said, "I believe we both know one another's moves too well and thus we are not being quite as challenged as we could be."

"Mayhap I had better spar with your wife and mayhap I would learn something."

"I believe she could teach both of us a thing or two."

Giric brushed dust from his tunic and looked back toward the castle. His wife was somewhere inside teaching his maid servants how to protect themselves and here they were outside practicing how to protect them all. Did he think bringing a Viking wife home would come without a price? Nay, but he did not anticipate having to go to war so soon.

The biggest question was who had sent the assassin? Giric could summon about five hundred men if need be and Osgar about three hundred more. Only the king could match those numbers unless other nobles banded together.

But it was those on the coast who had suffered the most at the hands of the Vikings, whose families had been murdered, women raped, and lives destroyed. Few inland could claim those horrors. So if not for retaliation, what? Why take issue with Giric's attempts at peace? And how did they acquire the king's assassin to do so? It made no sense.

"What now?" Osgar asked.

Giric scrubbed his hand down over his face. "Now we flush out the enemy. Once I'm satisfied those here are no longer in danger, I will travel to Dunnottar and seek the counsel of the king. I believe a rider would be intercepted and so we will wait until this threat has passed and make our way together."

"And your wife? What will you do with her?"

"She will be safer here once I have determined the threat is over."

"I believe she can defend herself on a field of battle, Giric, but there are dangers here she cannot foresee. Your brother for one. And who is this woman you allowed through the gates?"

"My brother will do as he is told. As for the woman, she is Lady Fraser. We both knew her husband and you know he was murdered. She had disappeared from social life and has now returned dressed as though attending the king's court at my gates begging to protect my wife. The woman knows much more than she is letting on and I intend to get to the bottom of it and I intend to take her with me to Dunnottar. The king must be privy to her knowledge. For I fear any attempt against me is a precursor to an attempt on him."

"Who would dare?"

"Many would dare, as you well know. It's a matter of determining who is most likely and why they would start here. Has there been any news from the north?"

"From Lewis? Nay. To my knowledge those peace treaties occurred without much objection."

"Then it must have more to do with this region as much as with me specifically. The question is who would benefit most from this continuing conflict?"

"I know not," Osgar said, shaking his head.

Giric scanned the bailey. His men sparred, others sharpened their blades, while others wrestled. They were as good as any soldier in the country and better than most. They'd had to be. Never was there a time when they could stand down, for danger had always lurked.

"I will put more thought to it," he said. Clasping Osgar by the shoulder he added, "We must bring our trust circle down to the basics. You may trust two people. Who are they?"

"You and your brother."

"You trust my brother?"

"You do not?"

"Nay, not in this case. He is opposed to this marriage and has been quite vocal in his opposition."

"All the more reason for him to be trusted. For if he was behind an attempt on yours, or your wife's life, would he single himself out as such?"

"Nay I suppose you are right. But he does not want her here."

"Nor do many, but here she is and here she will stay. Most of the people here know that and will accept it in time. I believe the person or persons behind this do not reside here or near here."

"Very well, I trust my wife and her sister and my sister."

"That's three. And you will still leave your brother out of it."

"Aye, for the time being."

"What makes you trust your sister?"

"She has always been loyal to me."

"So she says, but where was she last night when my cousin attacked your wife? As your sister, she should have been by her side all evening."

"She claimed to have a headache and retired early. She has a delicate constitution, you recall."

"Did she? So why did I see her roaming the gardens when I went to bed."

"Mayhap she couldn't sleep."

Osgar shook his head. How do you think you will ever solve this if you do not open your eyes?"

"Are you saying that my sister is behind this?"

"I am saying you need to look closer at whom you trust and why."

The man made sense. But there was no way his sister had anything to do with this. Mayhap a part of him knew his brother did not either, but his actions were suspicious.

"And you?" he asked. "Only two?"

"Very well. I trust you, your brother, and I trust Vigdis."

"But you just met her?"

"Says the man who met his current wife on the same day."

"Aye, but she has married me."

"That does not mean Vigdis and I do not share the same bond."

"So we agree we trust the women. Does that mean we do not trust that Gunnar has found another way to attack? In a sideways manner?"

"Nay, Gunnar has as much to lose here as you do. He needs this alliance as much as we do since he has threats from his own people as well."

Something clicked for Giric. "That's it then."

"What's it?"

Ignoring the question, Giric's mind raced to catch up to the conclusion. "But how would the Vikings have formed an alliance with the king in order to acquire his assassin?"

"Giric you've lost me."

"Do you recall what Gunnar said about the clan on the other side of the island trying to claim it and drive Gunnar off?"

"Aye, which is why we offered our armies as part of the wedding bargain."

"But what if the deal had already been struck?"

"With whom?"

"With the king. Not the king necessarily, but someone close enough to him to speak for him."

The wheels of the scheme turned over in Giric's mind so fast he could barely make sense of it. Giric had assumed he'd have the king's blessing to carry his plan through so he had not waited for the king's reply. What if a resolution had already been struck from the king's name and in his mind all was already resolved? But whoever resolved the conflict did not reveal that an entire clan would need to be laid to waste in order to instil peace. Surely the king would not condone such actions and so Gunnar's clan which included Giric's wife would need to be eliminated. His guts lurched at the thought.

He had to find his wife.

CHAPTER EIGHTEEN

She was quite pleased with herself by the time her lessons were complete and could see a marked improvement not only in the women's skill, but also in their attitude. Many stood a little taller and most of them smiled at her as they walked back to their duties.

"I shall speak with my husband about providing each and every one of you with your own concealable dagger," she said as they left the hall.

Ja, she was pleased with herself, to be sure. Somehow she would carve a life here and make this work, for her own sake as well as the women here. They needed someone to speak for them and to help them speak for themselves. There were still a precious few among the ranks who glared at her and she would accept that, regardless of her heritage, that might happen anyway.

Her new friend had long since retired to her chamber for an afternoon respite and so Saga now found herself alone in the hall. The clang of metal on metal still sounded from the bailey and so she decided to take this time to work on her own training.

Scanning the wall of weapons she realized that a lot of these were not practical, where were the long bows? Where were the daggers and short swords? For surely it was not practical for a castle's arms to be displayed on the wall. Nay, this must be for decoration. There must be an arms house somewhere close-by.

Saga finished scanning the walls and turned at a noise near the entrance to the hall. A slight flick of movement caught her attention and she froze. She wasn't alone. Reaching behind her she grabbed a spear from the wall and held it at the ready, never taking her eyes from the entrance.

The doors opened out, which, apparently, was the way of it here; in case of attack, it was harder to open a barred door with this orientation working against itself. And so the only thing on the wall with which a person could conceal themselves was the tapestries.

Saga approached with caution as she continued to scan the hall. With the spear she quietly lifted each end to ensure no one hid behind. And on to the next one she went until she was about twenty paces from the door and the entire right side of the hall had been cleared, including the hearth.

"You cannot best me one on one so you find solace in cowardice and hiding. Is that who I battle right now?" she asked hoping the taunt would draw out the person.

Saga swirled her spear around her head and repositioned it under her arm whilst drawing her dagger from her girdle.

"Come and show me how you can best me," she said.

Movement from behind her drew her attention back to the hearth and that's when she realized her grave mistake. She had not been seeking one attacker, but two.

As soon as she made this conclusion something pinched her neck. She dropped the spear and pulled the stick from her neck but kept a grip on her dagger. By Thor she would not go down without a fight.

"So you need to drug me to be brave enough to fight me, is that it? You are the worst cowards I have ever met," she said, her vision blurring.

"You cannot best me either way!" As she said this she swung her hand wide. A blurry image of a hooded figure appeared in front of her. She lurched forward and slashed at the air.

"You should have never come here," the muted voice said from behind her before kicking her in the back.

Dazed and stunned from whatever was on the tip on the stick, she stumbled but planted her feet more solidly on the ground.

"You had better stay back there," she said. "I will spill your guts where you stand if you come closer."

Try as she might to keep her head clear, Saga was losing hold on her consciousness. The figure in front of her was nowhere near as tall as she—the assassin was a woman. Saga knew a thing or two about fighting whilst having consumed too much ale and also assumed she did not have much time left before she succumbed to the drug entirely.

She turned to face the one behind her all the while keeping her focus on the one in front. They acted as she predicted. Their training was for stealth and not for one-on-one combat. They were waiting for her to fall so they could report their mission as successful. But not today.

Saga dropped into a squat and stuck out one long leg to sweep and trip the assailant behind her and turned to lurch for the one in front. She tackled her to the ground and pulled off her mask before rolling so that any attack from the other one would be shielded by her partner.

She'd been accurate in her assessment of these two. But the blade that ripped through the attacker on top went all the way through and into her body. Just enough for it to burn.

"No!" a voice shouted from the doorway.

A loud thunk was followed by the woman being pulled from Saga's body and in turn the blade pulled from her chest. She prayed to Odin it had not landed deep, but if this was her time for the Valkyries to carry her off to Valhalla then, by Freya, she was ready. She'd fought off these two assassins with skill and honour and she deserved her place at the feast.

"Saga, stay with me," the voice said.

She opened her eyes and smiled, or tried to smile, at Giric. He was so handsome. She reached her hand up to touch his face and realized it was covered in blood. Whose blood? Hers or the assassin's? Did it matter?

"You are so good," she said to him.

"Shhh, love. You will be fine. I will take good care of you."

A scream was followed by a scurry of activity.

"Get my brother," Giric shouted to someone.

Many voices surrounded her then. Too many faces for her to count. Some seemed there twice, but that was not possible. And where was Gunnar? She needed to see him. She wanted his blessing as she flew with the Valkyries.

"Gunnar," she whispered.

"I will send for your brother, love. I will get him here. Just stay focused on me. Do not leave me, wife. Do you hear me? That's an order from your husband and you may not disobey me."

Ire rose in her. She could disobey him if she wanted to. She tried to lift an arm to slug him, but it would only raise a little before falling back down. There was a great deal of pressure on her chest and she found it difficult to breathe. She opened her eyes to see Giric hovering over her with his hands pressed hard on her chest. Fear and moisture filled his eyes.

She smiled at him. He was so handsome, her husband. Her focus shifted to his breastplate. On it was the image of the serpent much like the one on her own shield. In her world it represented that which was sacred and rare and protected while also representing those who did the protecting.

Much was the same she suspected for Giric. He was to be protected, but also a warrior, like her. He would not want her to go to Valhalla. But he may not have a choice. Her parents were there among others of her kin. They awaited her.

Slay the serpent.

Her gaze shifted to his breastplate again. This time the serpent disentangled itself from the sword and regarded her. At first it spit and breathed fire, but she reached her hand out to it. Its piercing black eyes scrutinized her—as if to determine what made her up from the inside out. After an age, the serpent breathed out only smoke and moved its face so Saga could stroke its smooth scales. Despite the heat from within it was cool to the touch. She laughed, causing the serpent to veer up and grunt.

"Are you my Valkyrie, come to take me away?"

"No, Shield-Maiden. I am your guide back to where you belong."

"And where is that?"

"Back to the Scots-land of Alba. You have much work to do there."

"You are a serpent of Alba. You are not my kin."

Just then another serpent emerged in the scene. The one from her own crest and side by side, Saga could see the similarities. They were sisters.

"We were separated an age ago, Shield-Maiden. You must go back and repair the damage done so we may reunite for all eternity." Her serpent entwined its tail around Giric's and they lay down beside one another. "There is more at stake here than you realize."

The pain in her chest shot through her, causing her to gasp and arch her back.

"Hush love, the bleeding has stopped," Giric said above her.

When she opened her eyes, her hand was on his breastplate and the image was as it had always been. But what of her vision? What of the message she'd tried to understand?

"Saga, love I will need to move you, but I cannot do so yet. I have summoned our healer, but I need you to stay focused and stay awake, can you do that?"

The poison muddled her brain. She was not sure if she could do as Giric asked, but she would do her best. Why had it only occurred to her now that there were so many similarities between the images of symbolism between Giric's people and hers? It did not matter, she supposed, but she was determined to best this injury and return to him in full form.

Hands touched her body and within moments she was rolled onto her back. White hot pain stabbed her chest causing her to cry out. She was lifted and placed onto her back again. She opened her eyes a crack when she had the sensation of being lifted again. Her husband's face was above her and another man's was at her feet back on.

Saga felt herself drifting slowly away from the image.

"Keep your eyes on me, love," Giric said.

She tried, oh how she wished she could tell him she tried, but she was so tired and she could hear the first screech from the Valkyries. They were coming for her and she did not possess the strength to tell them she was not ready, that she wanted to stay here for another little while with Giric, and that she wanted to see her brother again. That thought too faded as she slipped into blackness where there were no Valkyries, no Valhalla, and no Giric.

∼

$\mathcal{A}$s they lifted Saga, Giric noticed the two assassins' lifeless bodies nearby.

"Osgar! Secure them!" He could offer no more instructions as he and Donnan lifted her up the stairs and away from prying eyes. She had fallen unconscious and would need immediate care if she was to survive.

At her chamber he placed the cot on the floor and lifted her body in his arms. To Donnan he said, "Help Osgar find out everything about those two responsible for my wife's condition."

Thankfully, Donnan left and did not object in any way. Giric possessed no tolerance for his brother's cynicism at the moment.

Once Saga was in bed and her clothes removed, Giric ushered everyone out of the chamber except for Lady Fraser, Freydis, and Vigdis. He would not even permit his sister entry for she'd begun shrieking from the moment she'd spied them climbing the stairs with Saga.

"You must heal her," he said to Lady Fraser.

"I will do my best, my lord," she said. "Did you bring the spike with the poison on it?"

"Aye, here it is. Be careful with it." Giric removed it from his pocket and placed it on the side table near the bed. Lady Fraser placed a drop of water over it and they both watched at how the reaction had no effect.

"Is that bad?" he asked.

"Nay, that is good. It means the poison is most likely plant based and so can be flushed out by getting her to drink water."

"Do you think they were trying to kill her or incapacitate her?"

"Considering her current state I believe they were trying to kill her, but misjudged the dose. They could not have guessed her size or strength otherwise she would not be breathing right now."

"And have you gleaned the poison?"

"Aye, but I want Freydis to examine her as well."

Freydis swiftly examined Saga and the spike. She touched it on the tip of her tongue despite Lady Fraser's urgings and smiled.

"'Tis belladonna, m'lord. Wolfsbane. Your wife will live but she will be weak for some time. I have potions that will help flush the poison from her body, but your biggest worry right now is if she was carrying a bairn. I know you are just wed, so 'tis probably too soon, but that amount of poison would surely kill a bairn though not your wife. She is as strong as any man I've attended, yourself included. She will live."

"Lady Fraser, go with Freydis, aid her in any way you can with her potions and I expect both of you to be here at all times whilst my wife recovers, is that clear?"

"And where do you go?" Lady Fraser asked.

"I go to send word to her brother. We have much to prepare," he said as he smoothed the hair on Saga's forehead and kissed her softly. "Get better swiftly, my love," he whispered. "I need my shield-maiden recovered and by my side for the coming battle."

At the door he turned and regarded both women. "You will tell no one of her progress. Do you understand? No one comes into this chamber and you do not leave it until my return. I will arrange for food to be delivered to you. Go and see to your potions and make enough for three days, or better yet, bring it all up here. I do not want anyone to know how ill she is or if she still lives. Do you ken?"

"Aye, my lord," Lady Fraser said.

Giric left and found Aislin outside pacing. "You will not

enter this chamber under any circumstances, do you understand?"

"Giric, will Saga live or not?"

"I cannot say that at the moment, but I need to go send word to her brother. This is a serious business, sister, and I need you to do exactly as I say. I want you to stay in the chamber across from this one and watch through the keyhole to see who comes and goes. I know this may mean some sleepless time for you, but it's important you do this. Can I trust you?"

"Aye, you certainly can, brother, I will have my meals brought up here and will not leave until you tell me to." That would suit Aisling, since she was not one to enjoy being around many people.

That meant three people were assigned a duty. Now for the rest of the suspects in a long line of who could have been involved here. Osgar had put some doubt in his head about his sister and he'd already had them about Lady Fraser but he was certain this business was beyond any agenda she may have. He absolutely trusted Freydis and also knew she always carried a concealed weapon as a good Norsewoman would. He also knew a thing or two about belladonna and by Saga's reaction, realized she should regain her strength within a few days. The only factor remaining for her safety was his presence, and he was determined to not leave her side until she was recovered fully. Unfortunately, he had to send word to her brother. Gunnar needed to know he was in much more danger than he realized and he'd have to see reason that Giric could not come to his aid right at that moment. Rather it was safer for Gunnar and his people to come to him. Though he realized there would be no way he'd leave the village without defences.

Nay, Giric needed to make a choice for all of them and he needed to make it swiftly.

At the bottom of the stairs he located Osgar.

"How does she fare?"

"She's been poisoned by wolfsbane."

"Christ's teeth, Giric. There is nothing to be determined from the assassin's bodies. More darts and some small blades, but all we could see was white foam at their mouths and that they are dead. Giric, who would send them?"

"I am starting to glean an idea. We need to send word to Gunnar. I cannot tell the man to bring everyone here for safety, but I believe his enemies on Islay are in a closer position to attack than he realizes. Either way, send word and tell him his sister has been poisoned but will live. Send this by someone you trust."

"I will take it myself. I do not trust a carrier pigeon for this. Is there anything else you would like him to know?"

"Aye. Tell him to trust no one. And take Vigdis with you to prove to Gunnar we are still on the same side. Keep her safe."

The two men clasped arms and parted. Giric was certain Osgar would get the message to Gunnar. The two had fought in battle many times and knew exactly how the other would react in each situation. The fact that Osgar could be walking into a trap would not be lost on him.

Giric made his way to the kitchen to talk to the cook. "I will be away for a few days," he said loudly. "Ensure meals are brought to my wife's chamber for her and her ladies and leave them outside."

"Aye, m'lord. I will see it done."

"See to it," he said and left the kitchen to make his way to the armoury.

Once there, he selected three daggers and an additional short sword. This would be more than enough for his purposes.

Giric mounted his horse and spoke with the guards on

the way out through the gate and tore off toward the main road leading west. Once far enough away from the castle, he dismounted and grabbed his horse by the reins to lead it off the main road. After about half an hour he came to a crofter's hut and tied the horse to a tree. He went inside and met Osgar and Vigdis.

"Now what?" they asked together.

"Now you convince Gunnar to come here. Once I'm certain Saga is well, I will journey to the king's side and converse with him. There is a bigger scheme at play here, and I intend to discover it."

CHAPTER NINETEEN

Saga opened her eyes and watched Lady Fraser fuss about the chamber. Her head hurt and her chest felt like a heavy stone lay atop it.

"Och, you're awake now lass," Lady Fraser said. "Did I not tell you I saw this vision? Of me tending to you on your sick bed?"

"Ja, you did. Where is my husband?"

"He has gone to send word to your brother."

"My brother? What kind of word?" Panic rose in Saga. If Gunnar knew she'd been harmed he would show up on the drawbridge with a mighty army ready to tear the castle apart stone by stone.

"Easy lass," Lady Fraser said. "You've had a rough blow and you need your rest."

"Why do you keep calling me that? You were calling me Lady MacDomnail earlier."

"Aye, I can call you that if you prefer. Your husband asked me to help attend to you."

"But why?" she asked. Was it the poison or had Saga lost all ability to comprehend anything?

"He fears you might still be in danger and so he wanted to be sure there was someone you could trust around you at all times. And that is me, lass."

"But you said you were a healer. And you said that in front of him."

"Now, now lassie, all will be well, you rest up a little and it will all be clear to you soon. Here," she said, "You must drink this."

The woman lifted something to Saga's lips that smelled off, sour even. The stench of it cleared the fog in Saga's brain a little as well as her eyesight. "You're not Lady Fraser," she said.

"I am, love. I am here to help you."

Saga's mind could not make sense of the woman before her. Her brain would not let her.

Just then the door opened and another woman entered. "How does she fare?" the woman asked.

"She is confused."

"She has been poisoned with a significant amount of belladonna, surely it will be a while before her mind clears."

"Aye, you speak true, Freydis. But if she is to recover fully, she must drink her tonic, otherwise the poison will not flush from her body."

"Hold her and I will try to get it in her."

Saga felt her arms being held down and her head lifted. The next cup placed near her nose did not smell the same, it was sweeter in nature and so she sipped some. The taste was more like bark and moss and so she drank deeper. The warm liquid flooded her veins and eased some of the ache.

She opened her eyes to see Freydis leaning over her.

"My friend," Saga said. "What happened?"

Freydis smiled. "You've been poisoned," she said. "I'm to attend to you until your strength returns."

"Thank Odin for you, Freydis," Saga said. And she meant

it. Her arms felt like dead weight. She tried to lift her head but could not. Had she been anywhere else, she feared she would not be breathing right now.

"And I thank Odin for you. He was watching over you, Saga."

Freydis' words mirrored her thoughts. Her mind turned over the attack. The moment she realized there were two assassins, she knew she'd been outwitted and that wasn't something she was used to. While she may have great strength, Saga thought on her feet and used her size and speed to her advantage. But she'd had none with these two. They were small and agile, and almost childlike in size. By her standards anyway. Most of the women here were far smaller than she.

She recalled the moment she'd waited for the Valkyries to come for her. She'd heard their screech and the horns of Valhalla. She'd been so close to that glory, but could not bring herself to leave Giric. And what of the serpents in her vision? The message mirrored Giric's intent from the beginning—heal the wounds of the land by forging bonds versus ripping them to shreds through the ravages of war. So what was her role here? How could she affect change?

Saga managed to pull herself to a sitting position with Freydis' aid. Once she was propped up, Lady Fraser brought her a bowl of broth. She sipped the warm fluid for a few moments and passed the bowl back to her. The simple movements sapped her limited energy. Saga lay back down and closed her eyes. Her body was relaxed now at least as the pain and ache had subsided.

Her thoughts drifted to Giric. She envisioned his strong arms around her and him nuzzling her neck. The image brought a peaceful weight over her as she drifted into the black once again.

~

*G*iric rode across the narrow stone roadway to the castle fortress of Dunnottar. Somehow it reminded him of the wharf at Lagavulin. Anyone wanting to gain entry to this castle must cross this narrow path. An army would never succeed. King Constantine had retreated there three years prior in order to save himself and the country from certain invasion from the English King Athelstan. Much of the country's business now operated from that location which meant squabbles on the west coast of the country often fell outside of the king's notice. But Giric was not about to let that sit. Great strides had been made over the past few years to find peace, but that peace rested on a fine thread.

"Who goes there?" a guard asked.

"Giric MacDomnail. I am come to speak with the King about the threat in the west."

The guard sized him up then reached out his hand. "Weapons."

Times surely had changed. Giric had been in the king's company enough times that he would have expected to be granted entry straight away. Then again, three years was a long time for a man to be cooped up in a fortress such as this with limited counsel.

Giric removed his broadsword and knives and handed them to the guard. He was led inside the main keep.

The place was eerily quiet. A castle of this size should be buzzing with activity from servants and guards alike.

"Where is everyone?" he asked the guard.

"Most of the staff were let go. Only the king's guard and his counsel remain."

"And his family?"

The guard turned and leaned toward Giric. "They are safe."

Giric didn't doubt it. The atmosphere in the castle and the guard's behaviour gave rise to a certain unease.

"This way," the guard said as he turned a corner leading to a winding staircase.

When they reached the top, two additional guards stood at attention before a large wooden door.

"Giric MacDomnail to see the king."

A man cloaked in black emerged from the shadows and slid his hood to his shoulders. His face was twisted into a permanent sneer.

"Who are you?" Giric asked.

"I am the king's seer," the man said. "You may call me Luther."

"Well, Luther, I am come to see the King about the threat in the west." There was no cause to keep that much information from the man. Aught else would be for the king's ears only.

"What threat?" Luther asked.

Giric laughed. "I am sure you are privy to King Constantine's concerns as related to this castle, but I am certain you are not aware of happenings in the rest of the country. My information is for him."

Luther stepped a little closer. The man was a bit hard to look at with one drooping eye and clenched teeth.

"What did you say your name was?"

"I am Giric MacDomnail, Laird of MacDomnail Castle near Prestwick. I am loyal to the King and you will let me pass." Giric had no weapons and so took a step forward to gaze down upon the man. His height was threat enough, but to add effect, he folded his arms across his chest and braced his stance.

Luther's gaze flicked across Giric's arms and back up to

his face. One of the guards cleared his throat which immediately affected Luther's demeanour.

"You may pass, Giric of Prestwick. I will accompany you to the King."

"You will not," Giric said. There was nothing trustworthy about this man and he was not about to bring him into his confidence.

"I speak for the King," he said. "I determine who sees him and for what purpose. If you want to see him, you will do so with my company and on my authority."

Giric laughed and turned away from the man. He stood in front of the guards and let his arms fall to his sides.

"I wish to see the King."

Without hesitation they stepped away from the door. Luther tried to skirt around Giric, but one easy shove pushed him back to where the two guards kept him at bay. Giric opened the door, moved inside and closed it firm.

The king sat near a large stone hearth staring into the fire. He wore thick fur in which his body appeared dwarfed. Across from him a large wooden table was strewn with masses of parchment, some big enough for a map, whilst others were strips of possible messages sent by pigeon.

"Laird Giric MacDomnail to see you, your grace."

King Constantine glanced over toward the door and grunted. He stared back into the fire.

"You are well guarded, your majesty. I trust you are in good health?"

Still no reply. Giric moved to the table and glanced among the papers. Missives and formally stamped documents lay about. A map showed the entire eastern side of Scotland on which several up arrows pointed toward them from the English border. Was this a previous threat, or a new one? Athelstan had been kept at bay before, but did this mean he had a new plan?

"Your grace, I come with news from the west."

Giric turned to find the king had emerged from his furs and now stood but a few feet away staring at the map.

"He is coming."

"Aye, it would appear so."

Within a heartbeat, the king appeared to snap out of his stupor and acknowledge his company.

"Giric?"

"Aye, your grace. I come with news from the west."

The king embraced Giric and stood back with a look of wonder on his face.

"I have not seen you in some time, Laird MacDomnail. How fares your kin?"

"My kin are well, your grace. I am come to share some news you need to hear."

The king clapped his hands and made for a side table on which a tankard and several goblets sat. He poured two nearly full and passed one to Giric.

"Come. Sit. And tell me your news."

They sat by the table as the king drank deeply. He was pale and smelled sour. Exactly how long had he been holed up in this chamber?

"I have taken a wife. A Viking wife." Giric was not one to mince words and wondered how long the king's lucidity would last.

King Constantine stopped drinking and placed his tankard on the parchments. He scratched his beard and nodded. The man Giric knew to be king was strategic and clever. Bits of him emerged at that moment.

"Viking. From where?"

"Islay."

The king nodded again and pushed some papers away from another map, this one was quite large and showed the entirety of Scotland and the northern half of England. The king circled Islay with his finger and drew an imaginary line toward Dublin.

"How did you achieve this?"

"I approached the Chieftain and negotiated a contract. We have an ally."

"But."

"But we have a problem."

The king smiled. "Of course we do."

"My wife was attacked."

"Makes sense," the king said. "I cannot imagine your clan approves."

"She was not harmed by any of mine."

"Then who?"

"I do not know. When I left Islay, my alliance with Gunnar was solid, though he has his own territorial issues to deal with and I trust your allies in Dublin are still sound.

"They are."

"Excluding mine and her kin leaves a rather large question mark, does it not?"

"Aye, it does. Tell me about the attack."

"Poison tipped darts. Two attackers gained access to the castle and there was one puncture on the side of my wife's neck."

The king's eyes widened. "Assassins." He stood and moved to the window to push open the shutters. "This place smells like my dungeon. Too long have I barricaded myself behind these walls."

The king walked to the door and flung it wide. "Have my bath prepared and a proper meal." He turned back to Giric and grinned, then back to the guards. "And assemble my council. We have work to do."

Giric noted the surprise on Luther's face before the door closed again.

"You know who is behind this?" Giric asked.

"I have a thought or two. Now go to tell the guard to find you a chamber and a meal. We will convene with my council and unravel this new threat together."

Giric bowed low and left the chamber. The king's response was more than he could have hoped for. He prayed Saga was recovering well and he prayed they could ferret out the instigators and executors of this crime.

CHAPTER TWENTY

Three days after the attack, Saga devoured the stew Freydis placed before her. She would have sworn it was a month full. And the fussing from Freydis and Lady Fraser was enough to drive her to madness. She wanted to see her attackers and examine them herself, but these women fawned over her as though she were a new babe.

"Another bowl?" Freydis asked.

"A bigger one. I will be out of this bed today and you will not keep me in it."

"Under any other circumstance, I would agree with you; however, you are not yet at full strength and I am certain I could restrain you."

Saga grinned. "Is that a challenge?"

"I may be weaker than you, but I am not daft," she said and grinned.

For all she had endured since coming to this place, losing her strength was by far the most difficult to accept. "How long before I am at full capacity again?"

"At least a sennight, maybe longer. But you have to allow

your body to rid itself of the poison. If you push yourself too hard it will take longer."

"A sennight! No, that will not do. I will go mad in the head if I am kept in this chamber another day. How will I find out who sent the assassins from here?"

"That is not your concern. Your husband will track them down and he will be sure they are brought to justice."

"And where is my husband? Off talking to the king as you say, whilst I'm here vulnerable and unable to protect myself or anyone else."

"You are not unprotected."

"I hope you do not refer to those children on the other side of that door," she said and pointed to the closed door.

"How do you know what is on the other side?"

"Because I am trained to know. I have ears that function quite well and I hear the fear in their voices."

Freydis shook her head. "You are not human," she said and laughed.

"I am blessed by Odin. He gives me the strength reserved for one son and the wits of the other. I will remain in this bed for one more day then all the guards in Alba will not keep me in it."

Freydis placed her hands on her hips. "Very well. If I only have one more day with you, you will not complain about your food or your drink. You will not scoff or bat my hand away. Do we have an agreement?"

Saga folded her arms across her chest and nodded. This was worse than any torture she could imagine. She was well enough to be up and around and was convinced staying abed only delayed the poison's effect.

"Here is your stew," Freydis said and placed a much larger bowl before her. The extra chunks of meat made Saga smile.

The door opened and Lady Fraser entered, dragging a large sword—Saga's sword. She was on her feet in an instant, and stumbled when the room spun. Freydis rushed forward and helped her back to sitting.

"I told you the poison still held its power over you," Freydis said.

Saga carefully stood again and reached for her sword. Lady Fraser dragged it across the stone floor and offered it to Saga. Her fingers curled around the grip and tightened. She lifted it a couple inches before it dropped to the floor again. Thor's teeth, the effort was overwhelming. She'd had this weapon since she was ten and even then could raise it over her head.

"I told you, not to overdo it," Freydis said and took the sword from Saga then leaned it against the wall. "Now do you believe me?"

Saga grunted and sat back down to eat her stew. By Odin, she'd have that sword above her head by the morrow even if it killed her.

~

The lords took their seats around tables framing the long central hearth in the great hall. These were men Giric had fought with and trusted, but there was a different air about them today. This was no jovial celebration like the last time they'd met and driven back the English king. He'd been fed and watered and was ready to seek their counsel, but he could not discount the fact that one or more here may have a different agenda and ally since they'd last met.

The king entered from the head of the hall and took his seat on the dais. All heads turned toward him whilst servants filled tables with drink and a feast. Giric had to give them all credit for preparing such a meal in a few short hours. King Constantine looked different from earlier that day. He'd obviously washed and donned clean garments. He now looked like a king with his amber tunic, wide belt and longsword at his side, his head adorned with a thin golden crown centred with a large red ruby.

"My lords, I thank you for your company. It has been far too long. I welcome you to my table and invite you to fill your gullets."

"We are honoured to be invited to your table, my king," a white haired, fat Kenneth Andrews said. "I admit, whilst I am pleased by the invitation, I was surprised by its coming."

The man was no warrior and fancied himself the king's most loyal noble. Giric groaned inwardly. He was the type of man who sidled up to the winner in any argument and asserted himself as their staunchest supporter. Giric wouldn't trust him the length of a shortsword.

"Aye, it has been long since we convened. I shall jump right to it, then. News has come to me we must assess from my trusted ally in the west, Laird Giric MacDomnail. You have fought with this man and his words shall be taken as truth."

Andrews eyed Giric who was sitting to the right of the king. It appeared he only just noticed his presence, perhaps reserving that attention for that which the king offered first.

"My lord, MacDomnail," Andrews said. "It is a pleasure to make your company for it has been some time since we have conversed."

"Aye, it has," Giric said. "Our king has much to share with you, my lord. Perhaps we may reminisce once he is finished sharing his news."

Andrews' brow knit. Giric didn't have time for niceties. Not whilst Saga was recovering from a deadly attack and those ultimately responsible were still at large.

"Of course, my lord," Andrews said.

The man was never one to allow the last word to go to anyone else.

"My lords," the king said. "Laird MacDomnail has recently secured a worthy ally in the west. He has taken a wife in the form of kin of the Viking chieftain, Gunnar of Islay. You all know I would support this marriage as it aligns with my own thinking of how to manage our former battles with these Northmen."

Giric turned his head toward those gathered. Some nodded while others, like Andrews, smirked.

"You're a stronger man than I thought," Andrews said. "I heard Viking wenches strapped knives to their thighs to keep a man from taking what is his right."

"And you're a denser man than I thought," Giric said. "To interrupt your king and insult an ally is ill thinking indeed."

The king slammed his hand on the table, making Andrews jump. "Enough! MacDomnail's Viking wife has been attacked and I do believe our biggest enemy has in turn shown some of their hand at long last."

"How so, your grace?" Andrews asked.

"The mode of the attack was by poison dart. Obviously not in normal use by the forward attacking Vikings, or strategic and well-planned Scots. Nay, that sort of slithering effort only comes from one source—Athelstan."

"How can you be so sure?" Andrews asked. The man was beyond daft.

"I have fought this man before, as have we all. You may recall some of my soldiers being unaccounted for during some of the more important battles. It was discovered, though I never spoke of it, that the king had secured a small group of highly trained individuals who liked to skulk about and poison their victims with measured doses of wolfsbane. MacDomnail's wife was poisoned in such a manner."

"But if they are so good then why does she live?" Andrews asked.

"Because my wife is not your average woman," Giric said. "I believe these assassins miscalculated the amount of poison needed to do anything more than disable her for a short time."

Giric enjoyed the way Andrews swallowed hard at his words. He also noted that Luther had slipped out of the hall shortly after the king revealed his suspicions.

"What now?" Andrews asked, seemingly interested in more than his own interests for the first time since the meeting convened.

"Now we strengthen our allies to the west and prepare ourselves for another invasion which will be as unsuccessful as the last. This news Giric has brought tells me the English are fearful of our alliance with the Vikings and seek to drive a rift between us. An attack on a Viking woman on Scottish soil is normally enough for bloodshed. MacDomnail was correct in bringing this to our counsel. I shall travel to Prestwick with the laird and formally bless this union and any others that result in our alliance. That will send a clear message to Athelstan that we are united against him."

Andrews stood. "My alliance is with you, your grace."

His declaration was met with a nod from the king and followed in affirmation by each other man around the table.

"Now, please fill your bellies. We have much to plan and I need your wits about you."

As side conversations broke off, the king leaned in close to Giric. "Did you notice who left?"

"Aye. Where do you think he went?"

"I've long suspected his loyalty to Athelstan, however I could not prove it. Whilst he viewed an aging and dissociated king over these past three years, I've been amassing a stronghold of weapons in a secret location. You are now one of three people who have this knowledge."

"I thank you for your trust, your grace. Do you think you should have Luther followed?"

"He's been followed since the day he showed up on my doorstep three years ago. It is interesting what one can glean when one appears detached."

"A clever strategy, your grace."

"Indeed. Now, you shall make haste back to your new bride, and prepare for a visit from your king. I expect a great feast in my honour and hope to meet the great Chieftain of Islay."

"That you shall, your grace. As I headed east to seek your counsel, I sent MacAlpin west to gather Gunnar and his clan. I anticipate they will already be at the castle when I return."

"Excellent. I will now take my leave. Please enjoy the remainder of your stay. I have much to plan."

"As you wish, your grace."

Once the king left the hall, most of the other members of the counsel scattered as well. Giric remained to watch the men until only he and Andrews remained.

"You are loyal to your king," Andrews said.

"I am."

"And he trusts you."

"Aye. With good reason."

"I am glad to hear it. I am aware he has disclosed our little secret to you. I do not know you well, but if the king trusts you, I do as well."

Giric couldn't have been more surprised. Andrews had all the outward appearance of someone who took advantage of his position in life and ran the other way at the first sign of trouble.

Andrews smirked. "The king is not the only master of disguise at Dunnottar, Laird MacDomnail. We have many enemies near and far and I saw through his guise from the beginning. In order to make it more believable, I offered to add to the complacency. I believe we have succeeded."

"And Luther? Do you not think he could be skulking about listening to every word we say?"

"I will be made aware of his whereabouts as soon as I leave this hall. Know this, MacDomnail, the king and Scotland are in good hands despite outward appearances. You have been brought into the fold where few reside. Do not break the trust that has been placed in your lap."

With that, Andrews arose from the table and left the hall, leaving Giric to ruminate on the conversation with both the king and Andrews. Aye, much was not as it seemed at Dunnottar. The question remained, were these men actually successful at plotting a future defence under the nose of Athelstan, or were they simply delusional from being holed up in the castle too long?

Either way, Giric had achieved what he'd set out to do and wouldn't waste another moment in returning to Saga. He could not wait to take her into his arms and show her how much risk he was willing to take to keep her safe.

CHAPTER TWENTY-ONE

The cool autumn breeze caressed her face. Saga had shrugged off Giric's order to remain in her chamber and climbed to the tower many times over the past few days in order to rebuild her strength; her reward being the view and the clean air. She appreciated everything Freydis and Lady Fraser had done for her, but her chamber was too stuffy and she could take no more lying about.

The servant girl, Aslaug, had been sending word to both Freydis and Saga, from Prestwick, saying she wanted to be more useful to them. Saga understood that she'd likely been coerced into executing her past crimes, but she was not yet certain what to do with her. For now she would remain under the watchful eye of the innkeeper. Time would tell if she could regain their trust.

The responsibility of the woman weighed heavily on Saga. Or perhaps it was the damned Scottish gown she'd been encouraged to wear. The ties at the sides were so tight they practically bound her and stifled her breath.

This tiny platform was her only respite. The view from the tower was stunning to say the least. She couldn't get enough of it. Surely there was no other place in this land that could offer more peace and quiet. She could think up here. She missed her home, that was certain, but primarily at the moment, she missed Giric which was what originally brought her up there. He'd been gone a sennight and she had lost count of the number of times she'd scanned the road leading to the castle.

The low thudding of horses' hooves caught her attention and her heart soared. Except the sound indicated many horses, but Giric had travelled alone.

Saga leaned forward and squinted at the spot where the road disappeared into the forest. A heartbeat later the unmistakable blonde headed figure of her brother, Magnus came into view. He was followed by many others. Saga wasted no time descending the spiral staircase and making her way to the entrance of the keep. She met Magnus at the exact moment he dismounted.

Without hesitation, he picked her up and swung her around. "I am glad to see you up and about. MacAlpin left the impression there may not be much left of you." He hugged her again. "I have missed you, Saga." He leaned back and stared hard into her eyes. "It is time to come home, now. Your husband has broken his vow to keep you safe and Gunnar is convinced that is enough for you to divorce your husband and come home where you belong."

Saga swatted his hands away. "I am going nowhere. This is my home now."

"Saga, you must see reason. At least on Islay you have your clan to protect you. Who here can save you from another attack? It is clear that these people do not want you here, despite what their laird may say."

"You are mistaken, Magnus. My husband has gone to secure the support of the king."

Magnus's jaw dropped. "He's not even here?" Magnus

moved away from Saga and kicked the dirt. "He left you? I cannot believe this! He made a promise to us and he's broken it."

"All is not how it appears, Magnus," Osgar said from behind him. "And you misrepresent what Gunnar ordered."

"What exactly did my brother say?" Saga asked.

Osgar came up to her and bowed. "I am pleased you have healed, Lady MacDomnail. These shores are better with you on them."

Two small arms wrapped around her waist as a sob erupted from her sister.

"I prayed to Odin you would recover. I hated leaving you, sister."

Saga kissed the top of Vigdis's head. "It would take more than a little poison to defeat me, you know this." She turned to Osgar again. "I ask again, what did my brother say exactly."

"Gunnar said if I am not convinced of your safety, I am to return with you," Magnus said.

"No," Osgar said. "Gunnar said you were to come here and consider the full explanation as to what happened from Giric and satisfy yourself with the overall security of the castle as relates to your sisters."

"Same thing," Magnus said. "I am not convinced and Giric is not here. End of investigation. Come Saga and Vigdis, we're leaving." With that Magnus reached for Saga's arm.

Saga reached out with both hands and shoved Magnus hard. "I am going nowhere. When my husband returns you may hear his explanation and he will provide you with a tour of the grounds. Until then, you will be provided a chamber and all other hospitality any guest would receive." Magnus had the look of battle about him, but Saga would not be swayed. "My sister and I will be in the great hall awaiting the noon meal if you wish to join us."

With that she turned and walked back inside the castle. Magnus had always overreacted, but this time he took it too far. He had no say over her life anymore, neither did Gunnar for that matter. She had every faith Giric would apprehend the culprits and her safety would never be in question again.

Saga swayed a little before reaching her seat at the table. Vigdis was there to help steady her.

"Magnus only means well, sister. And I have to say, I have never seen you so pale."

"Not you too."

"I would never be bold enough to tell you what to do, but you have to admit, the end result could have been much worse."

"I know that, but Magnus does not have the right to come here and demand I leave this place. Nothing is ever as it appears on the surface, Vigdis. You know that. I am confident all will be revealed when Giric returns."

Did she believe that? Mostly. Saga despised feeling weak because as was demonstrated, her weakness would lead to someone else controlling her every move. She would rather fly with the Valkyries than allow that to happen.

Magnus entered the hall and took a seat to her left. He said nothing as he filled his trencher with meat and bread and cheese. He glanced at her trencher then flicked his gaze over her face and shook his head.

"What?"

"You always could eat more than most men, now look at you. You eat no more than a small bird."

"Do you want a record of everything I ate since I arrived here, Magnus?"

"Mayhap I do. I am to ensure your wellbeing."

Saga placed her bread back in her trencher and leaned toward him. "If you do not cease to pester me about matters that are none of your business, I will drive my dagger into your guts and leave it there to fester."

"Well that's a good sign," he said with a tiny grin.

"Speak plainly."

"If you're threatening me, you must be feeling better."

Saga opened her mouth to counter, but before any words could emerge they died in her throat when she caught sight of Giric striding across the hall. She jumped up to meet him and nearly fell when the room spun around her. Giric caught her before she hit the floor. He swooped her up and without missing a beat, turned toward the staircase.

"Nay," she said. "I wish to remain here. I cannot take any more of that chamber."

Giric nuzzled her neck and whispered, "Not even with me there? I've missed you."

Saga sighed and wrapped her arms around his neck. Put that way, she supposed she could tolerate a little more time in the chamber.

"I missed you too, husband. Did you discover what you sought on your quest?" she asked as he kicked the door to their chamber shut.

"Aye, but now is not the time to talk about that. You are wearing too much clothes," he said as he placed her on the bed.

"As are you, my lord."

"Oh now I'm your lord. I thought you were never going to call me that."

"I changed my mind."

"I am pleased to hear that. And you're still wearing too many garments."

Saga wiggled out of her gown and removed her shift. She had always been proud of her body and for the first time felt a little self conscious with her weight loss.

Giric's gaze burned along her skin. "God's teeth! I will never tire of looking at you."

He stripped and took her into his arms. Her world righted itself the moment he kissed her. No matter what befell them in the future, as long as they had this, all would be well.

~

She had fallen into a deep slumber and so Giric quietly left the chamber. He was not used to tempering his lovemaking to her, but he was certain she was not yet back to full strength regardless of her pleading. He would take no liberties with her health and safety.

He made his way back to the hall to where Osgar, Vigdis, and a brooding Magnus waited.

"What news?" Osgar asked.

"How fares my sister?" Magnus asked.

"Your sister is sleeping and I have much news to impart. The king will arrive here within a fortnight and looks forward to blessing my marriage and the alliance we have forged." Giric looked pointedly at Magnus who folded his arms across his chest.

"Your marriage for now," he said.

"I beg your pardon?"

"I am here on behalf of Gunnar who is none too pleased at the lack of care put into my sister's safety. I must be satisfied that she is properly secure and there is no remaining threat else she is to return with me to start divorce proceedings."

Giric stood and placed his hands flat on the table. "I assure you your sister is safe with me and there is no remaining threat. Further to that, there will be no talk of divorce now or ever. We have been married before God and that cannot be undone."

Magnus stood as well. "We do not recognize your God. Only Odin can decide our fate."

"Enough!" Saga's shout from the other side of the hall caught Giric off guard. By God he would need strong rope to keep that woman abed to heal.

"You should not be up," Giric and Magnus said together.

"I will get up when I please, as I see fit. And I concur with my husband, Magnus. There will be no talk of divorce. This marriage has been blessed by both our Gods and that is the end of it. I appreciate you coming here to rescue me, however, as you can see, I do not need rescuing. Now, husband, will you please enlighten us all as to what you learned on your quest."

She sat next to Giric and folded her hands in front of her. He admired her strength. He prayed she never lacked it again, but if she did, he would be there to carry her.

"As I said, the king will be here in a fortnight or less to bless this marriage. He is more than pleased with our alliance and is interested in further securing it. He believes the assassins who attempted to take my wife's life were sent by Athelstan. He said he has seen that sort of attempt before and that is why our alliance is more important than ever."

"I don't understand," Osgar said. "Why would Athelstan try to kill Saga?"

"For the exact reaction Magnus has displayed. To divide us. He knows we are stronger together and that is a threat to him. News must have spread quickly about our marriage and as the king suspected, Athelstan's spies are never far away."

"All the more reason for Saga to return home."

"Nay. All the more reason for us to secure this alliance and ensure we are both well protected."

"Something we did not need before you came along."

"Oh, and the other inhabitants of Islay are all friendly now are they? And that's why Gunnar stayed at home and sent you to do his bidding?"

"I volunteered and no they are not our allies, but we know how to anticipate them. These assassins of yours have no honour."

"On that point we agree, Magnus. They have no honour, and their king has none. We will take stock of every man, woman, and child within these castle walls and the town. If there is anyone who does not belong, they will be brought to the dungeon and kept there until they can be properly assessed by the king. Magnus, you are welcome to stay here until the king arrives; however, he wants to meet Gunnar. I can send someone else with that message or I can send you. The choice is yours."

"I will go as soon as you show me how your security for this castle is set up. Gunnar will expect a full report."

"There is no better time than now." Giric realized Gunnar had been more than tolerant of him and his proposal than others of his clan. He dug deep to find the patience he would need with Magnus, but he'd come too far to stop now.

Together they left the hall and turned first toward the stables. Giric was proud of his horses and was even more so when Magnus started asking questions about breeding and training.

Next they visited the gardens and the kitchen, all well within the stone wall of the bailey.

"You plan to conquer your enemies by feeding them?" Magnus asked.

"No, but we are self-sufficient here and could survive a siege for several months."

Magnus scratched his beard. "That is all well and good,

but weapons are my language. I assume you have an armoury."

"Aye, in good time. Effective defences are not just about swords and axes." Giric didn't want to condescend, but Magnus was not understanding the greater picture.

As the tour continued, Magnus became more and more agitated so Giric conceded and brought him to the armoury.

"We keep all the weapons here for purposes of an attack or battle. Every clansman you encounter is responsible for his weapons, but my blacksmith is accessible to all who fall within my protection."

Giric watched as Magnus studied the longswords, daggers, axes, and crossbows in the long narrow chamber. Long minutes passed while the man assessed the hundreds of weapons before him. He lifted several swords and checked them for balance and swung them over his head. He loaded and unloaded some of the bows and came to several maces lined up together.

For the first time since they'd met, Magnus smiled. "I like these," he said.

"The mace has its purpose. It's particularly effective when its wielder is mounted."

Magnus held it up over his head then swung low. His eyes lit up like a child with a new toy making Giric grin.

"You may keep that one if you wish."

Magnus stopped and considered Giric. "I approve of your defences. And I accept your gift." He reached out his hand. Giric grasped his forearm as did Magnus; thankfully, that meant their bond was forged.

"You will bring my message to Gunnar?"

"He will return within a fortnight."

With that, Magnus left the armoury and Giric returned to the hall to his waiting wife and closest ally. When he arrived he noted Saga's absence and enquired as to her whereabouts.

"She has retired to her chamber," Vigdis said. "She bade our brother farewell and excused herself."

She went willingly? That was somewhat disconcerting and out of character. Giric took the steps two at a time to locate her.

He entered the chamber quietly and gently closed the door. She lay in a curled-up bundle in the middle of the bed with a quilt tucked in around her.

"Are you unwell?" he asked.

"The hall started to spin around me and I feared I would lose my guts so I chose to come here to rest to see if it would pass."

Giric stroked her hair. "This is difficult for you, my warrior wife."

"It is."

"You have my promise that no one will ever get close to you again."

"I believe you, husband. But a part of Magnus's argument is sound. Were I still on Islay, this would not have happened."

"How can you predict that?"

"Because on Islay, our threat was from our own kind. We know their ways and could sensibly defend ourselves from potential attack. This threat is new to me and I am trying to process it. I am used to an enemy coming at me front on, not from shadow and a poisoned dart."

"So you agree with Magnus, that you are not safe here?" Giric could not believe his ears. She sounded like she was giving up. This was not the fearless woman he knew. Giric's anger rose at that moment. He was now more determined than ever to push back the English king.

"I do not know, husband. I simply do not know."

"What can I do?"

"There is nothing you can do. I will need to reconcile this business for myself. I would like to be alone for now."

Giric leaned over and kissed her on the forehead then left the chamber. He stood outside for long moments considering her words with his guts twisting into knots. He'd been so driven to make this alliance work, he had refused to see any of the real dangers associated with such a strategy. His mistake was that he'd let his desire for his grand scheme prevent him from seeing some of the finer detail required for success.

Well, by God, he would not make that mistake again. The king would be here in a fortnight as would Gunnar and he intended to ensure every detail of their visit would be perfect, all security would go through him, and his wife would never feel uncertain of her safety again.

Giric made his way back to the hall to seek out Osgar so they could begin their planning. He suggested that Vigdis see to her sister and he sat with his friend.

"Have we made a mistake?" he asked Osgar.

"Nay, I do not believe so. But you have been driving this forward too quickly, my friend."

"Aye, I see that now."

"You would not take no for an answer. Your wife is a strong woman; to see her spirit broken is difficult to watch."

Giric's heart squeezed tight. Osgar was right. He'd been so intent on doing the right thing, he'd allowed the people he loved to get in harm's way to achieve it.

"You are right. Now how do we fix this?"

"You will listen to me?"

"Aye, I will listen."

Osgar grinned at him.

"Well?" Giric asked. "What are your suggestions?"

"I am enjoying the moment first."

"What moment?"

"The one where you admit you've been an ass."

"Are you done yet?"

"Almost."

Giric shook his head and poured some ale into a goblet then drank deeply. He would let his friend have his moment —he'd earned it.

CHAPTER TWENTY-TWO

The days passed by in a blur as the castle prepared for the king's arrival. Saga's strength returned slower than she would have liked, but it was her time with Giric that brought her spirits and determination closer to where she wanted to be. She turned in his arms and watched him sleep, memorizing the lines of his face and smiling while he quietly snored.

If only they could stay that way forever. But her brother Gunnar was supposed to arrive this day, and the king two days after that. She'd been aiding where she could in the preparations and truth be told, she was somewhat apprehensive of meeting the latter. Giric had been adamant that the king was in support of their marriage, but she would believe it when she saw it.

"You look concerned," Giric whispered.

Saga looked up into his eyes and tried to smile. "I am thinking about what the coming days will bring. We both want this alliance to succeed, however, so much can go wrong. I could never live with myself if anything were to happen to you."

He stroked her face with the back of his fingers and lightly kissed her lips. "Nothing will happen to me. The king comes to strengthen our alliance and forge a new one with Gunnar. Wars are avoided by the peaceful negotiations you will witness."

"Wars begin over less."

"Do not worry, Saga. I will be mindful of how much drink flows before any serious talk ensues."

"And what is that supposed to mean?"

"It means that men in their cups or horns do not make the best decisions."

"Are you saying my kin have a problem with drinking?"

"What? No, I'm saying any man who drinks too much should not be trusted with negotiating peaceful treaties."

Saga didn't like what she was hearing. Or was she being too sensitive? Just when she was about to offer a rebuttal, a wave of sickness washed over her. She put her hand to her mouth and swallowed hard.

"Saga, what is it?" Giric asked.

She shook her head and closed her eyes, but that made the room spin so she sat up. Giric wrapped his arms around her shoulders and put the back of his hand to her forehead.

"You are warm," he said. "Lie down again and I will get Freydis."

"I do not wish to lie down. The room spins more when I do."

"Do you think 'tis the poison still?"

"Nay, it is not the poison. I only feel like this when I wake in the morning and after a while it passes."

Giric rose from the bed, dressed quickly and left the chamber. Saga sat on the edge of the bed until he returned with Freydis.

"She says she is only like this in the morning," he said as they entered the chamber.

"Only in the morning?" she asked with a grin.

"I do not know what you find amusing," Saga said. "I feel like I will lose my guts if I move."

Freydis sat on the bed beside her, her smile holding. "Saga, when did you last bleed?"

"She has not bled since we arrived here four weeks ago," Giric said.

Saga pieced together Freydis' question and Giric's answer. Surely they could not mean what she thought. A babe was a blessing she had not considered would be bestowed upon them so soon.

"You are with child," Freydis said as she reached over and lifted Saga's breasts. "Tender?"

"Very much so," Saga said and peeped up to look at Giric. The smile on his face reached his eyes. "I did not know it would happen so soon," she said.

"For some it does," Freydis said. "This is a sign from Freya. She has blessed your marriage, Saga."

Freydis left the chamber then Giric took her place on the bed. He leaned over and kissed the top of her head. "I am so happy, Saga."

"You are not worried?"

"I am not. You are the strongest woman I know. Our bairn will be as well."

She rubbed her still flat belly and thought about that which grew inside. She had always assumed she would one day marry and have children, but both had been thrust upon her so quickly, she was not sure she had time to catch up. She looked up into Giric's eyes. Fortune had smiled on her the day he'd crossed the Firth of Clyde to land on her shores. The sea had given her a husband and now a babe, and she would be sure to thank the gods properly once her brother arrived. For the first time since coming to this place, Saga felt like she was becoming rooted here, as though the prospect of raising children with this man in this place was right and this was another demonstration.

Saga looked into Giric's eyes. "I already know it's a boy child."

He laughed. "You do? How do you know that?"

She rubbed her belly again. "I just do."

Giric kissed the top of her head again. "Well, my wife and my son, we need to get you dressed and fed. I will not have either of you wasting away."

Saga smiled at the thought of the extra care she sensed would be coming her way. Not that she wanted to be pampered in any way, in fact, she despised it, but for the first time in her life, she could think about more than what she wanted. If that meant letting someone do something for her, so be it. She would let him.

Giric and Saga reached the great hall as the servants were laying out the morning meal. She had to bite her lip when the smell of roasted meat met her. She tried to hide her revulsion, but Giric was too focused on her to miss it.

"Do you want to break your fast in our chamber?"

"Nay. I will survive it. The babe needs the meat as do I."

"Babe?" her sister asked from behind her.

Saga turned around to see her sister standing behind her. "I believe I am with child," she said, hardly believing the words herself. There could be no other explanation. She had not bled since before Giric arrived on Islay and that was six weeks ago.

Vigdis wrapped her arms around Saga and squeezed her waist. "Oh sister, I am so pleased! We shall make a blot sacrifice to the Allmother Frigg this day."

"A sacrifice?" Giric asked. "What kind of sacrifice?"

Saga laughed. She wouldn't expect Giric to understand the importance of asking Frigg's blessing, but she hoped he would not challenge her on it. The sacrifice at their wedding had been so quick that Saga wondered if Giric had missed it.

"We will slay an animal to honour Frigg and ask for her blessing for our child. The animal will be cooked and we shall all share it at tonight's feast."

"What kind of animal?"

"We usually hunt for a deer, but we do not have time for that this morning."

Osgar moved toward Giric then. "She can slaughter one of your sheep," he said to Giric. "Congratulations, my friend. I am certain we will all enjoy roasted lamb at the feast this evening."

Saga watched as Giric rolled the information around in his head. Her acceptance here hung by a thread, she knew it and he knew it. Performing a sacrifice in the manner in which she was accustomed, would be shocking to most of the people here so she would need to take care.

"I will help you," he said and took her hand in his. "If this is important to you, I will help you."

Her heart soared. Just when she thought he could not surprise her more, he did.

~

Saga and her sister pointed at the sheep and nodded their heads. Sacrificing an animal for the benefit of their child was such a foreign concept to Giric, he could scarce comprehend. His only reconciliation was that the animal would be slaughtered as they normally would, swiftly and cleanly, and that they would consume it. Whatever prayers Saga wanted to impart in that process, he could accept. He had to. This was part of her and so he would find a way to make it work.

"Have you made your selection?" he asked her.

"Ja," she said. "I have." Saga pointed to a sheep standing a bit apart from the rest of the group. It was a fair size, but wasn't as frisky as the others.

"If you are certain, I will have it done for you."

"I will watch," she said. "And I will send up my prayers to Frigg for our child."

"You are certain you are well enough to watch?"

Saga laughed. "Do you know how long I have hunted, husband?"

"I do not, but probably since you could first hold an axe," he said with a grin. Hints of the powerful woman he'd met broke through when she stood a little taller. He marvelled at the thought of her regaining her full strength.

Giric motioned for the herder to lead the sheep into the slaughterhouse. He held Saga's hand as the herder put the animal into position. He found it curious that the animal did not try to escape; it stood there as if it had already accepted its fate.

"We are ready when you are, Saga," he said.

She stepped forward while holding her sister's hand. Together, they lifted their faces and hands to the sky.

"Allmother Frigg. Goddess of life and love. Accept this offering as a token of our love for you and bless my child with your grace."

"Allmother Frigg," Vigdis said. "Accept this offering as a token of our love and bless Saga's child with your grace and carry the spirit of this animal to its great reward."

Long moments passed as they closed their eyes and smiled as if their goddess whispered sweet affirmation in their ears. After a time, they lowered their hands and heads and nodded to the herder.

"She is ready to receive our gift."

The herder sliced the sheep's neck and laid it on the ground so the animal would not panic as its lifeblood flowed onto the thirsty earth. Vigdis reached down and drew a small amount of the blood from the pool then brushed it across Saga's forehead and her own.

Giric was fascinated watching them and the connection they displayed between the animal and their goddess. The two women hugged as they walked out of the slaughterhouse together.

"Have the butcher prepare the meat and have it brought to the kitchen immediately," he said to the herder.

He followed Saga and Vigdis back to the great hall. While he had to admit, their ritual was not something he would seek out, there was a certain beauty and respect they showed to the animal for its sacrifice. And it would not be wasted, that was important. Animals were slaughtered regularly on his lands for feasting with no ceremony whatsoever. Yet he would take the time to visit the chapel later to say his own prayer for God's grace and blessing for their child. Surely all the Gods combined would heed their call for the safety and wellbeing of the child.

A commotion met them when they re-entered the great hall.

"Where is my sister?" a booming, familiar voice asked.

Saga ran toward Gunnar and wrapped her arms around him. Giric loved how free she was with her emotions. In his own world, one was taught to keep emotion in check at all times as it could be seen as a weakness. But these Vikings loved and lived with abandon. They were fierce in their battles and in how they loved.

"Welcome to my home, Gunnar of Islay. I hope you like it."

"'Tis more than a man needs," he said. "Only a man who needed to make up in other areas would need a dwelling this large."

Giric winked at Saga. "My endowments are well enough," he said. "Come and enjoy this feast and I will give you a tour."

"Feast indeed," Gunnar said as he took a seat beside Giric and across from Saga. "Exactly how many people are we feeding?"

"My family and I dine first, and the rest is shared amongst the castle staff."

"They eat after you like dogs?"

Giric had not thought of it like that and was slightly taken aback. It was one thing for Gunnar to degrade him on Islay, but another altogether to do it in his own castle and in front of servants.

"Every person here is a valued member of this household."

Gunnar eyed him for a moment then burst out laughing. "You really are much too serious, MacDomnail."

He'd almost forgotten how much Gunnar enjoyed a good jest and prayed he would keep it in check when the king arrived. Comments like that would not bode well for either of them and he would need to find a way to temper Gunnar's boisterous nature.

"My brother is not in his cups now," Saga said. "I see the worry on your face. You do not think he will get along well with your king."

"I don't think that at all. I am certain when the time comes for your brother to meet the king, he will pay the man his due respect and that respect will flow both ways."

Giric really did not want to get into this at the moment.

"You think I am unworthy of your king?" Gunnar asked in a voice that almost sounded hurt.

"No, Gunnar. I believe you are an honourable man and I am honoured to introduce the king to you. The path forward for us all is through this alliance. It is important, as are you, otherwise we would not all be here together at the moment."

"I am unwell," Saga said and abruptly left the table and the hall.

Giric did not follow her this time, rather nodded to Vigdis who left the hall behind her.

"What's wrong with her?" Gunnar asked.

"She is with child."

Gunnar sat back for a moment and howled in laughter again. This was shaping up to be a long day.

CHAPTER TWENTY-THREE

"*S*aga, I do not understand what has made you so vexed. Giric did not say anything about Gunnar, did not accuse him of anything."

"Nay, but he was thinking it. I could see it on his face." Saga was not about to sit around and allow her family or her people to be treated like an embarrassing relative. Nay, she would set Giric straight before his king arrived, or they would leave.

"Saga, come and sit with me," Vigdis said. "You must calm yourself."

She didn't want to calm herself. She wanted to grab the nearest sword and go thrash at something. Odin's breath, her emotions were all over the place. She must surely be going mad.

"Well, at least cease pacing. You're making me dizzy." Vigdis approached Saga. She placed her hands on her sister's shoulders and stopped her movements.

"Saga, if it is pent up energy you have, let us walk or ride. You are like a caged cat."

Vigdis was right. She was coming apart at the seams and

she had to find a better way to manage herself. She'd never been idle in her life, and the past few weeks had been more than a challenge. Now with a babe growing in her belly, she needed to set her pace up front. She'd seen other women at the castle, namely Giric's sister, who was fat with child and lazed about all day with servants waiting on them hand and foot.

She needed to clear her head and set some boundaries with Giric. Otherwise she may as well pack her chest and return to Islay. The mere thought made her chest tighten.

"A ride, you say?" she asked Vigdis. "I believe that would be a welcome distraction."

Saga and Vigdis left her chamber and proceeded to the keep and entrance to the stables. Giric possessed many fine horses, but Saga had been gifted the most beautiful mare she'd ever seen. Sif snorted and bobbed her head up and down as soon as Saga came into view, as if they'd already forged a bond. The stable hand prepared Sif and a small grey mare for Vigdis.

They rode for nearly an hour until they reached a high crag overlooking the glen below and the sea in the distance. Saga tugged at the hem of her gown to keep it from riding up her legs.

"'Tis beautiful here, Saga. Fortune has smiled on you."

She had not thought about her current situation quite in that way, but she could certainly admit to the beauty before her. She'd not imagined the mainland of Scotland to be so different from her island. But different it was. And was that such a bad thing? Differences were what made life interesting. She'd been so worried about holding on to her traditions and rituals that she could not see that exposure to Giric's world could help her find even better ways to live her life. Instead of fighting against that which was before her, what if she let a little in? In truth, she was a little more than curious about Giric's religion. Nothing would sway her from her gods, but she was curious as to how one single god could serve so many purposes. How could he be the god of love and war at the same time?

She didn't have the answer, but wondered if asking the question might help her adjust better to this new world. Too much change had been thrust upon her in a short span and the time had come for her to regain control of her world.

"You're smiling," Vigdis said.

"This place holds much beauty."

"Are you certain that is the only reason why you suddenly look at peace?"

She may not be completely at peace, but she had settled the clutter in her head. Saga had always navigated her life with clear direction. That's how she must approach her new world. If she was going to find her place here, she must be observant and use her senses to learn how she could combine two very different worlds.

"Come, sister. Let us return to the castle. I wish to know more about it and everyone who provides services to the laird."

"That is a smart plan, however, I am surprised at your transformation."

"As am I, but if I am to remain here, I must discover every secret of this place, else I will lose all of myself within it."

Thankfully, Vigdis remained silent during the slow trot across the winding pathway and onward to the stables. When they arrived, a concerned looking Giric met them.

"I was worried," he said quietly when she dismounted and approached.

She reached up and wrapped her arms around his neck, inhaling his scent and pulling him toward her waiting lips. She kissed him softly and tenderly as she wrapped her arms tighter around his neck. Giric wrapped his arms around her waist and lifted her as he deepened the kiss. His hot mouth pressed against hers and his tongue slipped inside to dance with hers. Her womanhood clenched when he groaned deep within his throat.

When he placed her back on the ground, he said in a breathless voice, "I am not worried any longer."

She smiled. "Nor am I."

They linked hands and walked in silence to the keep. Had they found their truce yet? Nay. But they would. Saga would be sure of it.

~

They returned to the great hall and to a confused looking Gunnar. The man's expression mirrored Giric's own thoughts. He could not fathom what had upset his wife, but he was pleased all appeared well again. The king was set to arrive on the morrow and he wanted this meeting to run smoothly for all parties involved. He prayed Saga was onside else she could convince her brother to return to Islay and they would be no further ahead.

"Exactly what is it you wish from me, MacDomnail?" Gunnar asked when they took their seats.

"I want an alliance between you and the king in order to strengthen our efforts against Athelstan. That's it. There is no hidden agenda here. I cannot speak any more plainly than that."

"And what part of that do you not like, Sister?"

Giric turned to Saga to see her frown again.

"I do not believe we have any business fighting someone else's war. The business between the English and Scottish kings is just that, between them."

Giric understood, he really did. "Saga, I ken you are

trying to protect your way of life and your people. But the situation is far more complicated than that."

"I understand well enough, Husband."

"Do you?" Giric asked, beginning to lose the remaining patience he had. "Your people took the land you now inhabit and it is likely it will be taken from you again."

"You've said enough, MacDomnail," Gunnar said.

Saga looked at him with wide eyes, her jaw agape. At that moment he was not sure if she was about to burst into a rage or weep. He was not sure which he would prefer and his heart squeezed when she chose the latter. Before he could say anything she ran from the hall and up the stairs—he hoped to their chamber.

"Well now that you've made my sister cry, I guess I have to beat you senseless," Gunnar said with a straight face.

"I sincerely hope you do not mean that," Giric said as Osgar moved a little closer.

Gunnar stared him down for what felt like an eternity before the corners of his mouth started to curl.

"I am not trying to hurt your sister," Giric said.

"Nay, it appears that it comes naturally."

"Gunnar, we are running out of time. The king arrives on the morrow and I need to be sure we have an understanding."

"That is your perception. We can return to Islay any time and defend our lands. And ja, they are our lands."

"By conquer, Gunnar. Do we really need to have a philo-sophical discussion about land ownership?"

"Mayhap we should. You are not native to your lands. The king granted them to you and the peoples who lived there before you were driven out. You are not better than us, though you appear to believe so. I understand why my sister is upset and it is because you have treated us like the pet you wish to display but are challenged to keep under the yoke."

"You have it wrong, Gunnar. I do respect you and your kin. Hell, I married your sister. What more commitment do you want?"

"You are committed to a cause that has some nobility, I will grant you that. But you cannot bend us to your ways. We are a fiercely proud people, and while I do agree that violence is not always the answer, it does serve a purpose when necessary."

"My cause is noble. Peace is noble and we must find a way to work together to ensure a tyrant does not take that from us."

"We already have peace. Why should we concern ourselves with your worry?"

Giric was not sure if Gunnar was baiting him or disagreeing with him. This was a far different conversation than the one they'd had on Islay a few weeks ago.

"Because if you do not, and the English are successful, they will not stop with the mainland of Alba. Unchecked, they will continue until they possess all there is to be had."

"Giric, I agreed to come here to listen to you and your king's proposals, and I am a man of my word. But I do not like what I see in my sister's distress and I do not like what I see in your approach. I can only assume the king will have his own thoughts on how we should proceed."

That was not a full agreement, but it was a small concession and he would take that if it meant keeping Gunnar here until the king's arrival. He'd not really considered that all parties would not agree to his suggestions. Perhaps Osgar was right. Perhaps he had not quite thought this through and the whole business was doomed to failure. And where would that leave him and Saga? Nay, he could not think like that. He must stay the course and remain vigilant when others around him lost faith.

"I appreciate your concerns, Gunnar. I will strike a

bargain with you. If you still feel the same way as you do now once the king's visit is complete, I will not stand in your way to return to Islay and I will not hassle you for your allegiance for the upcoming conflict. But know this, my wife will remain here."

"My sister will go wherever she pleases whether you like it or no." Gunnar downed his ale and loaded up his trencher as if to settle in for a long repast. "You still don't comprehend, do you MacDomnail?"

"Comprehend what?"

"Saga cannot be tamed."

Giric didn't reply to that statement. How could he? And was that what he was trying to do? Tame her? He didn't think so, but mayhap that was the impression he'd left with them all. With the king's arrival mere hours away, he had little time to do anything about it. So much depended upon this meeting and if Saga was upset, more than his marriage could be at stake. He needed to find her and do what he could to smooth things over with her else all could be lost.

His plan to seek out Saga was interrupted when Magnus entered the hall.

"I thought you did not wish to meet the king," Gunnar said.

"I have news that may impact your talks here," Magnus said.

"We're listening," Giric said. Why did he suddenly feel like a load of stone was about to drop on his head?

"You were right all along about Einar. He was playing both sides and he played me. Short-Beard had no intention of attacking you, in fact, he had intended to invite you to his hall and discuss boundaries for Islay."

Gunnar was on his feet in an instant. "I'll send him to Niflheim this day."

Giric didn't know where that was, but he imagined it was

not pleasant. "How did you discover this, Magnus? And how does it affect us striking an alliance against the English king?"

"Our kin caught Einar in Dublin with King Olaf, convincing him to act against us and the Scots and side with the English instead."

Giric glanced at Gunnar, his face was a deep scarlet, yet he did not speak. The man was always quick with a quip, but right now, he was frighteningly silent. Giric needed to think of something to get them back on track.

"Where is Einar now?" Giric asked.

"In irons on Islay. Bjorn will not sleep until I return. I came here to warn you in case any damage had already been done."

Giric thought back over the past days and weeks. Damage done? There had been an incredible amount of damage done and there were many prejudices to tackle and that would take some time. His cousin Naywin's reaction came to mind. What would it take for her to accept Saga? Would she ever? Was he asking too much?

But there had been progress too. Many of his serving staff now openly spoke with Saga and even Magnus' current demeanour was different from when they'd first met. This was the correct path. Gunnar would have to now see the value in this alliance. For all of their sakes.

"Return and keep Einar secure." Gunnar's voice was low and deliberate. "I will follow in a few days and then you and I will visit Olaf in Dublin and share the results of these meetings. Then we will visit Snorri Short-Beard, return his treasure, and shake hands or feast in Valhalla."

Magnus nodded and grasped arms with his brother. "I will await your ship on the horizon. Leave Einar to me."

"Your news is valuable, Magnus. Will you rest before you return?"

"Nay." he said with a grin. "I will take a fresh horse and be on my way."

Giric grasped the man's arms and said, "You are welcome to any but mine and my wife's."

It was the least he could offer. And now he must find Saga.

CHAPTER TWENTY-FOUR

Saga tore at her dress. She'd had it with all the transformations she'd endured and she'd had it with Scottish dresses. Struggling out of her gown and pulling at her pinned hair, she was in the middle of the chamber stark naked when Giric entered. His jaw dropped when he saw her.

"Saga, what are you doing?"

"I'm dressing the way I always have, in my own clothes, made by my own hand."

She pushed him aside and flung open the trunk that held her belongings. She grabbed her leather trews and fur vest, belt and boots, and ties for her hair.

She dressed as she had a thousand times before and cared not that this time she had an audience. As she donned each item, her heart lifted more and more. By the time she was clothed and starting to braid her hair she heard a sigh behind her.

"What is wrong now? Do you regret taking a Viking wife?"

She turned to look at him when he didn't answer.

"Well?"

"I do not regret one moment of my time with you since we met. You are in my heart for now and forever. But I do regret that you feel like you had to wear clothes that did not make you comfortable or feel like yourself."

How was it he could peer deep into her soul?

"These clothes represent who I am."

"I know that. And you are free to wear whatever you like."

"Even when the king arrives on the morrow?"

"Aye, especially then. I want you by my side, Saga. I want you to be proud to be my wife and of who you are and what we are trying to do."

She considered him for a minute or two. She'd never imagined life with him would be easy, but she'd never imagined she would be in danger of losing herself so completely. Well no more. She would be true to herself at all costs from now on. The babe that grew in her belly would need her and Giric's combined strength.

"Your brother feels that you are miserable and unprotected here. Is that how you feel as well?" he asked as he took a seat by the hearth.

"I do not feel either of those things. I have felt angry however, and confused. I do not ever want to feel like I or any of my kin are inferior to you, Giric. That is how you made me feel."

With each word, her resolve returned. This was her true self, standing up for what she believed in at all costs. Never again would she cower or run from a room because she didn't like what she heard. She was a shield-maiden of the north. A warrior who had a mind and a voice of her own and, by Odin, she would use both from this moment forward.

Saga stepped toward him and pointed her finger at his chest. "You do not get to decide alone what happens with these alliances. You invited us here and we will not sit by quietly whilst you negotiate on our behalf. You think we are untamed and unrefined and you are wrong."

"I do not believe that, Saga. I have always marvelled at the intelligence and patience your people uphold. Your hall, your dwellings, your ships, and your beliefs are all a wonder to me. If I have insulted you or your kin, it was not my intention, and I am sorry. Will you please forgive my arrogance?"

"I will forgive your arrogance," she said, jabbing her finger into his chest again. "And you will also apologize to my brother."

"Aye, I will do that. Can I ask you for something first?"

"What is it you want?"

"I want to kiss my wife. Nothing more, nothing less. There was a moment earlier when I thought I had lost you for good and I knew then I could never live without you. I am glad to see you dressed in a way that makes you happy. You have no idea how that makes my heart swell."

Giric gazed into her eyes. He'd said everything she wanted to hear and more. She would grant him his kiss. And demand an assurance that they would never again reach this level of disagreement.

Saga pulled him toward her and reached up to brush her lips across his. Softly and slowly, she drew him closer and deeper into her kiss. She wrapped her arms around his neck and held on tight as he slipped his tongue into her mouth and danced with hers. Giric's arms were tight around her waist as they shared their passion for long moments.

He broke the kiss first and leaned back to stare into her eyes.

"Do you know how lucky I am to call you mine?"

"I do know how lucky you are and will ensure you never forget it."

Giric slipped his hand into hers and led her toward the chamber door. Shall we go speak with Gunnar together?"

"I will be down in a few minutes once I finish my hair," she said pointing to the one braid that was half complete.

"Do you mind if I stay and watch?"

Saga smiled. She didn't mind at all, in fact she enjoyed it when he watched her. It made her nipples harden. This man could drive her insane with anger or passion and she wondered if she would always feel this way with him. She hoped what they had now never ever waned.

~

Watching her walk was a delight. More than that, Giric loved her strength, her compassion, and her goodness. He'd been such an arrogant arse that he understood now just how poorly he'd behaved. He'd been given a second chance with her and he was not about to foul it up.

Gunnar's grin stretched broad across his face as they entered the great hall. His trencher was full again and Giric was pleased that despite their differences, he felt at home enough to enjoy himself. It seemed the man had regained his composure from Magnus' news.

"There's my sister," he said, reaching for his tankard of mead. After taking a large gulp, he said, "This drink. What is it?"

"'Tis mead made from honey."

"It is better than any mead I have had. You will tell me how it's made, ja?"

"Aye, Gunnar. I will tell you how 'tis made."

Saga walked to her brother and hugged him tight. "Thank you for being here, Gunnar. This work is important to my husband, and also to us."

"Ja, I know that. But I was concerned that you didn't fully understand that."

"I do," she said and looked at Giric. "I have been trying so hard to belong here and lost part of myself along the way. I am back now."

"I am pleased to hear it," Gunnar said. "Now are we going to sit around and eat and drink all day, or are you planning to give me a full tour of this armoury I've heard so much about? Magnus practically drooled while talking about it."

"A tour it is. Magnus was quite happy with it, aye. In fact, I think that was the only time I've ever seen the man smile."

"He does not do that often. I blame it on the stick that remains firmly planted up his arse," Gunnar said and roared in laughter.

Giric liked how the man could entertain himself so easily. He was enjoyable to be around, and Saga was more relaxed with him here, as well.

Once their bellies were full, they all walked together to the armoury. Giric answered the many questions Gunnar had about the number of times the steel was folded in his blades, how the spikes were attached to the mace, how they kept the fires hot enough.

"We use more than peat. Coal burns hotter and for longer, but aye, peat is in enough abundance. Would you like to speak with the blacksmith?"

"I would like some of this coal for Ragnar."

"I'm certain we can make arrangements."

"This exchange of ideas and materials makes for a good relationship, MacDomnail. Are you certain you are not part Viking?"

Giric chuckled. Mayhap he has transformed somewhat as well. He understood the need for good bartering, but one thing both Gunnar and Saga had taught him was the importance of truthfulness and honour. These people were strong and resilient, but they were honourable to a fault.

"You will have to ask your sister if I am worthy of that title," Giric said.

"Not yet," Saga said with a grin. "You wouldn't last in a fight with me, let alone one of my kin."

Gunnar laughed again. "I am happier with this conversation than earlier, but I do have a need to release my bowels after all that meat. Where do I go?"

"In that structure right there," he said, pointing to the shack used by the villagers.

"Inside there?"

"Aye, you will see."

Gunnar went inside and after a time emerged with a wide-eyed look on his face. "That's the most ingenious thing I've ever seen!"

Giric laughed. "Aye, in that regard we are somewhat advanced. There will be a pot in your chamber you may use throughout the night so you do not have to leave your chamber should the need arise. The servants will empty it in the morning."

"You have people who carry away your shit?" Gunnar shook his head. "Just when I think I have you figured out."

Put that way, Giric supposed it was a little ridiculous, but that was the way things were done. It was incredible that something as simple as waste disposal was treated so differently between the two cultures.

"Tell me why you have need of such a large home?"

"Defence more than anything. If we were attacked, we would move everyone inside the keep and could sustain ourselves for quite some time."

"And why built out of stone?"

"To protect from the elements and fire. A wooden house would not last anywhere near as long."

Gunnar looked up the full height of the castle. "I want to see from the tower."

"The view is spectacular. The view runs all the way to the sea."

They climbed the tower steps, Gunnar marvelling all the way about the shape of the stones used for the circular staircase and the window holes.

As they stood on the tower overlooking the lands beneath, Giric's pride in his home welled within him. Aye, it was different from Gunnar's, but no more a marvel than his upside-down ship hall. They could learn so much from one another. The thought filled him with hope and peace. He'd wanted this for so long and he was on the brink of getting it all. Aye, he'd made some errors in judgement along the way, but he was more determined than ever to make this work; to listen to what those around him were saying, especially his wife. Her intelligence and wisdom went far beyond her years and he'd been a fool to brush that aside. He thought about the women who worked at the castle and those in his family. They were not given the same amount of voice or power as was displayed by Gunnar and his clan. What a loss. Giric planned to rectify that situation within his own household. No more arrogance. He would make his home a formidable fortress from the inside out.

CHAPTER TWENTY-FIVE

Saga fastened her golden brooches at her shoulders and smoothed her best green silk gown. Vigdis braided her hair and threaded fresh flowers through the braids. The king was set to arrive any time and Saga wanted to leave no one in doubt as to her heritage. If there were any in their midst who disliked her because she was Viking, they would have to deal with it. She would conform no longer.

"You look like a goddess," Vigdis said.

"As do you, sister. We both do our kin proud on this day."

"I believe your decision to wear your own clothes again was the right one. I could see you slipping more and more away from yourself as each day passed whilst wearing the Scottish garments."

"You should have said something."

"How could I? I barely recognized you during that time and was unsure if I would make things worse. I learned long ago that you learn lessons the hard way and in your own time."

Saga swatted at her sister's arm. "You know you can say anything to me. You are the only one I would allow that."

"I know, but I don't like upsetting you, whether it would end up in a physical altercation or no," she said, laughing.

"And I do not like to see you distressed either. Rest assured, I am myself again, fully and wholly."

"I am pleased to hear it. What do you suppose this king is like?"

"I imagine him to be strong like my husband, and powerful like our brothers. Giric has put much into planning for his arrival so he must be someone who commands respect. I don't think he has ever fussed so much for anyone," she said with a grin.

It was true. Giric had been nigh impossible to be around last evening. He had everyone including herself driven to distraction with his incessant points about where the garlands should go and who should serve the meals, and how well the chambers were made up.

At least the day was finally here. Come what may, she wouldn't have to hear 'when the king arrives' one more time.

A knock sounded at the door before Giric entered. He stopped inside the chamber. "You look beautiful, Wife."

"You look formal, Husband," she said. He wore his breast plate with the white serpent crest, the same one he'd worn the first day they'd met. His fur trimmed cloak flowed down his tall body and pooled on the floor. His longsword was sheathed at his side and his fingers were adorned with golden rings. On his head, he wore a thin crown of gold. He himself looked like a king. She wondered if he intended to outdo the real one.

"If you are ready, we should convene in the great hall to await the king's arrival. He has been spotted not five miles out."

This was it. She was going to meet the man her husband appeared to respect more than anyone. They walked together to the great hall. Once there, her breath caught in her throat at the beauty of the place. With such an amazing transformation in a few short hours, she was convinced, someone had stayed up all night long.

Thick garlands of green boughs were decorated with purple heather and strung all around the hall. The long table was adorned with silver goblets studded with rubies and so shiny, she could see her reflection. Large tankards of a red liquid and an amber liquid dotted the table's length. At the head was a chair Saga had never seen before. It was beautifully carved wood depicting two serpents intertwined. She gasped when she realized it was a near perfect image of the one at her home. On the chair sat a bright red cushion.

Dozens of large vases of flowers were positioned at many locations all around the hall. It was like something from a dream.

"Do you approve?" Giric asked.

"How could I not? Giric, it is beautiful!"

"You are beautiful. I am so proud to have you by my side and your brother here as part of these talks. I would like you to stay with me whilst we converse with the king."

"That is an odd thing to say. Where else would I be?"

Saga looked around the hall and realized there were some women present she had not seen before. It occurred to her that Giric was trying to be more inclusive of the women who lived in the castle and that it was not normally customary for that to occur. His sister was nowhere in sight. Neither was her brother. She wondered if Giric had purposely given him some sort of fool's errand to keep him away from the king.

"You are exactly where you should be," he said and kissed her on the forehead.

Before long, a messenger entered the hall to announce the arrival of the king.

Giric took her hand and led her to the entrance of the keep. A large tapestry covered cart was pulled by four horses.

Saga had never seen anything like it in her life. She could only assume a dozen or more people must be inside. When the footman placed a stool at the back and flipped back the fabric, she was certain to see many people emerge. Instead, only one man emerged.

If Giric's finery was impressive, this man's was downright overwhelming. From the large gem encrusted crown on his head, to his lavish fur trimmed robe, to the shiny gold chest plate, the man exuded extravagance. Two young men emerged from behind the cart to lift the back of the king's robe as he walked toward them.

Her husband bowed and she followed suit. She didn't know if she was supposed to or not, so she followed Giric's lead.

"MacDomnail," he said.

"Welcome to my home, my king," Giric said.

"I thank you," he said and turned to her. "I have met many Vikings, MacDomnail, but I have never seen one so lovely as this."

"Thank you, my king," she said, not really knowing how to address him.

He grinned and winked at Giric. "My king, is it? I approve of her wholeheartedly."

Saga wasn't certain if he was jesting or being truthful. She was usually a good judge of a man, but there was something a little off-putting about this one.

"Come in out of the weather and let us feast. Unless you wish to rest before we share a meal."

"Nay, I am ravenous and have been lying about for too many days in that damned cart. My guards insisted I travel hidden away like some frightened hare."

"I have to say I agree with them. Until we are certain of no further attempts on anyone's life from Athelstan, we cannot be too careful."

"Aye, we shall be careful. And I wish to hear everything about you, Lady MacDomnail. I understand your brother, Chieftain of Islay is here as well."

"He is inside and looking forward to meeting you as well."

Giric and the king walked ahead of her and into the great hall. Watching them both she was struck by the difference between them. Her husband was much taller and leaner. They were different in other ways too. Whilst Giric was like an open book when it came to his expressions, the king appeared more cunning, as though he missed nothing under his scrutiny. She wasn't sure if that warranted her to be more careful in his presence or more forthcoming. She would observe him more over the next few hours before making any kind of determination.

~

Giric was pleased by the king's expression when they entered the great hall. He practically stopped in his tracks when he saw the lavish decorations in his honour. Giric led him to the seat at the head of the table then turned to help Saga sit beside him and Gunnar across from him.

"My king, this is Gunnar of Islay, brother of my wife Saga, and chieftain of that realm."

"I am pleased to meet you, King Constantine."

"And I, you," the king said. "I appreciate all that you have done in my honour, MacDomnail. Truly, I have rarely seen such a grand display. Your wife is to be applauded."

"My husband oversaw every detail," Saga said. "This is all his doing. I cannot take credit for that in which I had no part."

"Well then my praise falls on your lap, MacDomnail. If

the food is as good as the presentation, I believe we will be successful in our endeavours."

"That is my hope," Giric said and squeezed Saga's hand under the table.

The servants came out with several platters of roasted wild boar, rabbit pies, stuffed salmon, pitchers of steaming gravy, and mounds of bread. The head servant served the king, then Giric and Gunnar, and then Saga.

Giric watched as those around him feasted. He ate what he could, but in truth his guts were full of nerves and he had difficulty forcing himself to eat. Gunnar was being his usual jovial self and Saga was engaging with both the king and her brother. Giric had decided to let them converse in an attempt for them to build some rapport which would make the meeting go much smoother in his estimation. He could not force these people to like one another, but if they came together naturally, the alliance would no doubt be stronger. The reality of the situation was that he'd worked hard to convince both the king and Gunnar to accept this alliance and they'd had time to consider the value. If all the collective gods were in agreement, this should be an acceptable union for them all.

"Your cooks are worthy of their efforts, MacDomnail. This is a sumptuous feast."

"Thank you, my king. I am fortunate to have such talented cooks and to live within such an abundant land."

"Do you approve as well, Gunnar of Islay?"

"Ja. I have never had such a feast in my life, though we enjoy ourselves immensely."

"You are being modest, Gunnar. You treated me to foods I've never heard of at your table. I am pleased you feel I have reciprocated with the same quality."

Gunnar looked around then back to Giric and winked at

the king. "You'll not find so many pretty things around my hall."

The king laughed out loud. "I would like to see your hall, Gunnar."

Gunnar stood then and lifted his goblet. "You are welcome, King Constantine. Please allow me to offer my alliance to you, but I cannot call you my king as my sister offers with her graciousness."

Giric stiffened. Had he let his guard down too soon? He'd thought the meal had passed well up to that point. His heart raced as he waited for the king to respond. Gunnar had offered his alliance, but appeared to revoke it in the same breath. He glanced at Saga who smiled at him. Did she know something he didn't?

"I don't imagine you would," the king said. "Your sister is gracious in her address, but I do not expect it of her either."

Giric was not following the logic of either man at that point.

"You may both address me as your grace and I relieve you both of any other primary fealty."

"Thank you, your grace," Saga said. "I am certain King Harald will appreciate your respect for our allegiance to him first."

Now Giric understood. He had not considered that Gunnar and Saga would still hold such an allegiance to the Norwegian King, but thankfully King Constantine was more sensitive than he.

"You are a gracious king," Gunnar said. "Considering the history of my people and yours, I am impressed."

"I want what MacDomnail wants, for us to work together to push the English back to their lands. Too long have they coveted what we have. Our feuds with your people can be abolished if we decide to work together toward that common goal."

"Are you proposing a fresh start and all is forgiven? I do not think everyone will find your forgive-and-forget approach so easy to adopt," Gunnar said.

"It will not be easy. Much has been lost on both sides over the years, but I believe you wish to live in peace as much as I do. I will marry my own flesh and blood to a Viking in order to promote peace and I am pleased MacDomnail has followed my lead."

"I admit, when his galley landed on my shores, I was not sure if he was the cleverest man alive, or the densest."

"Thankfully, you settled on the former," Giric said. He'd grown accustomed to his sense of humour and wasn't sure how the king would take insulting him.

"I didn't say I'd settled," he said and reared his head back in laughter.

The king followed and beside him, Saga let out a quiet laugh as well.

"You are too serious, MacDomnail," Gunnar said.

"He speaks the truth. Come let us be easy and enjoy the rest of this feast. We have plenty of time to hammer out the details of our agreement for the next few days. I need to return to Dunnottar within a sennight to prepare for talks with Olaf of Dublin. If we can solidify this alliance, we will have an edge Athelstan will not see coming."

Giric was more than pleased with the king's statement. He sat back and listened as the king asked Gunnar questions about life on Islay and exchanged some of his thoughts on how the Vikings on Lewis had merged cultures with the Scots who lived there. Dublin was slightly less successful, but this alliance would take time to nurture. One marriage at a time and one agreement at a time would have to suffice.

King Harald would never agree to a full-on alliance, but he had supported his and Saga's marriage since it was supported by King Constantine, and with that he would have to be satisfied for now.

The remainder of the feast went as well as he could have ever hoped. Gunnar was as entertaining as he expected, and the king appeared quite taken with him.

Before retiring for the evening, Saga leaned close and said, "I will be waiting for you, but I will leave you to your discussions now."

"Thank you, wife, I suspect your brother will keep us up for quite a while. Get some rest. We have the hunt on the morrow."

CHAPTER TWENTY-SIX

Saga opened her eyes and blinked a couple of times to understand what was happening. Her whole body tingled with anticipation and she was unsure what was the cause. A deep groan brought her fully awake and she recognized that Giric was nestled between her legs and flicking his tongue back and forth across her woman's bud. She arched into him as he pushed two fingers inside her and hooked upward as he stroked. She orgasmed almost immediately.

"My God, you're so wet. I cannot wait any longer."

Giric lifted his body over hers and pushed his hard shaft inside her swiftly, she orgasmed again as his thickness impaled her. Saga held on to his shoulders as he lifted her legs above his shoulders and pounded into her like his life depended on it. Higher and higher they climbed together until she met her final climax as he crested.

Bathed in sweat and breathless, she curled into him once he slipped out of her.

"I do love waking up in such a delicious way," she said.

"Mmmmm, you are delicious."

They lay like that as the sunlight filled their chamber. The king's visit was considered successful and her brother had left the previous day. Life at the castle would return to normal soon enough, but she and Giric had agreed to do as little as possible for the next few days. No one was certain what would happen if the English king decided to bring his campaign north, but for now an alliance between her people and the Scots was solid. Neither side had to fight alone.

"What would you like to do today?" Giric asked, interrupting her musings.

"I would like to stay here with you."

"All day?"

"All day."

"You won't get bored?'

"Nay. I do not imagine I will."

Giric kissed the top of her head. "I would like that too, but I have a surprise for you."

"Do we need to get up to see it?"

"Aye, we do."

Saga heaved a sigh. She snuggled closer to him and slapped his buttocks as he slid away from her and got out of bed.

"Come on sleepy-head. We cannot laze about all day."

Saga giggled as she got out of bed and donned her leather trews and fur vest. She loved wearing her old clothes again. She had noticed some sideways glances from a few of the women and men at the castle as she passed by, but she cared not. They would have to adjust to her ways as much as she did theirs. Her belly had not yet gotten bigger, but her body had thickened somewhat so she had pieces of cloth stitched into the sides of her trews to give her some growing space.

Once they were both dressed, he led her to the stable and helped her mount Sif.

"Where are we going?" she asked as they trotted away

from the castle. She noticed a satchel tied to the horse containing bread.

"Eat," he said. "We have a long ride ahead of us and you will need your strength."

She nibbled on the contents of the satchel as did he with his. They kept a steady pace though not a full-on gallop. After a couple hours' ride, they came to a clearing and a structure that looked somewhat familiar, resembling their god house on Islay.

Giric dismounted then came over to help Saga off her horse. He tied both horses to a tree and took her hand.

"What is this place?"

"Some of your people lived here a long time ago. Because it is a place of worship, no one wanted to destroy it after they left and so it has remained empty for many years."

Saga walked inside. Bones of various animals in tribute hung from the walls and an altar table, now dusty and dirty, signified where sacrifices would have taken place. The people who had worshipped here paid homage to Odin and all the gods in the same way she did.

"I wanted to make sure you approved of the way this building is laid out."

"Of course I approve. It is much like the prayer house at home. But why do I need your approval?"

"Because I plan to build one alongside my chapel."

Saga's heart squeezed. This was most unexpected.

"Giric, I do not know what to say."

"Say you like it, and say what you want done and how you want it to look. I have made many mistakes in my time with you, but I want to start fixing them at this moment. You are my life and my world and I want to spend the rest of our days together showing you how grateful I am to call you wife and share in your joys and triumphs and sorrows. I know how important your prayers are to you and I know how important it is for you to preserve your way of life. I want to help with that in any way I can. You have given up so much for me and I want you to know how grateful I am."

Saga's chest tightened and her eyes stung. This was more than she could have ever hoped for. She'd never realized until that moment how happy she was that he'd landed on her shores that day, that he came looking for an alliance and found her, that they found each other. Her life was full and her blessings were many because of him.

~

His wife intermingled with the other noblewomen around the table. She'd been singled out a few times with comments about her attire and he wanted to make sure she was not misunderstood or demeaned in any way. So he'd organized a feast including Osgar's family as well as his own to pay homage to Saga in formal acceptance of her as Lady MacDomnail.

He sat back and listened as they asked her many questions about her clothes and her weapons, marvelling in half shock when she explained how she'd been in battle and how common it was for women to be warriors. In turn, Saga asked many questions of them along the lines of what they did all day long if they were not contributing to the hunt for food or protecting the villages.

She laughed out loud when one woman mentioned stitching on pillows. "My apologies, I did not know such a thing existed," she said. "Do you not find that boring and overly taxing?"

Saga was genuine in her curiosity but the woman seemed to take slight offence to her comment.

"I find it quite relaxing in fact, and I suspect you would too if you were to give it a try."

The afternoon was somewhat painful, but it would be better for both Saga and the women with which she would socialize in the future if they better understood one another. She'd been in the company of her sister ever since coming here and now that Vigdis had returned to Islay with Gunnar, Saga would need companionship. He hoped in time she would find one of these women good company.

"I do not like any of them," she said as they lay in one another's arms later that evening.

"There must be some redeeming quality in at least one of them," he said, chuckling at her indignation.

"Nay. I would rather spend time by myself than mindlessly stitching pillows or talking about the weather or what other people are doing."

"You may get lonely after a time. I cannot always be your companion."

"I know you have things you will need to do from time to time, but you do not need to worry about me. I have plenty of ways to keep myself occupied and they do not include anything in the lifestyle these women share. I will hunt or ride when I am bored. In truth, I feel bad for them. Mayhap I should teach them how to wield an axe or sword."

Giric laughed out loud. He couldn't imagine any one of those women lifting a sword let alone raising it over their heads and striking anything.

"I will introduce you to my huntsman tomorrow." Giric drew a deep breath and let it out slowly. "I am the luckiest man alive. Have I told you that?"

"You tell me every day."

"And I will tell you every day for the rest of your life. I love you, my Viking shield-maiden. You excite me in ways I never knew possible. I would not change a hair on your head. If you do not wish the companionship of the women of your status, you may choose how you spend your time and with whom. I learned the hard way to never try to tell you what to do."

"I am glad you finally understand. There was a time I considered you to be thick in the head and worried you were not as clever as you initially appeared."

Giric pinched her bottom and she squealed. God, he loved the sound of her voice and the feel of her skin and the wild scent that always lingered around her. She was tame and untamed at the same time, and she was a mystery he wanted to spend his life unravelling.

"I love you, Saga. My Viking wife. I will always love you."

"And I love you, my stubborn Scottish husband who takes far too long to figure things out."

"Like what?" he asked, noticing how her hand had slipped down to stroke his manhood.

"Like the fact that I hold all of you in my hand and you have not yet flipped on top of me to give me what I crave."

"You are insatiable," he said.

"Is that a complaint?"

"Nay, it is one more reason why I am the luckiest man alive."

Giric did give her what she wanted, over and over until they both lay spent in one another's arms. He thanked his god and all of hers for the fortune that had brought them together. Come what may in the future, they would face it together and nothing, not even life or death could separate the bond they shared.

THE END

Pre-Order The Raven, Spirits of the Norse, Book Two

~

~

ACKNOWLEDGMENTS

My road to self-publishing has been filled with bumps and lumps and even some stumps. I could not have gotten here without some very special people and organizations picking me up when I fell and helping me focus when my muse decided to take a one-way ticket to Jupiter. I think she was on a drinking binge, but she won't admit it.

To my sons who watch me slip into an alternate human to create the stories I adore so much, you are the reason I want to succeed. I love you both so much for your endless support.

To Michelle O for offering editorial services to a stubborn writer. You make me readable. Thank you.

To Melanie and Vicki. Thank you for all of your encouragement and patience when I'm not sitting my butt in the chair and getting the words out. Mostly thank you for supporting my efforts to 'go indie'.

To Roy. You encourage me, you challenge me, you don't put up with my bullshit when I'm making excuses. Thank you for everything, always.

To Suzan. You've been on this journey with me a long time. I so appreciate your guidance and advice!

To Victoria Z. We got this, lady!!! #rockstars

To my beta readers, the above noted plus Maria, Sharon, Mari-Lynn, Kellie, Vanessa, Tina, Jill, Cynthia, Barb, Melba, and Glenn. Thank you for your feedback on the advanced read!!! XOX

Thank you to the Government of Newfoundland and Labrador and Titan Training and Consulting for your support.

To my readers. First of all, thank you for making The Serpent Reader's Choice Cover of the Month at Books and Benches for July, 2021! You have reached out to me many times over the years with helpful critique and kind words and your support has been unwavering. I sincerely hope you enjoy the first in this new series and I will continue to work hard to provide you with good quality entertainment. Please keep reaching out over all my platforms.

Much love to you all!!!

Kate/Debbie

ABOUT THE AUTHOR

Amazon internationally bestselling author of the award-winning Highland Chiefs series, Kate Robbins writes historical romance out of pure escapism and a love for all things Scottish. She thoroughly enjoys the research process and delving into secondary sources in order to blend authentic historical fact into her stories.

Ranging a thousand years, Kate's novels are filled with passion, adventure, and political intrigue.

Kate is the pen name of Debbie Robbins who lives in St. John's, Newfoundland and Labrador, Canada.

Stay up to date with new release information by signing up for my newsletter.

facebook.com/katerobbinsauthor

twitter.com/KateRobWriter

instagram.com/robbins.kate

bookbub.com/authors/kate-robbins

amazon.com/Kate-Robbins/e/B00FRHRUPE

linkedin.com/in/robbinsdebbie

Bound to the Highlander

Aileana Chattan suffers a devastating loss, then discovers she is to wed neighboring chief and baron, James MacIntosh -- a man she despises and whose loyalty deprived her of the father she loved. Despite him and his traitorous clan, Aileana will do her duty, but she doesn't have to like it or him. But when the MacIntosh awakens something inside her so absolute and consuming, she is forced to question everything.

James MacIntosh is a nobleman torn between tradition and progress. He must make a sacrifice if he is to help Scotland move forward as a unified country. Forced to sign a marriage contract years earlier binding Lady Aileana to him, James must find a way to break it, or risk losing all—including his heart.

From the wild and rugged Highlands near Inverness to the dungeons of Edinburgh Castle, James and Aileana's preconceptions of honor, duty and love are challenged at every adventurous turn.

Promised to the Highlander

Nessia Stephenson's world was safe until a threat from a neighbouring clan forces her to accept a betrothal to a man whose family can offer her the protection she needs. The real threat lies in her intense attraction to the man who arranged the match—the clan's chief and her intended's brother, Fergus MacKay.

When powerful warlord Fergus MacKay arranges a marriage for his younger brother, William, he has no idea the price will be his own heart. Fergus is captivated by the wildly beautiful Nessia, a woman he can never have.

When the feud between the MacKay and Sutherland clans escalates,

Nessia, William, and Fergus all must make sacrifices for their future. Longing and loss, honour and duty. How can love triumph under such desperate circumstances?

Enemy of the Highlander

Two years ago Freya MacKay walked away from the only man she would ever love, her family's bitter enemy, knowing her clan would never accept their love. A fragile alliance has been forged and now he has returned to warn of a terrible threat. Freya MacKay is torn between the familiar surge of passion he evokes and her promise to wed another man.

Ronan Sutherland has lost everything to a cruel uncle who will lay the entire north Highlands to waste if he is not stopped. There is only one who can help—but seeking alliance with his former enemy, Fergus MacKay, means encountering the woman who left him two years ago, breaking his heart.

A bitter feud keeps their clans at one another's throats and it seems nothing will stop one from destroying the other. Will Ronan ever forgive Freya for leaving him? Can he trust her again? Or will the decades of hatred and deceit between their families prevail?

Prisoner of the Highlander

Annabella Beaufort, cousin to the Queen Consort of Scotland, visits court in Edinburgh upon the queen's urging. She has little interest in this wild and rugged land and is pleasantly surprised to find Linlithgow Palace and King James' court quite refined. An attack on Edinburgh Castle by a savage Highlander results in her capture. This flaxen haired giant is like nothing she's encountered before, but her fear of him quickly turns to lust and she prays he will not also claim her heart.

Son of the great Alexander MacDonald, beloved Lord of the Isles, Angus MacDonald refuses to bend to King James' tyrannical rule.

After his father is imprisoned, he becomes acting chief. Unlike his father and his schemes, Angus will attack and bring this king to his knees. His attempt to release his father is thwarted and instead he abducts the Queen's cousin. His desire for her is intense and immediate, despite her flawed Sassenach ways. But he must keep her at arm's length regardless of the raging passion she evokes in him. She is his pawn—his prisoner—and he must always remember that.

Though they fight on opposite sides of the battle for power over Scotland, Angus and Annabella discover a fire that will not be ignored or denied. Will their loyalties to their families tear them apart? If he sets her free, will she return to him? Or will she in turn imprison his heart for all eternity?

~

Heart of the Highlander

Devastated to learn the betrothal to her beloved Rorie has been broken, Muren Grey vows to take control of her life once and for all. But independence is not an easy path in a world dominated by men. Can she love a man who wants to control her? Muren must gather her strength and find the essence of who she truly is—even if it means losing the only man she will ever love.

Rorie Mackenzie has inherited a clan he will do anything to protect. Drawn into the king's schemes involving Muren, diplomacy will only take him so far before he must make a stand, for her and for the Highlands.

Facing impossible odds from their world and beyond, Muren and Rorie seek the one power that can obliterate any barrier.

~

Highlander Bewitched

Stripped of her title and wealth at a young age, Gwendolyn MacGregor was put into service for the chief of the Chattan Clan. Determined to embrace her new life, she shed her noble expectations and even her religion. As a pagan wise woman, she developed a gift for channelling nature's energy and became a contented free spirit in every way—until she meets Calum MacIntosh.

Brother of the great MacIntosh chief, Calum MacIntosh believes virtue is the most important gift a husband and wife can bring to a marriage. He is prepared to join his name with another noble lady when the time is right, until his path crosses with the enchanting lady's maid, Gwendolyn. Despite his efforts to forget her, he is drawn to her as though an invisible tether connects them.

Caught between longing and duty, Gwen and Calum discover a powerful bond that will not be defined by social expectations or status—and will not be denied.

One Knight in Stirling

Sir William MacPherson is honoured by the queen mother's invitation to protect her from her enemies. The only catch: he must reside at Stirling Castle where he will encounter Coira MacLaren; the one woman who can bring him to his knees and keep him there. Her refusal of his marriage proposal a year ago hit him hard and he has not seen her since. Can he harden himself against her, or will their insatiable lust for one another burn them to cinders this time?

www.ingramcontent.com/pod-product-compliance
Lightning Source LLC
Chambersburg PA
CBHW021646110726

47902CB00007B/1848